LETTERS FROM THE SUN

Gregory Fladager

To my brother Chris

CONTENTS

Letters From The Sun

CHAPTER ONE

It was brief, like a flash of light, but I had already turned the page. I slowly turned back, thinking it was an illusion, but it was still there, glowing against the ancient brown vellum.

It was my first day in the Saint Sernin library in Toulouse, France, amid a vast collection of books and manuscripts, many dating back to the Middle Ages. I was not an academic but an artist gathering material for an article I was writing on the Languedoc. I'd wanted to begin with illuminated manuscripts, as they were some of the earliest regional art. Luck had played a part in my getting this assignment, as it didn't matter that I had never been to this part of France; in fact, it was a benefit. The editor wanted a first impression, emulating the experience many famous artists had when they came here.

As I peered at the speck, it seemed almost radiant on the page. It was not paper or parchment, but something like it, and only large enough to hold a single mark that looked like Hebrew. Christianity and Judaism have the Old Testament in common, and finding a Hebrew letter might not be that unusual in a historical library. I could imagine this bit breaking off a Talmud scroll while being studied by some scholarly monk before being tossed into the fire. Following their victory over the Moors in 1492, Queen Isabella and King Ferdinand had expelled the Jews, seizing their property and destroying religious texts. Whatever the circumstance, the small flake looked out of place.

At one time, the cover of the book had been richly decorated, but only a remnant remained on the hard leather, worn smooth by centuries of soft hands. It was an indifferent example of an illuminated manuscript, however, and I wondered why I had been given this particular volume. In any event, my time was about up for the day, and I left the tiny flake in place, but not before taking a picture on my phone.

I decided not to mention it when I returned the book to the assistant at the front desk, but instead asked if there was anything more colorful available. The clerk apologized, saying he had misunderstood. He thought the book would be of interest because it was one of the last remaining texts of the heretical Cathars, and only spared because it was a Church-approved version of the Book of Revelation.

I later learned the Languedoc had once been a haven for the sect that considered itself Christian, though not Orthodox. They believed each person had a direct connection with the Divine, without the need for an intercessory priest or pope. It was a belief fostered by Gnostic traditions in the early days of Christianity.

By the 1200's the popularity of Cathars had become a growing concern for the Church. After failing to convert its adherents, it branded them as heretics and launched the Albigensian Crusade. Nearly a half-million died in the decades long campaign, and the method used to extract Cathar confessions was the beginning of the infamous Inquisition.

Interest in the Cathars was having a revival of sorts after becoming the topic of several novels and popular movies. As a result, more tourists were coming to the region, some lured by legends of a secret Cathar treasure hidden in their final days.

I said I'd take another look at the book, while the clerk agreed to find something more visually dynamic.

We were in the quietest part of the Library, where it seemed nothing ever disturbed the rays of sunlight gently passing over the dark wooden floors, yet my heart was beginning to race as I headed through the church courtyard. I could still see the bright golden flake, with its single black letter, and my imagination was beginning to churn.

I had wanted to start my assignment in Toulouse because it was the ancestral home of the famous artist Count Henri Toulouse Lautrec. As an adult, he lived a bohemian life in Paris, but as a child, he lived in the Languedoc, the eldest son of a wealthy family with royal lineage. They had been the lords in the Languedoc for nearly a thousand years, and their name was consonant with its largest city.

I decided to first look for a book on Hebrew and its alphabet before going back to my hotel. I had to be quick, as the shops would be closing soon and the streets filling with residents out for their evening stroll, which was so much a custom in this city. I also had a new friend I wanted to meet.

I got into my car and was lucky to find a parking space close by a small, long-established bookstore on the edge of the old city center. The owner and I had become acquainted on a previous visit, and he recognized me when I came in. Yoseph was Jewish, and I knew he had studied their ancient language.

He gave me a friendly greeting, but I did not want to reveal my discovery so soon; instead, I said I had been thinking about our earlier conversation, where he was intrigued that the Hebrew name for God was 'I AM'. For instance, he had noted when Moses was questioned about leading the Hebrews out of Egypt, he answered, 'I AM THAT I AM' has sent me.'

I told him I was interested in some books on the Hebrew alphabet, which he willingly showed me. Looking at the 22 letters, I saw one resembling the mark on the flake, and it was the letter for Y. Yoseph explained that letter was particularly noteworthy because it began their word for God, YHWH. He said Jews traditionally never say the word, as it is too sacred, and it had been that way for so long the pronunciation was now in some debate.

He retrieved a leather-bound book embossed with gold letters, and it struck me how Hebrew words look curiously like a menorah, each letter a flame flickering above a candle.

Hebrew reads from right to left, the opposite of English, and the alphabet consists only of consonants. Yoseph explained the vowels might have been omitted because, at one time, Hebrew was the common tongue, and everyone knew how to pronounce the words. But, he said, it might also have been a way to protect the language from non believers, or the vowels were left unrecorded so a person could shape the meaning of a word, like in a song.

Yoseph then looked up and said, "Why are you asking about this? Did you find something?"

While I might have expected him to notice, I was still startled by the question; and, I wasn't ready to answer it. So instead, I told him I came across a possible reference to God or something else, and while it may be nothing, I wanted to pursue it a little further.

Being polite and perhaps hoping I would say more, Yoseph launched into the alphabet's history, from its possible Phoenician origins to present-day use. I learned that not only is Y the first letter for God and several other important names, but it also represents the number 10.

During this time, another customer had come into the shop, a man in his late 70's, with white hair and very neatly dressed. Yoseph went to greet him. When he returned, the man came with him.

"Let me introduce you to Karl Yunger," Yoseph said. "He's an old friend, and I mentioned your article to him. His family here goes back many generations, even before the Inquisition. He is interested in what you are doing."

I told him about the article and my time at the church today, including finding an unusual reference that may be to God.

"But it is really something of a fishing expedition," I concluded.

Karl had listened attentively while I was speaking.

"Was this a Cathar text?" he finally asked.

Surprised again, I said it was; and, only spared because it was a Church-approved version of the Book of Revelation.

"That's interesting," he replied simply.

Yoseph said that Karl had done extensive studies in the Talmud and other Judaic texts.

"He is also versed in the Kabbalah."

I sensed Yoseph had gone a little out on a limb mentioning that. The Kabbalah is one of the most enigmatic of Jewish writings, and some believe it contains the keys to divine order. For a long time, only special initiates were allowed to study it. Anyone can get a copy today, but there is still mystery around it.

Some other patrons had entered the store, and I was glad to let the matter drop. I sensed, however, that my earlier hunches had been correct, and I might be on to something with that small flake.

I soon left, taking some books on Hebrew and the Cathars. Yoseph suggested I might also be interested in the Knights Templar. I was aware of them, but my understanding was more storybook than reality.

It was past 6:00, and I was anxious to return to my hotel. I thanked Yoseph, and as I was heading out the door, Karl suddenly called to me.

"Look for the red dot."

I turned, but he waved as if it was unimportant.

"You don't want to be late," he said.

Back in my hotel room, I sat down and wrote a few notes about the day and then started flipping through the book about Hebrew. While the alphabet appeared arcane, its history was fascinating, though I didn't see anything about red dots.

The evening stroll is one of the most pleasant customs of Southern France and Mediterranean countries, and I was about to join it. The cool air and beautiful glow of sunset invites a change of pace from the heat and activity of the day. The street becomes as familiar as a living room with couples, grandparents, children, and lovers walking the plazas and thoroughfares. There is a sense of community that, as an American, I find appealing yet unfamiliar. Maybe it takes centuries of tradition to share the common bond.

I was also intent on seeing another writer, Juliette White, who I had met at an art gallery opening my first night in the city. She said some friends often gathered after work at a café in the heart of the old town area. I saw it as an opportunity to connect with the local scene.

During our conversation at the show, Juliette told me she grew up in the Boston area and had met her husband while traveling in Europe. He was Belgian, and they had a seven-year-old daughter, who was something of a wild butterfly. The girl, Artemisia, seemed to be always weaving through the crowd at the opening, holding a precariously overfull cup of fruit punch in one hand and a piece of cake on a napkin in the other.

The cafe was busy by the time I arrived. It wrapped around a corner location in the central plaza. There was an array of tables with umbrellas and a long mahogany bar just in from the street. As I stood looking at the younger crowd, I caught sight of Juliette with a small group, some seated at a table. She was in conversation and, when she saw me, she smiled and waved me over. I waved back, pleased at being recognized but also at her smile.

As I made my way through the crowd, she did, too, and we met in the middle.

"So you came," she said, apparently pleased.

"Well, I had a free evening," I replied.

"I was hoping you would. I wasn't sure if my daughter had scared you away. She is impossible in places like that. She ruined her blouse with that juice."

"Kids are like that. They really can't handle their drink."

"It wasn't wine," she said a little defensively.

"I was just kidding. Really, she's a lovely girl, lots of spirit."

"Yes, she's a handful," she remarked, then added, "I'm not sure I want to be a mother."

I didn't know quite what to say.

"She is with William tonight. I think they will be coming by later."

She brought me over to her table and introduced me to her friends. Denis was an accountant, and his wife Jeanette, Dieter, was Dutch, handsome, with bright blue eyes, wavy blond hair, and quite friendly.

Madeline was quintessentially French, slim, with dark hair

pulled back, and dressed in a dark smock-like dress over a white t-shirt. Her pale complexion contrasted with the darkening circles under her eyes, which were quickly sizing me up.

The group was discussing a street theater act. The small troupe was apparently the hottest thing in town, but Madeline was arguing they were not doing anything new to warrant it. Denis disagreed, philosophizing that they were bringing attention to the shattered human condition and relating it to the election of a premier whose base prejudices promoted social injustice.

The conversation was slipping in and out of English, but I tended to side with Madeline, probably because I find so little genuinely original. I was interested in seeing a performance, but unfortunately, the troupe was not playing tonight as the lead actor and his girlfriend were having difficulties. That, at least, was not original.

I struck up a side conversation with Dieter, who inquired what I was doing. I explained my article, and it turned out he had been to the recent Lautrec exhibition at the Tate in London, which I had seen, too. He was also well versed in the myths and history of the region, particularly about the Cathars and Knights Templar. I was beginning to realize this topic went deeper than I had suspected, and as in much of Europe, history's powerful undercurrents were alive in the present. Even this little street theater act was a form of public commentary dating back to the Middle Ages.

Juliette overheard Dieter and shifted the conversation to us. She was particularly interested in the Lautrecs.

Even though it had been 800 years since the Cathars purge, southern France continued to harbor an affinity for alternative views and expressions, particularly in the arts. I found something of that as I spoke with Juliette and her friends. Denis mentioned that Juliette knew one of the Lautrec's, the Count, who worked with her husband.

"Well, he is really my husband's friend. I've been to his house in town, but never the chateau, where I understand they have an amazing collection of Lautrec's childhood drawings and paintings that have never been seen in public," Juliette said. "That would make for an interesting article."

It appeared her knowing the family was about to open some doors.

Then Dieter and Jeanette said they wanted to come, too. It was becoming a crowd until Juliette told them we were first, and everyone laughed.

The conversation drifted on to other topics, and people began leaving. Meanwhile, Dieter said he would like to talk again, and we agreed to meet the next night.

Juliette was on her phone, and after a short conversation, she said her husband had to finish up some work and was dropping off Artemisia on his way to the office. A light grey Citroen pulled to the curb a few minutes later, and Juliette went over. She leaned in after he lowered the passenger side window, and they spoke briefly, but neither was smiling. She then opened the rear door for her little girl.

Artemisia was wearing an assortment of tights, a pink and silver taffeta dress, purple plastic slippers, and a little purse in one hand. She seemed somehow oblivious to her surroundings, alert, but in her own world. She was certainly dancing to a different drummer.

As everyone was leaving, Juliette asked would I care to walk to a park if I had time. She said she often went there with Artemisia to get away from the busyness of the city, and it had a wonderful old fountain.

CHAPTER TWO

Toulouse is a city of well over 600-thousand. The streets are often crowded with traffic, and its large areas of old-world charm abut contemporary glass and steel. The roads were narrow and lined with shops and residences in the old quarters, built when things were on a more human scale. I liked France, and even though it often felt agitated and crowded, there was still an appreciation of stepping back and taking a thoughtful view of life.

Artemisia was holding onto her mother's hand as she looked up and down, paying no attention to me.

"She is almost deaf," Juliette said. "I want to take her to a specialist."

"I am sorry to hear that. I just thought she was shy."

"I don't think that describes her. I'm worried I might be over-protecting her, and she'll have more trouble when she gets a little older."

"She looks fine to me."

"Thanks. I was serious about seeing the Lautrecs. I don't know what your time schedule is, and I would not like to interfere."

"That would be the opposite of interference. It's great you know one of the family," I replied.

"He knows my husband, they do some business together. I would like to do this, but I usually do not associate with William's friends much. I don't like them."

"You're that different?" I said joking.

"We have some mutual friends, but his family doesn't care much that he married an American, even if my father was French, and I don't care much for his family. If it wasn't for Artemisia he probably would have gone back to Belgium."

Her directness took me aback. The marriage was obviously uncomfortable, and she was not making any bones about it. Her husband had seemed nice enough, but I sensed a distance that left me feeling like a stranger.

"So why did you marry him?" I asked.

"I was on a trip to Europe right after graduating from college. I met him at a party, and at first it was, well, we couldn't keep our hands off each other. I should have let it go at that. I knew it was a mistake a minute after the ceremony. I went into the bathroom and cried."

I did not know what to say.

"I tried to make the best of it. Then we had Artemisia. He has provided for us well, and I've been comfortable."

"I think he loves you," I said, just guessing.

"He does, but I'm dying."

We walked for a while without saying anything.

"Today, I was reading about Lautrec. You know he grew up at Chateau du Bosc, but was often bedridden in childhood because of a bone disease. It may have been why he became an artist."

"I can relate to that," she commented, looking at her daughter, who had let go of her hand and run ahead as we entered the park. She was waving as if chasing butterflies, loosely holding on to her little purse.

"She is probably going to lose that," Juliette said. "There nothing in it but some crayons and a few sous. But then we'll have to look for it."

"Just so long as she doesn't drop it in the water," I said.

Artemisia had made it to the fountain and was leaning over and reaching into the pond trying to touch the water, her purse precariously balanced on the ledge.

She asked me how my article was going. I told her I had come across some interesting things in the church records, but just the experience of handling documents over 800 years old, so strong yet vulnerable, was worth the visit. While we have the idea the Middle Ages were a rough, if not brutal, period, I noticed the lettering was small and delicate, almost feminine.

"Well, they were celibate, those monks," she said. "Usually."

"I suppose they were written with great attention," I said. "Books back then were rare. Treasures really."

"Yes, I know. So what have you found most interesting?"

I decided to test the waters a little. She was perceptive and bright; I thought her opinion might be useful.

"I wasn't going to say much, but do you know anything about Hebrew?"

"No," she said.

"Well, I'm no expert," I began but started to get cold feet again. "I don't know if I should say this."

"I can keep a secret."

I believed her. Besides, she was going to try and get me in to see the Lautrecs, a gracious offer, and perhaps a social risk for her as well.

"OK. I came across this thing in one of the books, the Book of Revelation actually. It was a Hebrew letter, apparently a reference to God, but I'm not sure. It was out of place, and it didn't fit. This might sound strange, but it was so much more alive, brighter than the delicate but just dead parchment pages."

"What was it?" she asked.

"It was a little flake of papyrus, I think. I don't know what it was doing in that book. Look, I have it on my cell phone. I wasn't supposed to take a picture, but I did."

As I was pulling the photo up, Artemisia ran over and began tugging on her mother's jacket, looking about ready to cry. She was pointing at the pond. Indeed, her purse had fallen into the water.

She and her mother quickly went over while I tagged behind, fiddling to get the picture up on my phone. As I was doing that, a call came in. It was Wendy Mason, my editor in New York, and while it was about 8 p.m. here, it was before noon there. As I switched to the call, I wondered if I had just wiped out my picture.

"How is it going? Are you sipping Chateau Lafitte Rothschild as you watch the moon rise over the Rue de Arts?" Wendy asked in that no off-switch pace reserved for New Yorkers. "Or are you otherwise occupied?"

"I'm otherwise occupied," I replied.

"Ooh la la," She said in mock French. "Can you talk?"

"For a minute, but I am in the midst of arranging to get into the inner sanctums of Fortress Lautrec."

"That is an interesting way to put it," and I could see her smiling at her desk. "But seriously, that's terrific. Can you get pictures?"

"I don't know. I'll try."

"No one else would have that."

"If I can get them, I'll let you know."

"Good, and watch out, those French women will break your inner sanctum."

"Thanks, it is too late."

"Oh, really?" she said, "You were serious?"

"No."

"Too bad. Call me tomorrow."

Juliette and Artemisia were struggling to reach down into the pond. Her little red purse was shimmering faintly on the bottom.

The water was not very deep, but they were trying to avoid falling in.

It was a lovely old fountain with dark, worn stones patched with moss. The pond was a circle, about 20 feet across, with the water coming in at one end from a small stone well box with a tap people could use. Like most European fountains, it had once been the local water source for residents. While purportedly still drinkable, I doubted anyone used it now.

Artemisia had found a stick and was trying to hook the purse's almost invisible strap but mainly managing to push it further out into the pond.

"Oh, could you help?" Juliette asked when I came over. "I'd reach in, but maybe it would be easier for you."

I took off my jacket and rolled up my sleeve. The water was deeper than it looked, and as I reached down, I had to turn my head as it almost touched the surface. As I looked across the shimmering water, which appeared as red as the purse in the fading sunlight, I felt like a kid. A few drops splashed into my mouth and tasted like they had been soaked in fresh moss.

I was just able to touch the purse with my fingertips and move it close enough to get it out but soaking my rolled-up sleeve. I hoped I hadn't wrecked the shirt because while the water was clean, it had minerals that gave it a reddish tinge.

The ripples in the water reminded me of a parable by Mark Twain in his book Life on the Mississippi. He wrote how a crimson rivulet on the river looked beautiful to the passengers, but to the knowing eye of the riverboat pilot, that red smear hid a log just beneath the surface that could rip the bottom out of the boat, sending them all to their end. I took it as a caution. I was beginning to be attracted to Juliette, and I should probably be more careful.

Artemisia was happy to get her purse back as she began pulling out two small coins and three soggy crayons.

"Thanks," Juliette said. "I don't know if I could have reached it. We would have been here all night. She is very attached to it. It was a gift from her grandmother. I hope it's not wrecked it's quite old."

Then she said they had to go, but added, "I haven't forgotten. I will call you. What is your phone number?"

I gave her my number and said goodbye to Artemisia, who was still looking inside her purse. I do not think she noticed. As they walked away, Juliette turned and said, "And I want to see that picture."

After they were gone, I realized I had not asked for her phone number and then chastised myself for mentioning the Lautrec house to my editor.

I had no choice now but to hope it would work out.

When I was back in my hotel room, I began to read the books I bought from Yoseph. While I was coming to know the history of the Toulouse area, my primary interest for this trip had been writing an article and painting old buildings, castles, landscapes, villages, and the like: but, what I was getting into hinted at something more turbulent.

I did learn that Henri Toulouse Lautrec was related to Charlemagne, and his forebears had nearly been the royal family of France, at least until the Bourbons cut in. They had been wily and capable enough to survive several upheavals. Not only the Catholic purge of the Cathars, to whom they were supportive, but through previous generosity to the public, they were able to keep their heads during the French Revolution.

What was also interesting was the area's role in the early development of Christianity. Being close to Italy and the Mediterranean, the Languedoc was one of the first places it spread. It had become widely accepted within a few hundred years. By 1309 Pope Clement V of France even found it politically advantageous to hold his court in nearby Avignon, a move that did not endear the region to the church leaders in Rome, far from it.

Mixed into this were legends of Mary Magdalene and others fleeing here shortly after Jesus was crucified. It was a plausible story. The region was accessible from Israel, particularly by boat, and it would have been something of a haven. The Gauls had only been defeated following a long and hard Roman campaign, and while no longer rebellious, they had never fully accepted their Roman occupiers either. It was the same when the region came under the dominance of nobles from Northern France. The difference can still be heard in the regional dialect that gives the area its current name, Languedoc, after the language of the Occitan region.

It was in those early Christian years that the Cathar beliefs took root, and to which they later proved such martyrs.

When the Roman Empire began to crumble, Vandals from the area participated in its downfall by sacking Rome and carrying away its treasurers, not the least of which were sacred objects of the Hebrews that the Romans had taken from the Temple in Jerusalem. In the 700's, when Islam became a dominant power, the area came under Moorish control for several hundred years. However, Muslims were tolerant of Christianity and Judaism, and those communities thrived.

It wasn't until the Moors were pushed back into Spain and Portugal in the 1100's that Toulouse again came under Western influence, and the Cathars troubles began.

I was also finding perhaps less factual, more esoteric, aspects of the story. Numerology, lay lines, symbols, and mystic revelations, while as interesting, could not be so easily plotted as the record of conquest and politics.

Suddenly I remembered the cell phone picture. I was not particularly familiar with the phone's applications, and concerned about the results of my button pushing, such as taking that call while the photograph was still coming up. I opened the phone and clicked the menu. While I was scrolling, the phone rang again.

I didn't recognize the number, and as I fumbled to hit the right button to receive the call, I thought, 'That's twice today maybe I'm not supposed to have it.'

"Hello," I said loudly. "Hello, this is Bjorn." There was a moment of silence.

"Hello, this is Bjorn. Can you hear me?" I said again, perhaps just talking to air.

"Hi, this Juliette. Are you there?" came the unexpected voice.

I couldn't believe this either. I was excited to hear from her, particularly so soon, but also a little worried. My record with relationships was a road that needed some serious repair.

"Yes, I'm here. I can hear you. Can you hear me?" I said, relieved that at least the call had come through.

"Yes. You're very clear. Sorry to call you so late, but I think I've got us into the Lautrec's. I spoke with my husband after I left, and the Count was with him. He said he could meet us tomorrow at 2. Can you make it?"

"Of course, that's amazing," I said, startled at my good luck.

"He was reluctant to agree to photographs, but I told him that would be important. He's going to think about it, so bring your camera. I'm so excited."

"You do have connections," I commented.

"It was luck. Frankly, I don't like the Count much. He's like my husband, just business, without much else to show for it. I was surprised he said yes," she added. "Can we go in your car? I will have Artemisia with me."

"Of course," I said.

"In front of the fountain at 12. Don't be late."

"That's fine," I said, guessing I telegraphed my habits.

"Good. I look forward to getting to talk a little more as well."

"Me, too, and it will be nice to see your daughter again," I said, feeling the need for a little buffer.

"I hope she's not too much trouble. He doesn't know she's coming. Tomorrow at 12."

"Goodbye," I said, feeling very upbeat.

"Bye."

I didn't know what else to say. My article would be on the big map if I could get photos, at least in art circles. Not many publications would be able to get into those rooms, much less have pictures of artwork that had never been seen in public.

I decided there wasn't too much to worry about concerning a relationship: she was married, they had a child, and that was as far as that road went. Anything more would be in my imagination, and maybe hers. Safe enough, as travel goes.

CHAPTER THREE

As I sat on the bed, I began perusing Yoseph's other books thinking maybe there was something about red dots. The only thing I found, however, was a custom of tying a red string around your wrist while reading the Kabbalah. I was becoming doubtful there would be any mention of it.

I then picked up my phone to call New York about the Lautrec's, but only getting Wendy's answering machine, I left a message with the good news. Following the call, I looked for the cell picture of the tiny flake, and finally found it.

I enlarged the photo on the phone's screen, and while I thought I could detect something, it was too blurry to see much detail. I transferred the picture to my laptop but even on the larger screen it was still too hard to tell. I found myself wishing I had equipment like in the criminal investigation TV shows, where they instantly zoom in on a speck of dust. Come to think of it, the computer did come with a photo-editing program that could enlarge down to the pixel level.

I was beginning to feel like a covert agent, decoding microdots in a foreign hotel room with closed drapes. I only needed a sleek pistol, multiple passports, and a Swiss bank account containing euros, pounds, and dollars. In my head I imagined ominous music playing in the background.

When I magnified the picture, it appeared something reddish was in the upper right corner. It looked like a dot. My imagination was again beginning to run ahead, and I was even more interested in a second look at that old text tomorrow. I returned to Yoseph's books thinking maybe there was still something about a red dot. I fell asleep reading.

What I didn't expect was the red dot, Juliette, and Artemisia, making it into my dream. It was one of those where you never quite get what you're reaching for. I was at the fountain with the Revelation manuscript in my hand. Turning the pages, I had removed the papyrus flake, which I wrapped in my handkerchief. I started talking with Juliette and some of her friends, but as I sat down on the rim of the fountain, the papyrus flake blew into the water. I was afraid the red dot would dissolve, and desperately trying to grab it before it sank. Whenever I reached out with my hand, however, the movement would push it further down and, I began to lose sight of it. At this point, Artemisia was swimming under the water like a fish, and as her face came up from below, she scooped up the flake, and smiling, put it in her mouth. Somehow I was relieved because it was now safe.

When I awoke, I remembered the dream vividly and wrote down a few points because they would likely fade. I wasn't sure whether it was composed of anything more than worries and impressions from the day before. As my thoughts drifted, I remembered the part in Revelation where St. John was advised to eat the little book handed to him by the angel, "In the mouth was sweet, but in the belly bitter." Artemisia was smiling in the dream, so maybe she hadn't gotten to the bitter part. I had heard the passage was symbolic of being born, starting with the joy of great promise but becoming hard under the conditions of the world.

Out of curiosity, I decided to look at the picture on my computer again. Somehow when I fell asleep, I had left it on, and as the screen lit up, there was the blinking message about 'improper' shutdown, and if I turned it off, anything that had not been saved would be lost. Of course, it offered no other option than to turn it off, and the message asked if that was OK. I had not saved the picture in the photo program, and hoped it was still in the computer somewhere. I turned it off, cursing myself, and the geeks with their cynical 'OK' message. I quickly turned it back on, staring with fixed concern as it booted up.

The screen finally came to life, but having no idea if I had stored the picture, I wondered if it was even there. I checked the search menu and couldn't find it, realizing I didn't know what it was named. After a while, I began to conclude it was lost. I then opened my phone, and immediately it started flashing a low battery message. Having had enough of warnings I ignored it, and opened up the pictures. The photo was still there.

I admonished myself about needing to be more careful.

My time was running short, so I skipped a shower, put on clean clothes, did a quick shave, and was out the door, camera slung over my shoulder and the traditional narrow reporter's notebook stuffed into my back pocket.

It was a beautiful day, and the city was enveloped in an early morning glow that lived up to its nickname La Ville Rose, or The

Pink City. The local stone and brick used over the centuries were red in tone, and the same color had been incorporated into many contemporary structures. I wondered if there was any relation to the red dot.

I drove to the church administrative offices, went through the formal sign-in procedure, chatted with the clerk, and as I expected, was again enveloped in the quiet sanctuary of the records area. As I sat down, my heart started racing. I bushed my hand over the thick leather cover of the Cathar book, gently turning the stiff pages to the place where I had left the little chip. As a buffer to disappointment, I took the attitude that it would not be there, perhaps by some nefarious plot that had unfolded in darkened corridors during the night. Unknown church agents were scheming to deny the chip ever existed in hopes of seeding doubt when I found it was gone.

However, I was not to be disappointed as I turned to the seventh page of the book. The flake was where I left it and still bright against the aged parchment. I could not understand how anyone could have missed it. Yet, that was probably the reason. No one had looked at the book in a very long time. It was not something that would warrant very much scholarly or artistic attention. The lone illuminated letter at the beginning was not an outstanding example of the craft, and the text was quite orthodox. Even its age was not unusual amid the enormous collection. Other than its pedigree, there was nothing to make it stand out except for this small flake, at least to me.

As I examined it again, I was thrilled to see just what Karl had mentioned. There was a little red dot in the upper right corner that I had missed because it was on the edge; in fact, part of it had been clipped off. I had checked my camera equipment at the desk, and I did not want to risk another phone picture, so I looked hard at this little mystery, committing it to my visual memory rather than a digital one.

I had read enough on Hebrew now to get my bearings. The letter looked like a Y, and though I was taking a leap with my other suppositions, there was the red dot.

I was reminded of my dream and wondered if I should lick it. Perhaps it contained a magic potion that would send me into a state of divine hallucination, and God would be revealed through the magic of the ancient Cathars. I realized I was getting carried away.

Examining the book, I noticed the flake was on the seventh

page. As the Cathars were versed in sacred numbers and geometry, I thought that might be a clue. In the age of Cathedrals, the architects sought to incorporate the divine proportion into their buildings. But, of course, there was disagreement about the true proportion so many cathedrals were based on different formulas. Still, any building designed using a consistent ratio will have at least some uniformity and grace. I liked Michelangelo's answer, "Proportion is in the eye."

I decided to go in another seven pages, thinking perhaps that was the formula used here. But I found nothing. There were only 40 pages, and I tried various combinations of numbers. I wound up looking on every page and even the back and front covers but found nothing more. I thought of looking for chips in other books but eventually decided against it: not for lack of perseverance, but because I had a feeling I hadn't found the flake, rather it had found me.

CHAPTER FOUR

I went to the Park a little early following the church visit and called New York. Wendy was as excited about the prospect of seeing the private Lautrec art as I was. She spent time in the Languedoc and had even thought of doing the assignment herself. I liked her, she was a good editor, one of the best I'd had, and I did not want to disappoint her.

I hinted about my find at Saint Sernin and having stumbled into the area's mythic past.

"That is probably hard to avoid," she said lightly but a little cautiously. "Remember, this is about Lautrec, not you cracking the da Vinci code."

At 12:00 Juliette drove up, with Artemisia in the back seat. I hoped she could keep her occupied if things became involved and took some time.

"Hello. Have a good morning?" she asked. "Artemisia is not in school today, and I couldn't leave her. It could make things a little complicated. I didn't mention her to the Count either. If I have to, I will take her through the museum if you get tied up."

I was beginning to like her more and more.

"The morning has been OK," I said. "I'll tell you about it on the way."

The drive from Toulouse to the Chateau du Bosc is about 30 miles. The road flows through a region used for thousands of years by Roman armies, French crusaders, rumbling oxcarts, wandering Jews, singing troubadours, conquering Arabs, kings, Cathars, and those who painted the horses, bulls, and mammoths in the nearby caves of Lascaux. The notched stick of history is long here. If only hills and stones could talk.

While Toulouse lies in a river plain, to the east are mountains, limestone cliffs, and unique stone outcroppings. The imposing natural features made superb sites for castles and watchtowers, the high rocky cliffs making them almost impregnable. Streams and rivers cascade through the terrain, which helped the region, powering mills and machinery in the early industrial age. The water, fertile soil, and a long growing season also make it something of a

21

breadbasket and the home to many hot springs.

In the Middle Ages, these features gave the Counts of Toulouse some security when they began resisting an increasingly powerful and warlike Church. The Albigensian Crusade was ostensibly against the heretical Cathars, but it was also the prospect of wealth and land that helped bring forces to the Church's cause. Northern French nobles, and the King, saw an opportunity for the spoils of war a lot closer to home than Palestine.

"So, how was your morning," Juliette asked as we drove the smooth highway through a countryside dotted with vineyards and well-tended fields.

"I found that little flake again, right where I left it, and it was as bright as I remembered," I said. "And that friend of Yoseph's, Karl, was right. There was a little red dot, which I hadn't noticed before. I still don't know what it means."

"Do you have any clues?"

"Not really. I tried every seven pages, every 12 pages, and every 144th word, just a whole lot of combinations. I wound up looking at every page. The only thing I didn't do was turn the book inside out."

"They would appreciate that," she said.

"Tomorrow could be my last day there, and I might ask them about it."

"Hmmm," was all she replied.

"Before I do that, I am going to talk to Karl. Perhaps he will reveal the mystery."

"Don't give up," she stated.

Artemisia was going through a very well-worn book of her own in the back seat. She saw me looking at her while pretending she didn't, though her page-turning became much more deliberate. She seemed to be counting on her fingers.

"That is her book on sign language," Juliette said.

"But she can speak. I heard her," I said rather naively.

"Yes, but she has trouble hearing how words sound, which makes it hard. She knows how to read lips, so don't let her fool you, she knows what you're saying."

"It's more like she knows just what I'm thinking."

Juliette laughed, "Tell me."

By this time, Artemisia had leaned forward and put her head over the front seat. She reached out and touched my lips with her forefinger, gently tracing its profile. Then she touched her own lips.

"She likes you," Juliette said quietly. "She only does that with people she trusts."

Turning to Artemisia, she told her, "You should ask permission before you do that." Then after a pause, "I wish I could do more for her, but William insists she go to a Catholic school, but they are in the dark ages when it comes to this."

"I think she is doing OK," I said.

"Thanks, but advances have been made on how to teach the deaf to speak. As I said, I am not sure I am cut out for this."

We were now approaching the road into Albi and the Pont Vieux, the thousand-year-old bridge with eight high arches spanning the Tarn River. The city itself is a vision of the old world, with tiers of stone buildings, their red-tiled roofs rising on a steep hill to Albi's centerpiece, the Gothic Cathedral of Ste. Cécile. It is the largest brick cathedral in France and the only one with original polychrome painted statues still intact. Nearby is the main Toulouse-Lautrec Museum, housed in the 13th Century Palais de la Berbie, one of the best-preserved castles in the country.

I could imagine when troubadours thrived under the lenient hand of the Counts, and Albi was one of the most prosperous and cultured places in Europe. It has retained some of its former self, unlike the closed heaviness you can feel in sections of many medieval cities. Artists have always been attracted to the area. Pablo Picasso and Georges Braque came to escape the summer heat of Paris during their hot pursuit of cubism.

The Chateau du Bosc is just outside of the city. It was where Henri spent his frequently convalescent childhood, and the family gathered for hunting and riding expeditions amid their extensive holdings. It was an exclusive world. In Henri's time, a chest filled with money was by the front door, and when family or guests needed a little extra cash as they went out, which was frequent, they just reached in.

"Here we are, right on time," Juliette said. "We are supposed to use the side door, so we don't have to get involved with the 'viewing public'. We are supposed to meet him there."

As we pulled up to park the car, I was both humbled and excited. There were very few who had seen the family's private collection of paintings, books, and treasures, going back not just to Henri's time, but when centuries were counted in three digits and roman numerals.

I got out of the car and opened the door for Artemisia, who was wearing pink jelly shoes, a pale purple dancer's skirt, and two layers of yellow and white T-shirts. She had a green ribbon in her tussled hair and was clutching the red purse, her little chest by the door.

We went around the side of the building, which was sizable. It was built in the 1400's as a fortress, with four sides surrounding a quadrangle courtyard. It had been renovated into a residence as wars subsided, but windows were still few.

Many of Henri's artworks passed to the family when he died at the age of 37 from alcoholism and syphilis, exacerbated by his congenital bone disease. The family remains protective of its reputation, but Henri's prominence could not keep such details out of his public history.

Holding her mother's hand, Artemisia was swaying back and forth in her own world as Juliette knocked on the door. At first, there was no answer, so she knocked again, this time a little louder. We waited a moment and heard someone fumbling with the handle. Then the door opened a crack. Juliette said "hello" and gently pushed it open a bit more to peer in. Behind it, in a wheelchair, was an elderly woman in her mid 80's. She motioned for us to come in.

"The Count invited us today," Juliette told her. "But it seems he is not here yet."

The woman nodded, and when we were all the way into the foyer, she pushed the door shut with her cane. She smiled at Artemisia and then sat quietly looking at Juliette and me, not saying anything. Her eyes were bright, though she was thin and very pale. I guessed she'd had a stroke.

There was no one else around, and Juliette asked, "Do you know how long the Count will be? He said he would meet us here at 2."

The woman continued to just look, and then shook her head. It was an impatient shake, which I took to mean that she didn't know, or that she didn't approve of him being late, or maybe him.

She had not invited us to come in any further, though we could see a living room facing into the courtyard past the hall.

"Maybe it is better we step outside to wait," Juliette commented.

The woman started struggling with the chair's wheels, trying to turn herself around. I leaned over and asked if I could help. She grabbed the front of my shirt with a birdlike hand and pulled me closer, whispering in my ear. It was mostly a whistling sound, and I couldn't make it out. She pulled me closer and did the same thing again. I still didn't know what she was trying to say and glanced around to see any staff to help us.

24

The woman then looked at Juliette, and something in her eye caused Juliette to say, "I think she wants to go in the room behind us."

Working with Artemisia had given her a sixth sense when it came to the unspoken. The woman nodded her head more vigorously and tried to help me as I wheeled the chair through the doorway into the next room, which led to yet another.

There were paintings on the soft red walls, and the room was evenly lit from the windows facing the courtyard. I was impressed at how balanced and relaxed things felt. There were no stale corners as I'd experienced in other old buildings. Instead, this had been renovated to embody the regional light, beautiful and bright. The rooms were cared for, and it felt like a home.

She kept pushing the wheels, and we passed through the first room without stopping and into the next. Then I realized this was what we had come to see, the family library and private collection. The windows were draped to keep out curious eyes and protect the vulnerable artwork from direct sunlight. However, it was not dark, as the soft light from a few table lamps gave it a gentle glow. On the wall facing us was a large painting by Henri. It was a version of his famous circus rider, only the horses were larger, and the rider was black, not white. He made a series of the theme, sealing his reputation as a master draughtsman, particularly for the art of the poster.

Around the room were other paintings I had never seen in a museum or catalog, along with drawings and watercolors, some of which had personal remarks in the margins. There were also some of Henri's letters and a few childhood drawings. It was not just Henri on the walls, however. There were sketches by other family members of horses, hunts, and carriages, as they had a participatory love of the arts. Henri, however, was the only one who acquired artistic fame.

Juliette had wandered over to a small sculpture on a table; it was a Degas bronze ballerina, wearing a tutu, now a bit of faded pink gauze. It would be a prize for any museum in the world, and we couldn't resist touching it. I speculated Henri had acquired it directly from Degas. They were key figures in a group of avant-garde artists, including Gauguin, Van Gogh, and Cezanne.

The woman was motioning for us to come over, as Juliette and I were being entranced by the treasure trove. She had me push her to a table that contained a few leather-bound books. One was a Bible, and I was a little shocked when I realized it was as old as the ones at St. Sernin. I had been handling those with kid gloves, but this one was just lying on the table. Behind it was a bookcase filled with volumes that ranged across centuries, and the Lautrec's name was likely mentioned in many of them. They were originals by Voltaire, Dumas, maybe even St. Augustine. The titles covered the language spectrum, Arabic, Hebrew, Latin, French, Greek, and some I didn't recognize. I understood why they wanted to keep it private; it was their history, even though it was also the history of the country.

The woman had picked up the Bible, and I noticed Henri's name was on the inside cover, along with some papers. I assumed it had been his, though probably not the one he kept at his bordello-like studio in Paris. It had a hard leather cover, much like the one in St. Sernin, only the embossed and gilded letters were not worn off. I noticed a little flash of red as she opened the cover, and the loose papers fell out onto the floor. I was about to reach down to get them when she waved me off and began jabbing at the inside page while looking me straight in the eye. She was trying to say something and only stopped to see if we understood. Then she resumed her agitated fumbling and talking and looking. I had no idea what she wanted or was doing, and Juliette was also at a loss this time.

Then Artemisia, who had been sitting on a large leather couch, quietly came to her side. The old woman looked at her, and as she kept talking, Artemisia put her fingers to her lips, just as she had done to me in the car. Juliette was about ready to grab her arm when Artemisia said, "Look." Juliette was a little taken aback.

"What is she saying?" she asked her daughter.

Artemisia then began to speak in sign language. Juliette signed back. Artemisia shrugged her shoulders and began signing again. The woman was still pulling at the cover of the invaluable book, the hardened centuries-old stitches straining and cracking. I started to reach for it, but she nudged me away again, all the while repeating something.

"Artemisia can read her lips," Juliette whispered, and in some disbelief, added, "I think she wants us to tear the cover."

Her efforts were becoming more frenzied. Finally, she grabbed the aged cover and yanked it so hard all the pages ripped loose from the binding. With a loud crack the cover broke free, and was hanging only by a thin strip of leather.

Juliette and I were too startled to move. The book that had survived hundreds of years of wear and war and weather, the childhood Bible of Henri Toulouse Lautrec, was now a wreck. The woman kept pulling at the cover in desperation like she wanted to rip it apart. Then finally, she tore it open and stuck her thin hand between the layers. After a moment, she pulled out what looked like a sealed envelope. She looked at me with piercing, pleading eyes, and mumbled something.

Artemisia signed to me, and Juliette quickly translated, "She wants you to take it."

Hesitating, I slowly reached over and removed the envelope from her hand. She looked at me intently, but then her eyes became fixed, and a shadow seemed to pass over them. Giving a little shudder, a tremor began on the left side of her face, swept down her shoulder to her arm, and she slumped over, breathing heavily. She was having a stroke.

"We need to get some help," I said, but just as I turned to go out the door, the Count was coming in, along with a staff member.

"What..." he began to say.

"She's having a stroke," Juliette told him.

Then all hell broke loose. The Count began shouting for more help, Artemisia was crying, the old woman was trembling in her chair, and assistants came rushing in. Soon an ambulance was wailing up the road, with its horn pulsing like the Gestapo giving chase.

Juliette and I stepped to the side, watching. It was as if we weren't even in the room. Medical personnel rushed in, pulling supplies out of satchels, while tubes and wires seemed to spring from equipment flashing and beeping urgent warnings.

Juliette knelt to hold Artemisia, who buried her face in her mother's shoulder.

"I am going to take her out," she said.

I decided to go with them. There was nothing I could do except get in the way. As we made it to the beautiful red room, the Count came out with rapid steps looking very displeased.

"I'm so sorry, we..." Juliette began to say.

The Count cut her off angrily.

"What were you doing in there with her!"

"She answered the door, you weren't here," Juliette said, shaking a little.

"Couldn't you see she's an invalid!" he shouted.

He gave me a sharp glance, and then turning back to Juliette, clenched his jaw.

"I never want you to come back."

27

He then turned and walked away as stridently as he had come. Juliette's face was white, and as we passed through the brightly decorated red room and out the front door that held such promise just a few minutes ago, she started crying quietly. I put my arm around her shoulder.

"He's under a lot of stress, let it go," and under my breath, "the bastard."

The sun was shining in a clear blue sky, and a small crowd attracted by the commotion had gathered at the edge of the parking lot. The ambulance was parked by the side door, its lights flashing and radio crackling. We stood back and waited until they rolled the aunt out on a stretcher. She was still alive, and they were holding an IV bottle above her as they placed her in the ambulance.

The Count initially followed behind the stretcher and then went back inside, never looking our way. I could feel Juliette wanting to go over and say something, but he never gave her a chance. We returned to the car, and I suggested we stop in Albi for some tea, just to let things settle. We found a small café, and Artemisia, who had calmed down, ordered an orange soda. Juliette had a cup of tea, and not being a big tea drinker, I tried out the local bottled water.

"I really didn't understand his reaction, it seemed so uncalled for. All you tried to do was help," I said.

"Oh, it wasn't that. I know I should never have asked him, but I wanted to help you see the collection. It's always been strange, his business relationship with Bill. He was pleasant when I first met him, but at a conference he showed up in the lounge one night. He'd been drinking and Bill wasn't back yet. I think he was trying to pick me up, but with him it's hard to tell. I'm afraid he's the kind of person who has to destroy what he can't get."

"What can he do to you?" I asked rather naively.

"He has a lot of influence. I'm glad you were there," then after a moment, she asked, "I wonder what's in that envelope?"

CHAPTER FIVE

In the chaos, I had forgotten about it. It was in my jacket pocket. I took it out gently, trying not to damage the fragile corners. The envelope was obviously old and about six inches wide, eight inches long, and made of vellum sealed with wax. There was nothing written on the outside.

"Let's open it," Juliette said.

I was hesitant. It needed to be done carefully, and the only thing available was the butter knife on the table.

"Let's wait. I want to do this right," then I added, "Maybe we should return it. She seemed very confused, and we have no idea what it is."

"He told us never to come back," she said with a sly smile.

We agreed to do it in Toulouse, where I had a thin artist's palette knife that was less likely to damage the envelope. I thought it should be done by a trained conservator, but getting someone else involved would raise a lot of questions. I carefully put the packet back in my pocket.

I was disappointed at not getting the scoop for the magazine, and having the door slammed shut on whatever collaboration I might have had with the Lautrec family. I could not have done worse in that respect, though that might be OK based on meeting the Count. I would also be putting off my call to New York.

Still, I had been able to see the inside of the family library. Given what had just occurred, I had no way of using it in the article, but it was useful as background information nonetheless. There was also the envelope.

As we were driving home, I was thinking of the old woman.

"I wonder how she is doing?"

"I will find out, my husband will hear," Juliette replied. "But I can only imagine what he will hear about us."

It occurred to me if she and her husband were not getting along, and the Count was vindictive enough to exploit anything to satisfy his anger, this was quickly spinning out of my comfort zone.

"She certainly seemed intent on getting that envelope out and giving it to us," I said, partly to shift the subject. "It's almost like she planned it. But if she did, why us?"

"I don't know," Juliette replied.

While we were talking, Artemisia had leaned over from the back seat like before and reached out again to touch my lips with her finger, and then she unexpectedly did the same to her mother.

Juliette was about to correct her when she stopped short and said, "Thank you, Artemisia. Now I think I know."

At first, I did not understand what she meant. Did the woman tell Artemisia something in that brief time before she went unconscious? Had I failed to notice something, or was I simply too slow to comprehend what was unfolding?

"She trusted us," Juliette said. "I don't know if she knew we were coming, maybe it was an inner compulsion. She probably knew she didn't have much time."

Then turning to me with a determined look said, "We have to find out what's in that envelope. It's important, and she could not give it to her family."

Taken aback at that last thought, I couldn't imagine what it would be. Was it her final will, some dark family secret? Whatever it was, I had not come to France to get involved in personal or legal battles, particularly with the Lautrecs.

"So what do you think's in it?" I asked, putting my hand over the pocket with the envelope as if touching it might bring an answer.

"Something special," Juliette said.

The drive back to Toulouse found us silent, and in our private thoughts, as we passed through countryside that had seen its share of joy and tragedy, mystery, and political intrigues, and even this.

We wound up in rush hour traffic and did not get back until nearly six. Artemisia was hungry, and Juliette did not want to be home too late, but she was anxious to see what was in the envelope. She called her husband and explained what had happened, not mentioning what we'd been given. I didn't know if she had considered how her husband might react to her coming to my room, even with Artemisia, but I had.

"We could open it tomorrow, if that's better for you," I suggested.

"Why?" she said. "Let's open it now."

On the way to my room, she bought a container of fruit juice for her daughter, and Artemisia seemed pleased with that. Next, I pulled out my painting supplies and found the palette knife. The triangular blade was thin but not sharp and less likely to damage the envelope.

I took the envelope from my pocket, and the corners were a little bent as I'd feared, but otherwise OK. As we examined it to see the best way to proceed, I felt part sinner and part saint: after all, it did come from a Bible. I also wondered how I had gotten into this.

The envelope was made of a sheet of vellum and looked quite new. I noticed it had been soaked in beeswax, a remarkably ageless and waterproof material.

It was hard to tell how old it was from casual observation. The ancient Greeks used colored beeswax for their paintings in a method called encaustic. As a result, portraits made 17-centuries ago look as if they were made yesterday.

"You really think we should do this?" I asked one more time.

Juliette didn't even bother to answer.

I carefully slipped the blade under one of the flaps and ran it along the seam. The seal broke with a gentle crack, freeing the vellum from centuries of bondage. A flower-like scent arose as the natural fragrance of the newly exposed wax filled the room.

"Sweet," Juliette said, smiling.

Artemisia had come over to watch and nodded her head in agreement.

I was glad the seal had been so easy to separate, and the envelope was still intact. I lifted the flap, but the vellum had become stiff with age and offered some resistance. Fearful of it breaking along the fold, I paused for a moment, but not seeing any other option, I bent it back. Juliette's face was now close to mine as we both peered inside. She looked over at me briefly and then back. I felt a double pleasure, and possibly double trouble.

The envelope was somewhat translucent, and a pale glow lit the interior. A sheaf of paper with golden brown edges, perhaps four sheets in all, was securely in place. I tried to gently bulge the envelope to make some space, but the sheets didn't move.

Suddenly I felt a quick movement and, looking down, saw pink liquid spreading under my elbow and advancing quickly under the envelope. I jerked my hand upward, pulling the envelope out of the way. Juliette gave a start, and both of us jumped back as fruit juice slid across the table and began dripping over the side.

"Artemisia!" Juliette cried as she grabbed the juice container and turned it right side up, splattering some of it.

Artemisia looked stunned and helpless and about to cry. I got up and stepped away from the table while holding the envelope high as Juliette found a towel and began wiping up the juice.

"You have to be more careful," Juliette told her sternly, and then turning to me, she said, "I'm so sorry."

I was disappointed, but not surprised, to find a couple of red beads on the once pristine envelope. I used a tissue to carefully wipe them off, hoping the wax would protect the sheets inside. The juice came off easily, but left two droplet stains. I could only imagine what a conservator would say, but it was too late. The 21st century had left its mark, with red dots no less.

"It's OK," I said, trying to downplay that I was feeling a little sick. "It's not much, and it was an accident."

"Maybe we can get the spots out," Juliette said without much enthusiasm.

"Perhaps, but let's not try it now."

After a moment, Juliette said with a little grin, "Thanks for not getting mad."

That took the edge off. I sat down, and Juliette brought Artemisia back to the table and told her to just watch. Artemisia was noticeably relaxed.

We quickly found our heads together again, peering into the envelope. This time I was more successful at loosening the sheets and slowly began pulling them out. I could see they were not made of paper, but papyrus, giving me images of the Dead Sea Scrolls crumbling to dust under my touch. Yet, these pages were remarkably durable and felt almost fresh. I imagined that had something to do with the protective wax envelope.

It took about five minutes to remove the four pages. They were indeed writings, crisp black marks on the golden-brown surfaces. The letters appeared to be Hebrew, but somehow not quite. Each sheet varied in size, and some looked more like personal letters or notes than texts. On the bottom of one was the letter Y.

"I think these are letters from God," I joked, but Juliette didn't laugh.

Whatever either of us had been expecting, it wasn't this, and then Juliette's phone rang. It was her husband, wondering where she and Artemisia were. We had lost track of the time, and now she had to go. She said she would come back tomorrow, but it would have to be in the evening.

While I was sorry to see her leave, it gave me an opportunity to examine the letters more deliberately. I soon had the pages spread out on the table, making sure not to disturb their order. Writing covered most of the first sheet, another page was about three-quarters full, and yet another was smaller like a letter or note.

From the characters, I had the impression that three of the sheets were written by the same hand, masterful yet simple. None of them had the small, almost effeminate writing I had seen in the Bibles and books at the church; of course, this was not Latin either. Then there was the last sheet, which was more unusual. It was broken into three columns, and there were marks, little dots, by some of the letters. It had an almost rhythmic spacing, reminding me of a poem or sonnet.

As I looked at the sheets, I kept being drawn to the last one. I could not read it to save my life, yet I had a feeling I knew what it said. It wasn't so much the words as an overall impression. My mind seemed to clear, and my perspective changed. I became aware of feelings and thoughts, not all of them pleasant that I'd had for a long time. The moment passed almost as quickly as it had come, and I didn't quite understand what had happened; yet I was aware something had changed, like comparing the reality in a dream to that of waking.

I can't remember what I did for a while after that. I eventually decided to take photographs of the documents. I pulled out some of my lights, and with my good camera, I took close-ups of each page so they could be easily read. I thought I would e-mail them to a con-servator friend, who might even know how to read them.

I gathered the pages, still making sure they were in proper order, and placed them between pieces of museum-quality matboard I used for watercolors. I had some glassine I used to protect my paintings, and I put a sheet between each of the papers. These I placed into a large envelope, including the vellum packet, and all of it went into my locking leather briefcase. I was beginning to worry that the exposure to air, moisture, and light, would cause rapid deterioration.

When I went to bed, I looked through the books I had bought from Yoseph, and realized why the letters looked a little different than Hebrew, they might be Aramaic.

CHAPTER SIX

I was awakened by a phone call from Wendy in New York in the morning. I had no idea why she would call at this hour; it was nearly midnight there. She was excited about the Lautrec prospect, and as I hadn't called, she was eager to know how it had gone. I think she'd had a few drinks, too. She was very disappointed by the news. While I told her what had happened, I did not mention the envelope, though hinted I may have something else. I am not sure she believed anything could have been better than the Lautrecs. We agreed I should try and mend some fences, and she suggested I keep Juliette out of the picture. I said I would see what I could do, but neither of us believed there was much hope.

As I was dressing, I suddenly remembered I had agreed to meet Dieter at the Café last night, which I had completely forgotten. I did not have his phone number and could only hope he hadn't shown up either. I wanted to crawl back into bed and get up on the other side. Yet I also felt an unusual detachment and that somehow it was OK.

Once out the door, I headed straight for Yoseph's bookstore. He was not open yet, so I went to the café across the street to wait. It was a chance to gather my thoughts, and I was starting to consider the lost Lautrec story, the parchment envelope, and Juliette and Artemisia, when someone sat down beside me. It was Karl Yunger.

"Hello," he said. "May I join you?"

Karl was as carefully dressed as he'd been the other day, and his eyes were ageless, in contrast to his neatly combed white hair.

"Have you had any more adventures at the church?" he asked.

I told him I had again found the little piece of papyrus with the letter Y, and in fact, it did have a red dot on it.

"So, what does it mean?" I asked.

"It means you have found something," Karl said after a moment. "So, tell me a little more about what you are doing here."

We talked for a good part of the morning. He was interested in where I'd grown up, what I had studied in school, and my work as a journalist and artist. He was particularly interested in my reporting, so I told him a few of my better stories.

Karl had never been to the US, but as a child, during World War Two, he learned English as a runner between the French resistance and the Allies. He also helped hide German Jews who had fled from the Nazis to France. It is not unusual for people in Europe to know several languages, and Karl was fluent in French, German, English, Hebrew, and who knows what else. The Germans had persecuted his family, too, but they avoided deportation with the help of friends who opposed the Vichy government's policy of handing over French Jews.

It was hard to tell just what he was after with me. The papyrus chip was obviously of interest, but he seemed to be looking for something more. I could sense the gears whirling in his head when he suddenly said, "I think you should look inside the book."

At first, I did not know what he meant until I realized it was the Cathar book in St. Sernin.

"But I did, I went over every page, and I couldn't find anything. Not that I really knew what I was looking for."

"No, inside," he paused. "The cover."

I was taken aback and immediately thought of the Lautrec Bible. How could he know?

"But that would destroy it!" I said. "I'm not sure the church would appreciate that, and who knows where I'd wind up."

Karl just smiled. "I wasn't suggesting you take it apart. But look at it closely."

He told me there had long been rumors that someone, possibly a Cathar, had hidden some priceless secret writings. Where they might be, and what they say, had been lost. Whoever hid them may have died, or been killed, before being able to pass them on.

"That's why you were interested in the Cathar book in the cathedral," I said.

He nodded.

"Maybe we should just ask the Church to look into it if it's something that concerns them. They probably know about it anyway. "

"They do, and they don't," he said.

I gave him a puzzled look, and Karl said nothing for quite a while.

"It's only been in my family. You are the only one outside of it that has been told, ever. But, you have found something that no one ever has. A key that will unlock a great mystery."

It was my turn to be quiet. I could tell that this was serious by the timber of his voice, eyes, and posture. Now I understood why he had asked all the questions about my journalism career. I had told him I had worked with confidential information as a reporter and once even broke that confidentiality, and it was something I would never do again.

"I understand," I finally said. "So that's the red dot?"

"Yes," he said quietly.

"And the Y?" I asked.

"It's a name," he answered, "No one knows whose, but the Cathars went to their deaths protecting this."

This was a centuries-old family legend, and I knew from experience that it was sometimes better to leave such stories alone, as hard facts have a way of turning them into disappointments. Yet, there was the red dot at St. Sernin. There was also the Lautrec Bible. Part of me suspected I'd already found something Karl was looking for. I wanted to tell him about the letters, but first I had to ask Juliette. They were as much hers as mine, if ours at all.

I also wasn't about to damage the Church's book but thought it wouldn't hurt to examine it a little more. So I asked Karl to tell me everything he could. I did not want to go further into this situation blind. I also hinted I had something to tell him, but it had to wait as others were involved.

It was his turn to say, "I understand."

I never went into the bookstore. While we were talking, Yoseph had come and opened up, waving to us from across the street. By now, he would be very curious about what we were discussing, but I thought I'd leave that to Karl.

CHAPTER SEVEN

I drove to St. Sernin thinking of what I might find, but first, I wanted to ask Juliette about Karl. Once at the church I called her, but before I could say anything, she said things were not good with the Lautrecs.

The Count had called her husband after we left. The elderly woman was his aunt, and she had suffered a stroke, and this was her second. She remained unconscious, and the doctors were not optimistic. To make matters worse, the Count was now accusing us of theft. He had found the torn Bible and claimed I had taken advantage of his aunt's condition to rifle through the Library. His version was she had caught me with the Bible and tried to get it back. In the ensuing struggle, the book was damaged, and the exertion brought on the stroke. He said he also had a witness.

"You're kidding," I said in shock.

"No," she said. "I told you I did not like William's friends."

"Does your husband believe this?"

"I told him it was a total fabrication, but all he was concerned about was his business relationship with the Count, and our reputation. He told me not to see you again, and that he would get me out of it."

"That might be a good idea," I said.

After we left the Chateau, I did not have a good feeling, but I never imagined it would turn into this. The Count was malevolent, and I had walked right into it. This was a serious criminal charge if he pursued it. I could be arrested, and with his connections, anything might happen. At the least, it could mean the end of my assignment.

"William can't tell me what to do," Juliette said. "I still want to come over tonight. They don't know about the envelope, and I want to see the letters. We can talk more then."

I wasn't sure if she knew how serious this could be, particularly should the aunt die, but I was thankful she was undaunted.

I was very worried about the envelope now. How would I explain it to the police? To them, it would confirm the Count's story about the theft. Nonetheless, it would have to be returned. I began to think I should go into St. Sernin to pray rather than search for more documents.

At the front desk, the clerk told me he had retrieved several of their finest examples of illumination. I asked if I might be allowed to see the Book of Revelation again. As I waited, I could hear the birds outside and the fountain in the courtyard. Perhaps this whole Lautrec thing would blow over.

When he brought the book, I again half expected the chip not to be there, but it had not moved, and continued to glow with its faint red dot. I examined the front and back covers, and while I knew a little about the craft of bookbinding from one of my artistic tangents, I had never come across anything quite like it. On first look, the binding was relatively simple; however, on closer examination, I saw it was put together where one pull on the right thread would release the pages from the heavy leather cover, just as had happened with the Lautrec Bible. There was no standard for bookbinding in the Middle Ages, as each book was made by hand and essentially one of a kind.

As I studied the cover, it seemed slightly thicker than might be called for, but heavy covers were used back then to keep the parchment from curling in the damp. Both books had similar engraved markings, and it was possible they were related, but I didn't feel like taking any more chances. Karl was going to be disappointed.

I closed the book and paused. It was strangely like the night before, when I knew what was in the last letter even though I couldn't read it. I put my hand on the cover. The faint sound of birds and the fountain came again from the courtyard. It felt as if I was looking at the book through someone else's eyes. The clerk came in and was about to tell me they were closing when he, too, paused and stood silently. After a long moment, I handed him the book. He simply nodded and left, neither one of us saying a word.

When I left the building, I did not see anyone, and standing in front of the fountain, listening to the water and the birds, I was troubled yet calmly detached. It was Friday, and if I thought of returning, they would not be open again until Monday.

I drove back to the hotel to be there when Juliette arrived. She had not given a specific time, but I assumed it would be after five. Once in my room, I unlocked the briefcase and took out the carefully wrapped letters. I did not remove them from the package I'd made, not wanting to expose them to light and humidity more than I had to.

I decided to call my art conservator friend, thinking he might be of help. He worked from his home in Oregon, restoring old master paintings and documents, and it was likely he would be in.

"John, this is Bjorn," I said when I got him on the phone.

"Bjorn, what a surprise. How are you doing? Where are you, close by?"

"I'm good. No, I'm not in town, in France actually. I'm writing an article for an art magazine."

"That's wonderful," John said. "You know I lived in Paris for five years, that's where I trained for my restoration work."

"Hmm, that's right."

I had forgotten he had done that and a Paris connection might be useful.

"Listen, I've something to ask. I've come across some documents that are quite old. I can't read them, and I know little about this stuff. I was wondering if you might be able to help?"

"Sure, I can try," he replied

"This has to be confidential," I added cautiously, not knowing what the ethics were for conservators.

I then told him the story about the elderly woman at the Lautrec's and the Count's possible threat. He was thoughtful for a moment.

"Sorry it's such a mess. There is increasing concern about the removal, or theft, of antiquities these days. I'd be very careful, you might not want to take them out of the country," he said.

"I'm sure I will have to return them, but before I do, would it be OK if I emailed pictures to you? I'd really like to know what they are."

"That would be fine, and if I can't help, I know others who could, even my teacher in Paris. He's been doing this for nearly 50 years."

"Could I send them to you now?" I asked.

"Yes," he said.

I sent the pictures and then called him right back. As he pulled them up on his computer, I could hear little murmurs.

"Where did you get these?" he finally asked.

"The woman pulled them out of the cover."

"It looks more like Aramaic than Hebrew. I don't know the language, but I can recognize it. It was used in the Middle East between 200 BC and 300 AD, if I remember right. It's the language Jesus spoke. If these texts are that old their condition is amazing. It makes me think they are fakes," he said.

"Could be," I replied, even hoping they were.

"I'd like to show them to someone. He could translate them, and knows more about that era than I do. I mainly restore artwork."

"That would be fine, whatever you think," I replied. "Just don't tell him where you got them."

"Of course," he said.

As we were talking, every so often, I could hear him murmur "wow" or "Jesus," or an expletive, obviously looking at the pictures. We left it that he would call me when he had something.

Juliette finally came and apologized for being late. Artemisia was with her father tonight, but she first had to pick her up after school and take her home.

We talked about the situation with the Count. The aunt was in the hospital and still unconscious. William, meanwhile, had spoken with the Count, telling him that Juliette barely knew me and had been as shocked as anyone about what happened. I was made out to be the perpetrator, an unscrupulous American writer who had used Juliette to gain access to the Library, and get a hot story.

The witness turned out to be a staff member who said he saw things from a distance, but Juliette said she did not think anyone saw us, and he said it just to please the Count.

"William doesn't know that I'm here," Juliette concluded.

"What did you tell him?"

"Nothing, he sometimes doesn't ask."

"Oh, that reminds me, I was supposed to meet Dieter at the Café yesterday," I said.

"Let's take a look at the letters, and if there's time, maybe we can go there after," she said.

I carefully unwrapped the package, and spread the papyrus sheets on the table one at a time. They continued to look as fresh as when we first removed them from the envelope. The inked letters were black and sharp, and the papyrus was as flexible as paper. She examined the pages closely, lightly touching one or two.

"What do you think they are?" she finally asked.

"Last night I emailed a few pictures to a conservator I know in the US. He says the writing isn't Hebrew, but possibly Aramaic, which he said would date them between 200 BC and 300 AD, give or take. They appear in such good condition he suspects forgeries, but I don't think so. If the writing is Aramaic, he knows someone who can translate it."

"Can he be trusted?" she asked.

"I think so." She gave me a querulous look. "He's a friend, he won't tell anybody where they came from."

She nodded, "OK."

"We are going to have to give them back," I said.

"That will not be easy, and worse, confirm what the Count already believes," she replied.

"We still have to do it. He may not buy our story, and it could make matters worse, but I don't want this to get more out of hand."

"There might be another way, "Juliette said slowly, and then outlined what she was thinking.

While William had told her not to do anything more around the Lautrecs, she genuinely cared for the old woman and wanted to visit her at the hospital. Perhaps she could slip the envelope into some of the aunt's things. The lady seemed a bit eccentric, and her family might not find it too unusual when they found them.

"I don't think that would fly," I said.

"It might be worth a try," she replied.

While it was a bad idea, I also didn't look forward to explaining the envelope to the Count, much less the police. If no one ever knew, what harm could it do? Despite my concerns, we agreed she could take the envelope and see how it went. Chances were she would not be allowed in the room.

"There's another matter," I said. "I met this elderly Jewish man at Yoseph's bookstore who was interested in my research, and yesterday he confided in me a family secret that I think is important."

"You mean Karl?" Juliette said.

"How did you know?" I asked in surprise.

"I know Yoseph," she said smiling. "He apparently saw us at the café the other night, and this morning when he was unable to get a word out of Karl, rightly or wrongly, he called to ask if I might inquire what you and Karl talked about. You have his engines running, which is not easy to do. I told him no, of course, but since you brought it up...."

This was getting complicated, but I liked it.

"Well, I was going to tell you anyway, but it is strictly confidential. You can't say anything, and that means even to Yoseph."

"Promise," she said, continuing to smile, knowing I was a little baffled by her.

I told her Karl's story, of how the Bibles at the Lautrec's and St. Sernin seemed similar, and also about the little red dot and letter Y.

"I think they are all related," I concluded.

Then I ventured to tell her of my experience with the letters.

"This might sound a little weird, but I had a sense last night like I understood them, one of them anyway, even though I can't read the writing. Then this morning, a similar thing happened with the Book of Revelation at the Church. I suspect there are letters hidden in its cover, too. The feeling is like remembering something familiar, I can almost hear the words. If that makes any sense."

"It does," she said and fell silent.

I found myself being drawn back into the memory of a profound lightness and ease I had had with the letter. After a while, and even though it felt like pulling back from a dream, I said, "I didn't tell Karl about the packet, wanting to speak with you first, though he suspects I have something."

"You are a good reporter. Soon everyone in the world will be in your confidence on this."

"You'll be the first to know," I replied, and we laughed.

"So, which letter was it?" she asked.

I pointed to the last letter, saying it was probably just me, and might not be anything at all. Partly out of respect, and curiosity, I left her alone with the letters and went down to a corner shop to buy some cigarettes. While I had quit, the events had stirred the old habit. Juliette was sitting quietly on the couch when I returned.

"So, what do you think?" I asked as I sat down beside her.

She remained quiet but finally said, "I heard voices, maybe just one. I couldn't tell if it was mine or someone else's."

"Interesting, isn't it?"

"I'm not sure I want to give them back."

It was my turn to be quiet, but I knew what she meant. There was something magical about those ancient letters lying on the table. I suppose part of it was simply the feeling very old objects can evoke. The tangible connection with so much history, so many ages under the pen. But it wasn't only voices from the past, there was also a heightened sense of the present that seemed to clear and soften the air in the room.

"We don't have to give them back, tonight anyway," I finally said, then added, "Are you done, should we put them away?"

"Yes," she replied. "I'm not sure how much more I could take."

We carefully placed them into the waxed envelope and back into my briefcase. However, I could have looked at them for hours, and part of me was already anticipating taking them out again.

"What was it you wanted to do?" Juliette asked. "Go to the café and meet Dieter?"

"Yeah, but if you have to leave, I can go alone."

"I have time, but might not stay," she said and then asked, "Should we tell Dieter?"

"I wouldn't. There is an old ranch saying, "Shoot, shovel, and shut up."

She looked quizzical, then grinned, "Did you translate that from the texts?"

"Yes, so we'd better follow it."

CHAPTER EIGHT

As we made our way to the café, I explained how I'd missed Dieter the night before and was unsure he would be there tonight.

"Well, if he's not, we can still have a glass of wine," Juliette said.

"That would be nice. Sure you don't have to get home?"

"No."

Dieter was there and waved off my apology. It was a gentle summer's night, and the pink glow of the sunset had faded into deep violet. The murmur of voices was accented by the occasional clink of glass and buzz of a passing motorbike.

"So, what do you think of a trip to the Languedoc?" Dieter asked. "It might help with your mystery."

"I think I'd like that," I replied.

"Would you be free to go on Monday? I will have to make some arrangements. There are friends I'd like you to meet. They live in the area and have a great deal of knowledge." Then he asked, "How was your trip to Lautrec's?"

Juliette and I looked at each other.

"It was adventurous," Juliette said brightly. "The Count threw us out."

"What!"

"He wasn't there when we arrived, but we were greeted by his aunt. She took us to the library, and then, poor thing, proceeded to have a stroke."

Dieter just shook his head.

"When the Count came home he blamed us for some reason, and now Bjorn is persona non-grata. Me, too, but William managed to get it all pinned on Bjorn. Very gallant of him, his business relationship remains intact."

Dieter wanted to know the details, and we took turns explaining, with each of us making the story a little more outrageous.

Dieter finally said, "The Count is a powerful man. It's probably a good thing you're getting out of town. We'll hide you in one of the Templar castles."

"I might need it," I said.

After saying Dieter and I could work out those details, Juliette began to leave and asked me to walk her to her car.

"I won't be gone long," I told Dieter.

"Just come back," Dieter said with a twinkle in his eye. "I have a lot I want to tell you."

I walked Juliette to where she had parked at my hotel.

"I think I will visit the hospital tomorrow," she said. "Would you come with me?"

"That could be dumping gasoline on the fire."

"I would feel better going with you," she continued. "You don't have to go up to the room."

While my better instincts were against it, I could see she would like the support, so I agreed.

As we reached the car, I said, "I hope your husband is OK with you being out this late."

"It's fine," she replied, and as she opened the car door she leaned across and kissed me, saying, "I'll call you tomorrow, around 2 o'clock."

It was just a light touch on the lips, but her directness caught me off-guard again. I told myself it was no more than a simple gesture of affection, and as I walked back to the café, I did my best to forget about it.

"She's a beautiful woman," Dieter said with a little grin as I sat down,

"Yes, and she's married," I said, hoping to end it.

"I think she likes you," he continued to press. "Are you going to do anything about it?"

"She has a child, Dieter. I'm not getting involved in that."

He raised his eyebrows politely and then said brightly, "Let me tell you about Languedoc!"

He proceeded to convey some of its history, along with his experiences in the place where we were going, Rennes le Chateau.

"While it's not obvious when you are there in the landscape, there are five places that form the points of a star, a pentagram. You know the pentagram is a sacred symbol since Egypt or before. The Church says it is of the devil, but..." and he waved his hand in dismissal.

Then he drew a map of the area with the five places, Blanche Fort, La Soulane, Chateau de Templar, a hill by the motocross, and Rennes le Chateau.

"At the center of the star is a natural rock outcropping called la Pique. It is difficult to get to, you have to push through and do some

45

steep climbing. From there, however, you can see to the five places. Some think this is make-believe because the star's shape is not perfect, but it was not an accident."

Dieter was getting a little loud, so he lowered his voice.

"The Cathars knew, the Templars knew, these were natural power points, and that is why they put some of the buildings there."

He then described an experience where he saw the sight-lines between the points light up, forming the pentagram.

"There is more there than meets the eye," he concluded.

Dieter believed the Cathars had retained an innate knowledge and connection to the land, which he said Western society had lost. I was intrigued by his conviction, and while his experience was out of the ordinary, I did not dismiss it as not everything fits into neat little boxes. I was also intrigued that so many artists had come to this region. I could feel an intangible quality that was very attractive, and it made me eager to get into the countryside and do some painting.

It was getting late. Dieter and I agreed to leave on Monday, around 2:00, and stay about three days. He said he would talk to his friends and we would stay at their home. The afternoon departure would allow me to make a last visit to the St. Sernin library.

"Do you have any good boots," he asked as we stood up to leave. "The hike can be a tough one, and expect some rain."

I was prepared, but I needed to get a raincoat I wouldn't worry about damaging.

"I have one you can use," Dieter said. "I will call you if anything changes."

I decided to walk through the little park before going back to my hotel. It was a beautiful night, and listening to the gentle splashing in the pool helped settle my swirl of thoughts, and a pink tinge rippled on the water.

My first thought back at the hotel was to look at the letters again, but I decided to wait, and instead, I went on the Internet to look up Cathars, Knights Templar, and Rennes le Chateau. What I found piqued my interest.

The long-running Albigensian Crusade ended in 1244 at Montsegur, the last Cathar stronghold. After a nine-month siege, 200 Cathar "parfaits," or purified ones, surrendered, knowing they were to be burned at the stake. Notably, even some of the mercenaries defending the pacifist Cathars voluntarily went with them. There were too few stakes, so they were all burned in one huge pyre. To the disbelief of their captors, the Cathars were singing joyfully as they were being led to their deaths. The Cathars believed in a form of reincarnation, and dying by fire was the penultimate purification that gave final release from the cycle of life and death on earth.

The night before, however, four men carrying backpacks had scaled down the high cliffs protecting the castle, slipped through the siege line, and vanished into the dark. They were never caught, and what was in those packs remains a mystery.

Some speculate they contained sacred Cathar texts, or the Holy Grail, or something the Church would go to any length to suppress, a record of the reputed bloodline of Jesus. I learned the Merovingians, whose dynasty was centered in the region, had a vague claim to be descended from Jesus through a child by Mary Magdalene. The Nazis also searched the area seriously during WWII, believing they would find the Grail, but their effort was as fruitless as the others.

In any event, rumors of a Cathar treasure continue to circulate. I didn't put much weight in such legends and stories, but I was beginning to think whatever the truth was, there were some things the historians had yet to discover. That reminded me of the envelope, and I wanted to take one more look before giving it to Juliette. Then my phone rang. I didn't immediately recognize the number, except it was from the U.S.

"Hello, this is Bjorn."

"Bjorn, this is John. I have some news."

"Hey, John, what's up?"

"Those letters you sent me, well, I had my friend look at them. He thinks you might have a find, though in all probability they are forgeries. He would have to see the originals to know for sure."

"What does he say they are?"

"He wasn't definitive, but the writing is Aramaic, early first century, the same time frame as the Dead Sea scrolls. The style, the word usage, everything, fits for what they know of that era. He was impressed."

I wanted them to be fakes. It would have made it easier to give them back.

"What do the letters say?" I wanted to stick to my point.

"Umm, let me look here at what he said, which wasn't very much. One seemed to be taken from the Book of Revelation, like the first couple verses. Another might pass as a personal letter. This is what he wrote about that."

"Mary beloved I come to you in the cool of the day reminding you of the silent longing of your heart in the secret place where you are I AM in love Y"

"He told me they didn't use much punctuation back then, and it is only a rough approximation. Another had some sayings, a bit like the Sermon on the Mount. The last letter was very unusual, and it could be read in so many ways he was unable to translate it."

I knew about that last one.

"They are the Lautrec's, I shouldn't even have them." I finally said.

There was silence on the other end of the line.

"You stole them?"

"No, but it could sure look that way."

"Uh oh," he replied.

Mocking a plaintive voice, I said, "I told you it was complicated,"

"Bjorn, you have to get it straightened out."

"Yeah, but I don't want to get crucified in the process. I came here to write an article, make a little money, and get a free trip to France. Now I'm in some da Vinci code mess."

"What are you going to do?"

I could feel him backing off, and fast. We knew each other, but not well enough to put so much on the line.

"If they were stolen, or somehow forged, no one is going to touch them. It could ruin their reputation," he explained.

I doubted this would ruin anyone's reputation, and more likely it might help it. However, I could understand his concerns, and I wanted to keep the connection.

"Perhaps what you've found out will help me get everything cleared up," I said. "Don't worry, if there's a problem I'll keep your name out of it. But, if they are real, the point is that they need to be handled properly."

I then added, "I'm going away for a few days. Let's just stay in touch."

"OK," he said, "Let me know."

This was becoming more difficult, but at least something had been confirmed, and while not totally, it was enough for now. I regretted not getting the exact translations, but it didn't surprise me that some were religious; after all, they were in a Bible. The question was how to get them back to the Count and avoid any legal trouble. I felt like letting the chips fall where they may, but then again, it might be more prudent to wait and let him cool down.

I decided to take another look at the writings. Carefully removing them from my briefcase, I unwrapped the delicate letters and spread them out on the table. Now that I knew what they probably were, I could at least pretend I knew what they said.

The sweet fragrance of beeswax again surrounded them. I picked up what I now called the last letter and once more had that gentle, subtle sensation. I leaned back into the couch as I held it. My thoughts drifted a little, and I seemed to be taken back in time. I imagined a crowd on a hillside, looking up at a man I now vaguely thought of as Jesus. I could hear him speak, but the words didn't matter, and none came to mind anyway. It was simply presence.

Shaking my head a little, I placed the paper back onto the table. What John had told me had now influenced my daydream.

My attention was drawn back to the other writings. I figured the shortest one was the personal letter. It was then that I noticed the mark at the end. It was like the one on the tiny chip I'd found at St. Sernin, but here it was like a signature, but no red dot.

I was now wide-awake and interested in returning to St. Sernin to examine that volume one more time. I thought I was beginning to connect the dots, so to speak: the Cathars secreting out precious documents, the Lautrec family line going back to that era, the Church inadvertently keeping a coded Cathar book. It all made sense, and everything fit, or did it?

Was I getting sucked into fantasy because of a speck in a book, an old man's story, and an invalid woman's hysteria around some family letters? I came here to write about an artist visiting Languedoc.

As I mulled things over, I absently began looking at the other two documents. They were both about the same length, and I couldn't tell which would have been the possible St. John writing or the Sermon on the Mount. In a way, it didn't matter which was which, except the St. John piece, if it were by his hand, would be an artifact of inestimable value, and here it was simply lying on a hotel room table. If it was his, it should be in a climate-controlled vault the size of my hotel room and guarded by security 24 hours a day.

What timeworn wisdom lay in those words? You can't beat two-thousand-year-old advice. Or was it only as profound as the ancient Egyptian papyri lauding beer?

I decided whatever the facts, the truth was probably in the middle. The letters could have enormous value, but then again, maybe not. The volume at St. Sernin was likely not that intriguing, but it was worth another look. I would withhold judgment on Karl's family story for the moment.

In any case, I needed to avoid more trouble with the Lautrecs. Juliette's plan of slipping the packet into the aunt's things was suspect. Yet, it might be the simplest way of returning it. I needed to tell Juliette what the letters might be and went to bed, hoping a direction would become more obvious after we talked.

As I lay down, I was still thinking about the letters, and that people were feeling the same feelings, thinking the same thoughts, and telling each other the same things, so long ago. A skilled artist made the 15,000-year-old cave paintings at nearby Lascaux, showing a common thread as far back as you wanted to go.

CHAPTER NINE

I awakened to a bright, beautiful morning. The sun was streaming through a gap in the curtains, and the black briefcase was illuminated like an altarpiece. My heart froze when I realized that precious light might also be heating the wax to melting temperatures. Leaping out of bed, I shut the curtains and felt the case. It had not been in the sunlight long and was only warm.

As I opened it, I could imagine the letters that had survived the millennia reduced to a fragrant lump of wax. How stupid to leave it there, but a cursory examination showed no damage. Before I could lock the case, there was a knock on the door. It was Juliette.

"How are things going?" she asked cheerfully.

"Other than just about frying the letters, everything is fine," I replied as I reached for a bathrobe. "I left the briefcase on the table last night, and this morning it was directly in the sun."

A look of concern crossed her face.

"Were they damaged?" she asked.

"No. Take a look."

I brought the packet out and gave it to her. She held it as gently as if it was a fragile piece of glass.

"I've been thinking," Juliette replied. "William told me the aunt is no longer in intensive care, but apparently not yet lucid. The Count, meanwhile, is livid and has not changed his mind about seeking charges against you. I tried to get William to talk to him out of that, but he's not going to do anything to counter the Count. It's business, as usual."

This put a clamp on my idea to go to him directly, at least for the moment.

"I came early to tell you I still want to visit the aunt. Whether we give her the packet or not, I'll still bring it, and see if it seems right. Who knows, she might even be awake."

I remained skeptical but felt a little better about going.

"So we'll go this afternoon?" I asked.

"Yes. I'll have Artemisia because William is going to the office as soon as I get back."

"So, it's still 2:00," I said.

"A little before. It will take about 20 minutes to get to the hospital from here. It's Saturday, traffic should be light," she said.

I thought about it for a moment and then said, "OK."

I had a lot to tell her about the letters, so we sat down, and placing the packet on the table, I again carefully unwrapped it.

"This one may be an early copy of the Book of Revelation, very early. Who knows, maybe it is in John's own hand," I said, pointing.

Juliette's eyes widened.

"I'm just imagining, but if it is, that would make it one of the most valuable letters in the world."

"I bet it is," Juliette remarked, surprising me with her assurance.

"This one he thinks is a personal letter," I said, then pointing to the paper with the possible signature. "And, look, its signature is the mark I found in the manuscript at St. Sernin. There's no red dot, but it's the same mark. Interesting, huh?"

"Is it related?" she asked.

"Who knows? The Lautrec family line goes back a long way, a thousand years or more. Their forebears were sympathetic to the Cathars, if not Cathars themselves, and may have secreted away some documents, but that is all conjecture."

I then turned to the remaining letters.

"This one, which I like the best, apparently was written in a way that can have a lot of interpretations. The translator called it unusual."

Juliette was getting excited.

"Maybe we shouldn't give them back," she said. "If they are that significant why don't we just turn them over to the Louvre or National Library?"

"Juliette! We'd have to tell them where they came from. Can you imagine what the Count would do to us then?"

"OK," she said. "But quite frankly, while he scares me a little, I don't care what he does or thinks."

"Let's hope the hospital thing works," I replied, not believing I was now defending her plan.

We carefully placed the letters back into the waxed packet and then put the packet in a plain envelope. I knew our fingerprints were all over it, but I hoped that wouldn't matter.

"If the aunt isn't conscious when they find this, they are not going to know what it is," I said, beginning to have second thoughts again. "They will question it."

Placing a hand on my shoulder, Juliette smiled sweetly and put the envelope in her handbag.

"Too late now," she said. "You know, I could have called, but I wanted to come over."

"It is a little early," I replied, readjusting my bathrobe.

"I like being here with you," she continued.

"Yes, and we'll have some more time this afternoon," I said, trying to deflect the pressure I was feeling.

"No, I mean really. It's pleasant," she said. "I woke up this morning, and my first thought was coming over."

I could tell that despite her boldness, this was not flirtatious talk on her part.

"I have to admit I was pleasantly surprised," I said.

"I was wondering how you'd take it. Though you could have offered me some coffee or tea."

Before I could apologize, she laughed and said it was too late now, and she had to go. Picking up her handbag, she gave it an extra squeeze and said,

"I'll see you at 1:30, meet me outside."

As I opened the door, I thought of kissing her goodbye but hesitated. We looked at each other, and then she extended her hand. Laughing, we shook.

"I guess that means we're partners," I said.

"Yes," she replied.

Watching her go down the hall to the elevator, I wondered if I'd missed an opportunity. She looked back before getting on, and then the door closed.

I had a few hours before Juliette returned and decided to make some progress on my article. Before leaving New York, I had agreed I would make paintings, and photographs would be optional. When traveling, my medium of choice is watercolor because it's quick to dry and easy to use in the field. The paintings could be small, the size of a large postcard, which meant I did not need an easel and could work almost anywhere; however, I still consider it serious work. I grabbed my backpack containing paper, paints, and supplies and headed into the streets.

The old part of Toulouse is the more romantic part of the city, with many of the buildings made with the local red brick. My first thought was to head to Yoseph's bookstore, where I could paint from the little café across the street. I hoped I would go unnoticed, at least for a little while.

I crossed the thoroughfare and headed down when I noticed a

small crowd gathered in the middle of the block. As I approached, I could hear the voices of performers. I nuzzled my way in, thinking these might be the street actor friends of Juliette and the others in the café.

I couldn't understand a word of what they were saying in French, but the onlookers were attentive and seemed amused. The man was in white face paint, wearing a long black coat, black pants, and a white shirt. His shoes were long, square-toed, and black. He looked straight out of a Daumier print, with one arm waving wildly. His girlfriend was the other performer. She had blackened her eyes and was wearing a white blouse under a dress that came to mid-calf, exposing her bare feet.

I heard the word 'America' and the name of the new French premier. After a minute or two, I could feel nervousness in the audience. It was no longer laughing as much. One viewer shouted something, but the Actor kept right on performing. The shouter made another comment, stepped forward, then suddenly turned and jostled his way out of the crowd, cursing.

When there were only a handful of people left the Actor popped out a flattened black top hat, and in a grand sweep, bowed his head almost to his knees. The few that remained applauded and smiled, some dropping a coin or two into the hat.

'Tough way to make a living,' I thought. Unfortunately, I did not know enough French to introduce myself but hoped they might speak English.

"Bonjour," I said and hesitated a little before asking, "Do you know Juliette and Dieter?"

The Actor, who was still wound up from the performance, said yes in that French way of implying…and?

"She was talking of your performance the other night, and thought it was very good."

"Thank you," he said. "And you?"

"I don't speak French, so I have no idea what you were saying, but it looked impassioned." I then added, "That one guy didn't seem too pleased."

"Ahh, at least he heard enough to get mad," he said as he picked up his hat and nodded goodbye. "Thank you for watching."

I stood there as he and his girlfriend walked away, he still talking and gesticulating. I would like to have painted that, though it was probably too brief, and I wanted to see them perform when there was a little more time.

I continued to the little café outside the bookstore, looking for some view or angle that caught my eye. The sun was getting higher, and the strong light tended to eliminate any subtlety of color or form.

After ordering a coffee, I sat down and looked to see if this offered a view worth capturing. I was on the shady side of the street, and the bookstore opposite was bathed in mid-morning light. The recess of its front window and eves gave the inside a dark, inviting look, however. The few books in the display would add spot colors. Also, something about the golden pink color of the door, its glass panel, and large rectangular shape offered enough edginess to make an interesting composition.

I pulled out my paper, taped it to a small board, and holding my pocket-sized watercolor kit in one hand and my brush in the other, I licked the dry sable tip to a fine point, a habit, before dipping it into the water. The color flowed onto the paper, deep Prussian blue, bright vermillion fading to pink, and Naples yellow and turquoise blending into the chrome green that drove Van Gogh mad. Sometimes pictures paint themselves, the magic happening without thought, the brush moving rapidly from paint to paper. I was finished in about ten minutes.

You can't tell what a watercolor will finally look like until it dries. It passes through phases where you wish it would stop, only to be even more pleased when it shifts again, as vague colors come alive when they set. You wouldn't change anything and wonder how it happened.

As I was packing to leave, I saw Yoseph standing in the doorway of the bookstore. At some point, he had noticed me, and now that I had seen him, he smiled and waved.

"Come over when you're done," he called.

I paid my bill and crossed the street. Yoseph had gone back inside and was waiting at the counter.

"How is it going?" he asked, and then looking at my bag, "Were you painting, can I see?"

"I was painting your storefront, it's not fully dry yet."

I showed him the watercolor, and he looked at it for a long minute.

"I recognize the books," he said smiling.

"If it makes it into the article, which I think it will, your bookstore will be all over America."

Yoseph just laughed and said, "Is there some way I can get a copy?"

"Sure, I'll send you one, or several."

"How has your story been going?" he asked, but still an obvious inference to the little chip.

"It has been a whirlwind."

"And out of the whirlwind?" he replied, quoting Job.

"I wonder if dervishes experience that?" was all I could think to say.

"Perhaps," Yoseph said, smiling again.

I had anticipated his inquiry. And while I wasn't going to tell him about the letters from the Lautrecs, I did want to tell him about my latest find at the Church.

"I found a red dot."

Though his demeanor did not change, his eyes could not conceal his interest. He waited for me to say more.

"The dot was on the little flake I told you about. Karl may be on to something with that, but I still don't really know. I haven't connected all the dots," I added with a half-smile.

But Yoseph was not smiling. Karl had must have told him something.

"Is there anything I can do to help?" he asked.

"You've already helped a lot," I replied. "I am going back to the Church on Monday to have another look. I'll let you know what I find."

He nodded as if little more needed to be said.

"I'm also going to the area around Rennes le Chateau on Monday afternoon. I met someone who will show me around for a few days. He seems to know a lot about its history, the Cathars, Knights Templar, legends, all that."

"Yes, it's very interesting," Yoseph said. "I have some more books on that. Let me show them to you."

He led me to a back bookshelf, and I was impressed how many there were, most quite new.

"People have been fascinated with this region lately," Yoseph said, almost sounding like a travel agent.

On the other side of the shelf, there were books on the Knights Templar, some much older.

"Interest comes and goes," Yoseph explained. "Here is one you might find interesting."

He handed me a leather-bound volume, and by chance, I opened it to a page showing a drawing of la Pique. I looked at a few more pages and saw a pentagram.

"It looks almost alchemical," I said.

"You know the Moors occupied Spain for several hundred years, and they were great students of alchemy. Many Europeans were interested and came through here on their way South."

"Do you know what the pentagram means?" I asked.

"Why don't you read about it," Yoseph said.

"I think this book is out of my price range."

"Don't worry," Yoseph said. "You've been a good customer, it's a present."

He dismissed my protests, and I told him I would enjoy reading it.

"You might," was all he said.

I did buy another book that gave a more standardized history of the region, then I looked at my watch and realized I'd lost track of time. I needed to hurry back to meet Juliette.

As I was about to leave, I said, "So, you know Juliette?"

"Yes, she's a good friend," he said, and then with a quaint

grin, "You'll have to tell me about your trip with her to Lautrecs."

"When I come back," I said, waving goodbye.

Obviously, people liked Juliette and perhaps even knew of her discontent with the marriage. I was beginning to feel more at ease about people noticing us. Juliette was waiting outside when I got back to the hotel.

"I was wondering if you were going to show," she said brightly as I jumped in the car.

Artemisia was in the back seat, holding a beat-up doll. She looked at me and then went back to playing.

"Sorry I was late. I was at Yoseph's bookstore and lost track of time."

"That's easy to do there. I bet he was very interested to see you."

"I told him about the red dot, but not about the Lautrecs." I then added, "He gave me a book."

I pulled it out of my bag, "I haven't had a chance to look at it, but it might give some insight into what Dieter has been talking about. It has a picture of la Pique."

By this time Artemisia had leaned over the front seat, her face very close to mine. I showed her the picture of la Pique and then turned to the page with the pentagram. She reached over and put one finger on it.

"Don't touch, honey," Juliette said.

"I don't mind," I said. "Books are meant to be touched," then turning to Artemisia, added, "and fruit juice is meant to be drunk."

She giggled. It took us about 20 minutes to drive to the hospital, and traffic was light as Juliette had predicted. Once in the parking lot, she turned to me, "I can go in alone, and you stay with Artemisia, or we can all go in together."

"You should go alone, we'll wait in the lobby."

As soon as we went inside Artemisia started tugging toward the elevator.

"She wants to ride," Juliette said. "She loves elevators. It may have something to do with her ears. It would be good if you were close."

I had thought a low profile would be best, but I could see she was a little nervous, and Artemisia might be difficult. I had little experience minding children, but I agreed to come up. Once in the elevator, Juliette said she would only leave the envelope if the aunt had personal things in the room. Otherwise, she would hold onto it.

The nurse at the front desk was courteous and efficient. After a brief conversation, Juliette was handed a clipboard to sign in, something I should have anticipated but didn't. Others would see that she was here.

After she wrote her name, the nurse looked over to me.

"She wants you to sign in," Juliette said.

"Do I have to?" I said as unobtrusively as I could. "I could go downstairs."

Juliette spoke again to the nurse. I understood enough to know she was explaining I didn't speak French and was just a friend visiting from America.

After a moment, the nurse took the clipboard back. Juliette came over and said, "You don't have to sign in, but have to stay here. I will take Artemisia with me."

I didn't like us drawing this much attention and felt I should have followed my first instinct to remain in the lobby. I began to doubt the whole plan but it was too late now.

I smiled at the nurse. There was no place to sit, so I leaned against the wall. The floor had little activity. An older patient with a walker passed by slowly, her blue hospital gown sagging over thin shoulders. An orderly came off the elevator, chatted with the desk nurse, and then he walked briskly on noisy white sneakers down the corridor. A short while later, he came out of a room assisting an elderly man, talking to him cheerily and giving assurance. They passed by without saying anything to me.

I was becoming more uncomfortable after Juliette was gone for about ten minutes. I also remembered I don't like being in hospitals. I once visited a friend who had back surgery a few days before, and his pain seemed to fill the room. It was so intense I felt nauseated.

Finally, Juliette and Artemisia came out of the room. I couldn't tell what had happened. Juliette thanked the desk nurse, signed out, and nodded to me as she headed for the elevator. She waited for the doors to close, saying nothing for a moment after they did.

"I didn't give it to her," she finally said.

I didn't know whether to feel relief or disappointment.

"What happened?" I asked.

"I'll tell you in the car."

Artemisia had brought her doll and was talking to it with her fingers on the way down. When the doors opened, Juliette and I walked out, and as we stood there waiting for Artemisia to follow, the doors of the next elevator were just closing. It was the Count. We looked at each other, but before anyone could react, the doors bumped shut, and the lights above the elevator showed it was starting to go up.

Juliette and I looked at each other.

"That's not good," I said.

We didn't have to tell each other to hurry as we walked to the car, with Artemisia having to run a little. Juliette swung the car out of the parking lot and onto the main street.

"Well, say something," Juliette said with exasperation.

"I'd say we're in trouble."

"What do you think we should do?" she asked.

"There's not much we can do. Though it's a good thing I wasn't in the lobby when he came in."

I didn't want to say 'I told you so,' but couldn't help but think how stupid I was to imagine this would work.

"I'm sorry," she said like she read my mind.

"The Count is going to talk to your husband, you know."

"I'm not worried about that. I hope he loses that account, and I'm not worried about being with you."

She was a step ahead of me.

"It's probably fortunate you didn't leave the envelope," I said, going back to the immediate problem. "What happened?"

"She was asleep. I looked around, and while there were flowers and a few things on the table, there was nothing of hers I could put the envelope in. She woke up when Artemisia bumped the bed. It took a moment, but she recognized us, and of course she couldn't speak."

Here she paused for a moment.

"I decided to show her the envelope."

I said nothing, so she went on.

"Her eyes grew wide, then she started mumbling. At least that's what I thought until Artemisia leaned close to her and somehow was able to understand, saying 'She wants us to have it, mommy.' The aunt nodded, then fell back to sleep. That's when I left."

I thought for sure the Count would now go to the police. Who knows, he might even claim we had gone in to silence her. I had been somewhat hopeful, but everything was falling apart, the job, the truth of the letters, and I might wind up being prosecuted and going to jail.

"I guess we'll just have to wait and see," I finally said.

Artemisia had been sitting quietly in the back seat, and then she leaned forward and began stroking her mother's hair.

"I really feel sorry for the poor woman," Juliette remarked.

She then reached into her purse, took out the envelope, and handed it to me.

"I think you should keep this. The aunt wants you to have it."

I had no idea what to do next.

"We'll be OK," Juliette said after a minute. "Why don't we stop at the Park, maybe get some ice cream."

Looking over the seat, she asked, "Would you like that, Artemisia?" Artemisia clapped. "I think I have a plan."

We found a parking spot and then stopped at a gelato stand

on our way to the Park. Artemisia wanted strawberry, Juliette chocolate, and I took orange. Soon, Artemisia's fingers were pink. There were more people in the Park today, and the few ducks in the pond were quacking contentedly as people threw breadcrumbs. Artemisia sat on the edge of the pond wall, licking her fingers.

"I really don't know what to do next," I said. "If I go to the Count and give him the letters now, he's not going to believe anything I say, and it will only further his animosity."

"The aunt looked like she's recovering," Juliette said. "Maybe she will tell him. We might be making more out of this than it is."

"No, we're not. At least not at the moment," I replied. "But I don't know what else to do except keep going. I'll be with Dieter at Rennes le Chateau for about three days, and maybe things will be clearer when I get back."

"Well then, here's my plan," Juliette said. "Give the letters to Karl."

The idea stunned me.

"The Count doesn't know we have anything. He's just mad at you about his aunt, who he probably wants gone anyway. Everything would be his."

I hadn't heard Juliette talk like this.

"Karl would know exactly what the letters are, and in the world he lives in, they would know what to do."

"But we don't know what they are, really," I said.

"Yes, we do."

She held my gaze for a long time, and I knew she was right, more than I had wanted to admit.

"OK," I finally said, "but let me think about Karl. It could be a plan B."

"What's plan A?" she asked with a wry smile.

"Maybe plan B," I said.

We watched Artemisia play with the ducks as we talked about small things. I thought of coming back later and painting.

Then Juliette said, "Let me drive you back to your hotel."

CHAPTER TEN

Returning to my room I took the packet and put it back in the briefcase. Juliette's idea of giving it to Karl seemed like a good one, but I was still worried about what the Count might do, particularly if his aunt passed away. While she had improved, another stroke could do her in. If Karl had the letters, and the police investigated, he might get involved, and I didn't want that.

There was also a chance the aunt would recover enough to clear up the situation, and I realized Juliette's desire to stay close was wise. I decided to wait and see how things were after I returned from my trip.

It was before 5:00, and still too soon for the early evening light that I wanted for painting. I wasn't tired, so I lay down and started flipping through the book Yoseph had given me. It was written around 1930 and was a mix of the occult and history, religion and philosophy, with a focus on the Middle Ages. I read more than I could follow about the intrigues and speculations about the Cathars, Knights Templar, and the formation of the Catholic Church.

I read the pentagram was based on the mathematical 'golden mean' or "divine proportion." Early philosophers considered it, along with the associated pentagon, something of a perfect figure. In pre-Christian times it was a symbol for divinity, and so became a sign of paganism, or Satan, to the Church.

There was a formula on how to draw one to any scale, a secret of medieval craft guilds. I tried it, and was impressed by the natural repetition of the proportions. I could understand why the ancients might read more into it as they searched for the mathematical building blocks of the universe. The golden mean is also a constant in the proportions of the human body, and artists have long appreciated that fact. Mathematicians, meanwhile, are still seeking the universal constants.

The light was now coming in low through the window, and I headed out to the Park to paint. There was a crowd there, and as I drew near I could see the performers I met earlier in the day, only now there were four of them. Going to where the crowd thinned I found an angle that gave me a good side view, and started painting.

I still could not understand what they were saying, but by their antics, I could tell they were parodying something. One of the actors had a drum, along with other instruments to the side. He was occasionally beating a short tattoo. Another had a simple brass horn, which she was blowing erratically. It was deliberately unsettling, but the crowd seemed to love it. I began to feel that in Toulouse, where troubadours originated, street-theater is not something apart from everyday life, but an extension of it, and every topic is fair game.

As I became absorbed in the atmosphere, I found I was painting with unusual colors. Instead of Prussian blue, I was mixing pink, and instead of cadmium yellow, a grey-blue color I used so infrequently I had forgotten its name. The painting sparkled as under rose light. The Actor's white shirt rippled on the paper as he raised his arm, fist clenched. When they took their bows, the viewers applauded and laughed, and I had finished.

I sat down on the stone ledge of the pond, setting the painting between my feet as it dried. Then I noticed a square-toed black shoe on either side of the picture. I looked up, it was the Actor.

"May I see?" he said.

"Yes, of course," I replied a little startled. "It's not dry yet."

He sat down next to me, and I could feel the warmth of his body, along with a faint smell of sweat. He had been working hard.

"It's me," he said looking at it. "Or what I would like to think

65

of as me."

"I rarely use those colors, you changed my palette."

"Do you sell them?" he asked.

I was tempted to give it to him, but I knew I wanted it for my story.

"I would, but this is for a magazine article I'm writing."

"What's it about?"

"Painting in the Languedoc."

"You do not need words, this says it all."

I took the compliment to heart.

"It's good to see you again. Are you going over to the café?" he asked.

"I am now."

We walked over to the troupe. They had gathered their things and were talking loosely amongst themselves.

"This is…" he said, and then paused, "I don't know your name."

"Bjorn."

"Hi Bjorn, I'm Stephane," he said. "Hey everyone, this is Bjorn, he's a friend of Juliette's, and has decided to join us. He is a painter who will make the world a better place."

The drummer beat his drum, the woman tooted her horn, and Stephane said, "To a better place, the café!"

They all cheered, and walking arm in arm marched off toward the café singing, swinging me along with them. Stephane had his arm around his girlfriend, they seemed to have patched up their differences.

The café was lively, and I had almost forgotten it was Saturday night. The actors moved into the crowd with ease and quickly secured two tables at the back. Dieter emerged from somewhere and came over.

"Hey my friend," he said in greeting. "Good to see you here. What have you been doing?"

"Getting ready, I've been reading up on la Pique and pentagrams."

He became serious for a moment, and then brightened.

"We can talk about that later," he said. "This is not the place. This is a party."

We clinked our glasses together.

"I saw the Count today," I remarked.

"What! How did that go?"

I explained what happened. Dieter just rubbed his head for a moment.

"Well, you made it out alive."

Then someone touched me on the shoulder.

"I see you found the troupe," it was Juliette.

"They were in the Park when I was painting," I said in surprise. "I didn't expect to see you here."

"Were you expecting someone else?" she parried with an impish grin.

"My expectations have been fulfilled," I replied.

"Good," she smiled and sat down beside me.

"I thought you'd be at home after today."

"I was hoping you weren't at the hotel," she replied. "William is with Artemisia tonight."

The way she said "tonight" sounded like she might not be going home at all.

The party was boisterous, and while I understood very little of what people were saying, I could tell it was often political. At one point Stephane produced a guitar and started playing while a couple danced nearby in the corner.

Juliette turned and looked at me, "Would you join me?"

Stephane was playing a slow song. I had avoided physical contact with her until now, but my guard was dropping.

"Yes, let's," and as we stood up I added, "I'm not much of a dancer."

"Then I'll teach you. This is an easy one."

She drew close, putting her hand in mine, and her head on my shoulder. It was like holding a flickering warm flame. She made no effort to pull away when we came close. I told myself 'one dance', because I was afraid where two might lead. I knew she was not afraid.

Others joined and left the group throughout the evening, its size ebbing and flowing, but the energy never subsided. The actors were animated and always in motion, as bottles of wine kept appearing on the table. Juliette and I danced again, but to a faster tune, and I felt something had passed.

It was around 2:00 when people started drifting away. Dieter left earlier but told me everything was set for the trip and his friends were expecting us. We agreed to use his car, but I would drive over to his house. I then asked Juliette if she'd like to go for a walk before going home.

"I'm not going home," she said. "I'm staying with you."

CHAPTER ELEVEN

The next morning I awoke early. It had been a long time since I had shared a bed. To see Juliette's bare shoulder and her hair tousled on the pillow made me want to lie there and stay still in the white morning light.

Juliette stirred and rolled over toward me, her bright blue eyes looking into mine. She smiled, stretched her arms out, and rolled further, enveloping me.

"I guess this means you're awake," I said.

"How can you tell?" she replied.

"Because," I said, tickling her ribs, making her start.

She swung a leg over my waist, and sitting up, slid forward just enough. I reached up, and she pressed against my hands. It was noon before we got out of bed.

Juliette had told me it had been a long time since she and her husband had relations, and while this was the first time for her outside their marriage, he had been with other women. They did not talk about it, and she no longer cared what he did.

I was unsure how far Juliette wanted to pursue our relationship; after all, I was leaving in a few weeks, but I knew it was only a matter of time before she left him.

"Would you like some coffee?" she asked, already at the counter.

"Just some fruit," I said. "I can get it."

I sat down at the table, and peeling a banana, asked, "Why don't you come with Dieter and me?"

"I'd love to, but I have things to do, and Artemisia has school," she replied. "You know, I am not as free as you are."

I knew her answer before I asked, but I needed to make it real.

"We can do this," she added with confident ease.

Then sitting down across from me, she said plainly, "Don't worry about things so much. What are you going to do this afternoon, paint?"

"Yes, in the park. I should also start writing my article. I was thinking of it as an artist's journey, you know colors, places, thoughts, other artist's influences."

"You should write about your real experiences," she said.

"This is for an art magazine," I cautioned her. "It's not Rolling Stone."

"Most artists are very literary. You don't need to be superficial, it should match your artwork."

Europeans generally appreciate art and take it seriously as a part of life. In the United States, it's not as important, and paintings tend toward romanticizing or decoration.

Juliette began to get ready to leave. She slipped into her clothes, and as she put her purse over her shoulder, she said, "I might not see you before you go, but here is my cell phone number if you need to reach me."

"I'm glad we did this," I told her.

She kissed me full on the lips.

"I'll call you," adding, "tomorrow."

She then quietly closed the door.

You can plan for relationships, but not love. It was obvious I was beginning to fall for her, but I also questioned whether the barriers were too numerous.

I spent the rest of the afternoon painting in the older parts of the city. Ancient walls, churches, and historic buildings attracted my eye, and by the time I returned, I had four more paintings in my backpack. It had also given me space to think. I tried to put the pieces of the puzzle together, but it was too early, and there were still too many unknowns. I thought about what Rembrandt had said, "Do each day the work at hand, and the mystery will reveal itself."

I got up early on Monday and headed to St. Sernin. I wasn't sure what I would accomplish there, except there could be a connection between the letter with the St. John writing and the Cathar Book of Revelation. I was hoping something might jump out, as had the speck.

I went to the library desk, where there was a new clerk. I asked to see the Revelation book, and he looked it up in the files.

"That volume is not available," he said.

"But I just saw it on Friday," I replied, taken aback a little.

"I'm sorry," the clerk said. "Would you like to see something else?"

"No, thank you." I then asked, "Do you know why it was withdrawn?"

"I don't know. Perhaps for conservation, the older volumes are inspected from time to time."

I wondered if they would find the little flake or the letters that might be hidden in its cover. But, on the other hand, I was glad I still had the photograph.

"Is the other clerk here today?" I then asked. "He was very helpful, and I would like to thank him."

"No, he's gone," the new clerk said coolly.

"You mean he's off today?" I asked, noting his choice of words.

"No. He's gone."

"I suppose it's none of my business, but was he dismissed?"

"Is there anything else I can help you with?" the new clerk said, ignoring the question.

"No, I apologize. You've been most gracious."

I left feeling uncomfortable with the exchange. I had planned to paint the quaint courtyard with the fountain but instead walked to a nearby bridge to get a view of the whole cathedral. Maybe I was overly cautious, but I did not want to risk any confrontation on church property.

I then drove to my hotel to finish packing. I began thinking of places in the room where I could hide the letters. I didn't feel safe leaving them there while away for three days. I could not come up with anywhere a thief might not look, and it was too late to get them to Juliette. I then thought of leaving the briefcase with Yoseph or Karl. However, I wasn't ready to tell them about the packet, and they would suspect something. I decided to take the briefcase with me. At least Dieter's home would be reasonably secure, and he wouldn't inquire.

Within an hour, I was there. It was a two-story house in an older residential area. Dieter showed me around, including a larger room where he meditated and practiced a form of martial art. There were wooden swords, staffs, and other objects, ritually placed along one wall. He was obviously proud of his home.

"I have lived here for 20-years," he said. "I try to maintain a certain atmosphere. I sometimes violate it, but then I feel bad for days."

He then invited me to a small garden area along the side of the house, bringing out two beers and some bread.

"We need some sustenance for our trip," he remarked, laughing.

As we talked, I asked if I could keep my briefcase at his house while we were away. As I expected, he didn't ask what was it contained but said he had the perfect place. He led me into his attic, where he pushed open an inauspicious ceiling panel. There was a deep cavity behind it that Dieter discovered when making some improvements.

"I keep a few important things in here," Dieter said. "You just never know."

"So long as you can find it again," I joked,

"Of course I can," Dieter said somewhat defensively, and I concluded this was a special spot.

When we came down, Dieter said he was ready to go. My car would be safe parked in front of his home, where large trees lined the street. We were taking his older model blue Saab, and the seats and controls reminded me of the cockpit of a plane.

"Saab makes jets," Dieter said, noticing my interest. "This baby flies."

He then excused himself and went back into the house, saying he just wanted to double-check the atmosphere. It was a bit odd, but it reminded me of an old Russian custom where everyone sits down briefly just before leaving on a long trip, to settle things visible and invisible. Americans seem to have lost connection with such practices.

The motocross took us southeast into a region of increasingly mountainous terrain. It was a beautiful drive, and Dieter's car did seem to fly through the landscape.

We passed cities like Castelnaudary and Carcassone, which played significant roles during the Albigensian Crusade. Then, we drove through Limoux and into the rural countryside. Rich rolling valleys surmounted by white stone ridges, deep ravines carved by rushing streams and rivers, scattered farms and villages, all graced by the snow-capped Pyrenees in the distance.

The place Dieter was taking me was once the home district of the Merovingian dynasty, the family that claimed some link to Mary Magdalene.

It was here Dieter had seen his pentagram. Rennes le Chateau was one of the key places, with some others being Blanche Forte, La Soulane, and a high rock outcropping called la Pique. He explained all this as we wound through tree-covered mountains. It felt restful, belying underlying energy and a turbulent past.

It was obvious Dieter had a special connection with the area, and as we approached his friend's driveway outside Rennes le Chateau, he stopped before we reached the entrance. We both got out and stood looking down over a bowl-shaped valley that stretched for miles.

"This area has been inhabited for at least 70-thousand years," Dieter said. "The churches, old watchtowers, and Templar forts were built on sites of previous buildings, which in turn were on older sacred sites. It has always been a special place."

"It does have a gentle, almost feminine feel to it," I commented.

"Yes, with la Pique in the middle," Dieter laughed as he got back in the car.

I decided to walk the short stretch to the house. The driveway was made of greyish white gravel from the region's limestone, and I picked a piece up as a memento. It still felt warm from the afternoon sun. Dieter's friend came out to greet us. He had grey flecks in his dark beard and bright eyes beneath heavy eyebrows.

"Peter, this is my friend Bjorn," Dieter said.

"Bonjour," Peter said with a smile. "Bien venu."

"Merci," I replied.

"He doesn't speak much French," Dieter said in English.

"Well then, welcome, please, please, come in. Would you like some coffee or tea?" Peter said as he opened the front door.

Dieter reached into the back of the car and produced a bottle of wine, which he handed to Peter.

"Ah, c'est bon," Peter exclaimed, holding the bottle out as he read the label. "This is from here, so why wait to open it."

We stepped inside the single-story white stucco house, which smelled of wood smoke and flowers. It was apparent they had lived here for many years. Well-worn coats and boots lined the entryway, and an old black Labrador walked slowly toward us, wagging her tail.

"This is Sophie," Peter said.

I knelt and scratched behind her ear, and in a moment her head was nuzzled against my chest.

"You know the true language," Peter said, walking into the kitchen.

The kitchen was bright, simple, and led to a stone patio. We were soon outside, sitting at a wooden table, the wine sparkling and glowing pink in the waning afternoon light.

"So, Dieter tells me you are interested in seeing some sights," Peter started.

"And maybe doing a little painting," I added.

"You know Picasso painted not far from here."

"Yes, in Gosol and Ceret."

"Maybe you will be the Picasso of la Pique," Peter remarked with a twinkle in his eye.

"I'd like that, but not much chance."

"Peter can take us to all these places," Dieter chimed in. "He knows them very well."

"That's tomorrow," Peter said. "Tonight we eat."

We soon heard a car coming down the driveway. It was Peter's wife, Marianne, returning from work.

"Dieter!" she cried as she came onto the patio, and they hugged.

"This is my friend, Bjorn," Dieter said.

"I'm glad to meet you. Did you have a good trip?" Marianne asked, shaking my hand.

"It was a beautiful drive, and I appreciate you letting me stay."

"Have you seen your bedroom? We only have one extra, so you and Dieter will be together."

She suggested we unpack the car and then showed us our room.

"Bjorn, why don't you take a look around before supper," Peter said after we put our things into the room and came back to the patio to finish our wine. "Dieter and I are cooking tonight. We have a few things to talk about, and Marianne would like to take a walk before we eat."

Marianne looked thoughtful for a moment, and then said, "Maybe you'd be interested in seeing the cave, it's not far."

The idea excited me. The area was riddled with caves conjuring pre-historic times and secret hiding places; and, it would be going inside the land itself.

The path began near the foot of a nearby hill, and Marianne said we would be back before it became very dark. As we circled the hillside, it appeared as if we could see the whole world. There were groves of small oaks reaching down, and I could hear a stream running below. A light, warm wind blew as the sun settled over the crest of the hill.

We soon came to a ravine carved out of the limestone, and I spotted the mouth of the cave. It was just above us and easily reached.

"I will show you in," Marianne said.

We climbed up to the entrance, which had an opening about four feet around. It looked to extend back only about 15 feet, and I thought I could see the end.

Marianne sat down and made no effort to enter. After a moment, I realized she would wait while I went in alone. As I looked about, I could imagine someone looking over this valley, standing in this exact spot, 20,000 years before. It seemed timeless.

I crouched and went in slowly, entering a spacious chamber. The floor was sand and rock but relatively flat. There were no signs anyone had been in, at least for a while. The air was warm, moist, which I didn't expect in a cave, and had a slight smell of sulfur, which I assumed came from the limestone. As my eyes adjusted, I could see the wall I had taken to be the end, angling up and extending further back. First, however, I sat against it, looking toward the light from the entrance. It was quiet and still, except for an occasional hush of wind from outside. My ears were ringing in the silence, and I couldn't resist going further.

I began thinking how entering a cave might be a kind of ritual, like returning to the darkness of the womb. As I went up the inclined back wall, I couldn't see anything but a dim light behind. Climbing further, I was now higher than the entry chamber, and the air was getting even warmer. The cave walls were becoming more constricted, and the ceiling was lower. Suddenly they were gone, and I could feel I was in an open space. My heart raced a little. It was now totally dark, and I had no idea of the chamber's features. I coughed to hear an echo but still could not tell. Wanting to find a rear wall, I crawled in several more feet but then gave up, having no idea how far back it went. I was concerned I might even lose the opening where I came in. I rolled onto my back, staring into the void and listening to my breath in the dense quiet.

I didn't want to keep Marianne waiting, but she had seemed content to wait, so I decided I could stay a little longer. I kept my eyes closed even in the blackness and soon realized the loudest noise was the racket of my own thoughts. Then slowly, like water flowing into powerful darkness, they quieted, leaving me with only the stillness. It reminded me of when I was a child in bed at night waiting to fall asleep.

I was completely at ease, but there was something else, though I didn't know quite what. I lay there for some time, but as I was about to leave, I finally stretched out both my arms and was startled when one hand bumped against a back wall, and the other splashed into hot water.

I jerked my hand out of the water and jumped into a crouched position. Reaching out, I again touched water. Then I understood the slight mineral smell that permeated the cave was from a hot spring. Sitting back I gave a deep sigh. It had been quite a shock, and I'd have to ask Marianne.

As I slowly made my way out, everyday thoughts began to return. At the bottom of the incline, where I could again see outside, I paused. The sky had grown darker, but I felt lighter. I could see Marianne sitting in the same place where I left her, with her dark wavy hair framed in the deepening blue.

"I wasn't sure you were going to come out," Marianne said with a smile.

"Sorry to keep you waiting."

"No," she said. "I enjoy it here."

"So, it's a hot spring?" I said inquisitively.

"It's many things," she said somewhat enigmatically. "But yes, there are hot springs and caves all over the Pyrenees. I like to think of this one as mine."

"Do you go in it?" I asked.

"Yes, but mainly on special occasions. There are others we use more frequently."

Half of me was still in the silence of the cave as we walked back, the path now barely visible. Dinner was waiting, and Dieter was in good spirits. I presumed there had been more than one bottle in the back of the car.

"Did you make it to the cave?" he asked boisterously.

"Yes," Marianne answered simply.

"Did you go in?" he continued looking at me.

"I did," was all I said.

Dieter became subdued and said, "It's a special place."

I hadn't intended to cut him short, after all, I would not even be here if it wasn't for him, but I appreciated Marianne not letting the experience be dissipated with loose talk.

Peter then looked at me and said, "Marianne is queen of the cave."

Marianne's eyes flashed, and tension quickly filled the room. There was a pause, and then we all laughed. On impulse, I raised my glass, to which everyone else did the same.

"To the cave," I said respectfully.

"To the cave!" they all repeated enthusiastically.

I turned to Dieter and said, "Thanks for bringing me here."

He smiled and punched me on the shoulder. The rift was mended.

The conversation soon turned to my article. Peter and Marianne were good hosts, and their keen observations kept me talking. I eventually told them what I'd found at St. Sernin and the odd disappearance of the first clerk.

"It's not so odd," Peter said. "You obviously found something."

"I guess we'll never know," I said.

"Are you going to put it in your article?" he asked.

"I'm not sure, what would I say? I really don't have anything," though I did have even more than I wanted to admit.

"You have to put it in," Marianne injected.

"That could cause some problems," I noted.

"You have to put it in, people need to know about it," she reiterated.

"Yes, you should," Peter said.

They were apparently familiar with controversy, and not afraid of consequences.

"Well, I was thinking the article would be about all my experiences, not only the artistic ones."

"That's good," Marianne said.

That night in our room, a more sober Dieter asked about the cave. I told him about going to the first wall, then crawling up its face to the larger space, and lying in the darkness next to the pool.

"It was as if I was in a tomb, or maybe a womb," I commented.

"Did anything happen?" he asked, obviously thinking of something specific.

I paused and said, "I came to the conclusion that I didn't have to do anything. I already am."

Dieter looked deep in thought.

"Does that make sense?" I asked.

"I think that's it," he replied.

CHAPTER TWELVE

Everyone was up early in the morning, and a welcoming sun shone into the kitchen. Sophie was soon nudging up against me.

"Will we be taking her with us?" I asked.

"No," Peter said. "We'll be climbing in places she couldn't follow. She's content being here."

There was a little time before breakfast, so I gathered my backpack to paint a quick picture of the house. It was a classic country cottage with white walls and a red roof, surrounded by bushes, flowers, and trees. The painting came easily. As I was finishing, Marianne was driving out and stopped to talk.

"Nice picture," she said. "How are you feeling this morning?"

"A little resurrected," I replied.

"I thought you'd understand," she said smiling. "Not many people know about it. It was probably a bear cave, and during Neolithic times it could even have been used as a ritual space, initiations perhaps."

"I could believe that."

"I have to go to work, but we'll have time to talk more tonight," she said as she drove off.

Dieter and Peter were already eating by the time I got back.

"Eggs are on the stove," Dieter said.

"There's something we want to ask you," Peter said as I sat down.

"You've heard the story about Rennes le Chateau and Sauniere?"

"A little, not much."

"What do you think?"

"Well, I don't think he was a saint."

Peter grinned. "Nor do I."

They had been talking about it when I was out painting. One story is while renovating the old chapel, Sauniere discovered some ancient writings about Jesus that controverted core Catholic doctrine. He then used the letters as leverage with the Catholic Church, and came into a substantial amount of money. Others say he never found anything and simply made out selling extra Masses in violation of Church rules.

"The church was built on a pre-Christian site," Dieter noted. "It's a point in the pentagram."

"I'd like to visit it," I said.

"That's where we're going first," said Peter pointing to the village. "It's right there."

We packed a few things, and in Dieter's car, we headed into Rennes-le-Chateau. It's a small village, with about a hundred residents, a hotel, restaurant, and a few shops that cater mainly to tourists. The church is on the edge of town, and a little ways away is a crumbling tower complex that was once the Chateau.

The church is about average size for a village, and its mix of construction struck me as we went in. Some parts are dated to Merovingian times, while others are of more recent construction. Fourteen standard plaster panels showing the Stations of the Cross had been added as part of Sauniere's renovations. He had a few painted in garish colors, causing some to believe they contained clues to his mystery. Overall, the interior had a theatrical appearance, and Dieter soon suggested we leave.

"It feels a little second rate," I commented after we were outside.

Dieter shook like he was casting something off, saying, "It's still a powerful spot."

As we were leaving, we passed a man in his mid-50's, thin, with a small mustache, and wearing a red plaid vest and blue coat. I thought he looked stereotypically French. He caught my eye, looking aggressive, almost angry.

Peter noticed and said softly, "I don't think he liked your comment."

We walked over to the ruined Chateau. It had a sense of nostalgic abandonment common to many buildings across Europe. The tower and walls had been a stronghold that later became part of a home, but both purposes had crumbled. I liked the visual composition, however, and did another quick painting. We then stopped at the café for coffee.

There were a few tourists around, and as we discussed our next move, Peter nodded at another table.

"That man's following you, Bjorn," he said with a mischievous grin.

I looked over, and the Frenchman in the vest and coat was glaring at me again.

"Maybe he doesn't like Americans," I said, feeling a little uncomfortable.

"Well, don't worry, he's not going to be following us where we're going."

Our next stop was Blanche Fort, which was not a building, as I expected, but a mountain. It is still forested, and the white stone crest commands one side of the valley.

"The going gets rough in some places," Dieter said. "But there are lots of caves."

We parked the car and started up the trail that led to the summit. For the most part, it was not a strenuous trek but quite long, with several switchbacks as we ascended the mountainside. It was past noon when we reached the summit.

On our way, we had clambered around looking for caves. Dieter found one he was interested in exploring, and we both entered. The damp smell of stone and earth rose as we worked our way into the dark. While it was taller than the cave by Peter's house, it was also narrower, more like a crevice. Dieter had brought a flashlight, and as we went beyond the reach of daylight, he turned it on, the beam nervously glancing off the rough limestone. At one point, the rock became blackened and pitted, with the look of being deliberately enlarged. After that, the tunnel went back another 100 feet, following the natural course.

Suddenly Dieter stopped and put his hand to the wall.

"Look!" he said in excitement.

As he focused the light on the spot, there was a faint outline of an equal-armed cross. It did not appear to be natural, but it was hard to tell in the dim light on the blackened wall.

"That's a Templar sign," Dieter said. "They used this cave."

One of the nine founders of the Knights Templar was a Lord from this area, and nearly a third of the Order's vast landholdings had been in the region, so it was very likely.

We quickly made our way out and told Peter, then all of us went back in. Peter said he had heard of Templar Crosses on the mountain, and he knew of one in the valley below. The Templars were trained strategists and often hid caches of weapons, money, and supplies as a military organization. A few of the local Knights escaped on the day the Templar Order was destroyed by King Charles II, and there was likely enough in this cave to set them on their way. Peter doubted it was a new find, however. Archeologists and treasure hunters had been exploring this mountain for a very long time, and the cave was not unusually difficult to locate. Dieter was still excited, as it further confirmed his belief that this was a power spot.

I found something else, though. After my experience in the cave the night before, I sensed a similar quality here. I surmised it was also a place of retreat, not in the military sense, but a more spiritual one. I think Dieter did, too. He was picking up small stones here and there as if looking for something. I took a few minutes to paint the entrance, hoping to capture the sense of place. What came out was a picture in dark and light greys, with a faint accent of green. The darkness of the cave entrance was powerful, almost forbidding, and quite in contrast to the dappled light that was dancing across it.

At the top of the mountain, the broad view encompassed the whole valley. Given the perspective, it was not surprising to see the stone remains of what had been a watchtower. In the center of the crumbled walls was a cistern, large enough to have supplied the occupants with water for weeks at a time. Peter said this had been a viewing post used by the Templars and others.

As we ate lunch, I began ruminating on the cistern. I couldn't imagine how such a sizeable pit was filled. Hauling water would not have been easy. When I mentioned it, Peter smiled and said, "They used rain, like what's coming in."

Afternoon thunderclouds were building over the distant Pyrenees, and some were beginning to float into the valley, making large dark patches on the bright countryside below.

"We'd better start down," Peter said.

Dieter wanted to stop by the cave again as we went down but decided there was not enough time if we were going to visit La Soulane and La Pique.

"I can come back to the area," Dieter said to me. "You may not have another chance to see some of these places."

It took about an hour to hike down the mountain. When we reached our car, another was parked on the side of the road about 50 yards away.

"Isn't that the man from the church?" Peter said, peering over.

We all turned, and there was the Frenchman in the red plaid vest and blue coat standing by a white, four-door Renault. He still had that glaring look.

"Hey, you there!" Dieter called out in an aggressive Dutch voice.

The man stood for a moment, deliberately staring back. Dieter began walking towards him, and the man opened the driver's door and quickly got in. When Dieter kept coming, the man swung the vehicle into a U-turn and headed back down the road towards town.

"You sure you don't know him?" Peter asked me.

"No," I said. "I've never seen him before."

"Well, he certainly has taken a liking to you."

Dieter came back and said if the guy kept following us, he would confront him.

"He's probably just a weird local, "I commented, hoping to ease the situation.

"I've lived around here a long time," Peter said. "I've never seen him."

The whole thing felt a little odd. I began to wonder if he was sent by the Count to check on me, but something said that wasn't it. So I decided I would be a little more cautious making comments in public around here.

"Let's go," Peter said. "We're running short on time."

As we headed back into town, we wondered if we would see him again, but it seemed he'd had enough for one day. We then drove to La Soulane, another point in Dieter's pentagram.

"So, what do you think he's after," Peter finally said.

"The Frenchman? I don't know. I got into a little trouble in Toulouse with a member of the Lautrec family. We call him The Count, and I hear he's a real S.O.B. It might be related to that, but I don't think so. This guy, he kind of reminds me of a cop."

"The French connection," Peter said with a wry smile.

"Yes, he is cocky, like a cop," Dieter said. "All the more reason to
face him."

"Have you been doing anything else?" Peter asked.

"You mean other than finding the Holy Grail," Dieter commented.

"No, this person was not from the Church," Peter said. "They would not be so overt. Though he may think he's trying to protect the faith or something. One thing is for sure, he's not in the hotel business, unbelievers are good business around here."

La Soulane is a stone outcropping almost hidden in a tangle

of woods. At its crest, which is not high, a few rocks come together to form a point like a pyramid, which was beginning to take on a slight rosy hue in the slowly changing light. You could see a little of the countryside through the trees, but the place did not appear to have much that would make an impression. Dieter, however, again said this was a power spot, noting how some tree trunks were very crooked.

"That's a sign," he commented.

We did not spend a long time there, but Dieter stopped for a moment at the bottom and stared as if something was in the air. The sun was getting lower, and the clouds beginning to blush, casting a reddish glow onto the hills and treetops. The cool of the day was approaching, when everything grows still and quiet as if preparing for the night.

"Did you see anything?" Dieter asked as we were driving away.

"No," I replied. "Though it did get very still for a few moments."

"Yes, that's when I saw it. There was a circle of red light around the hill. The circle is of the feminine."

"Then I guess our next stop should be la Pique," Peter remarked cheerily.

La Pique is a narrow ridge rising a few hundred feet off the valley floor, surrounded by a copse of woods. A well-worn path leads to the top, but Dieter and Peter wandered about, so we did as much exploring as walking. It was secluded off the trail, and a gentle breeze occasionally stirred the leaves. Dieter was still looking for something and would stop to pick up a small rock, but as often as not, he put it right back where he found it. As we reached the summit, a large bird was circling high above, rising on the air currents. A view of the valley and mountains stretched all around, making it another good lookout point. However, it was hard not to notice the thoughts that came to mind: a magical spot, only to have been the center of such brutal contention. As Dieter had done at the church, I tried to shake them off.

The sun was now setting in a glow of gold and blue. The storm that had threatened earlier never materialized, and only a thin bank of clouds on the horizon was left to catch the sun's last rays. I pulled out my paints to make a little larger picture, about 9 by 12 inches. I worked quickly using a larger brush, and the painting turned out quite bright, with a white glow on the crest of la Pique nearly pushing the clouds aside. It was not exactly what it looked like, but how it felt.

Dieter had walked to the point overlooking the valley, and taking a few steps back, he pulled a handful of white stones out of his pocket. He carefully placed them on the ground, creating a small circle, and then put a dot in the middle. Then, with his arms outstretched, he said a few words as a prayer. I didn't understand the language, but it wasn't Dutch. We all stood in silence for a long moment before starting to walk back down.

I didn't know where Dieter was getting his ceremonies, but they seemed to fit. However, I wondered if he saw the pentagram again, as this was where it had appeared before. I asked him about it as we approached the car.

"No, I did not see it," he said. "I think it was only for that time, like the red circle was for today. It is still there, though. It's real."

Peter reached the car first, and looking around, called back, "The coast is clear!"

Dieter and I laughed.

CHAPTER THIRTEEN

On the drive back to Rennes le Chateau, Peter explained some of the valley's history and the sites we had visited. Visigoths from the area had sacked Rome in 400 AD and returned with many treasures. Some believe the plunder included sacred items from the Temple in Jerusalem, which the Romans had stolen when they destroyed the city quelling a Jewish uprising in 70 AD.

Following the Visigoths, the Merovingians emerged as the leading group, and their court flourished along with the economy. The warm climate was perfect for growing woad, the key ingredient in making a rich blue dye, and by the 1100's many of the merchants had become very rich, primarily from the cloth trade.

Bordering Spain was still under Muslim control, and their revolutionary advances in mathematics and the sciences were well known, attracting students and practitioners from all over Europe. Though widespread by this time, the Catholic faith was not the overbearing force it was in Rome. Jews, gnostic Christians, and native beliefs were not discouraged and even welcomed. The notched stick of history was long here.

"If only the hills and stones could talk," I said.

"But they do," Peter said. "You just have to know how to listen."

As we made our way back to the sprinkled lights of Rennes le Chateau, we drove through town and again passed the café and the Church.

"Isn't that the car we saw at Blanche Forte?" Dieter asked.

We slowed down, and it seemed to be the same white, four-door Renault.

"A Renault for Rennes," Peter quipped. "Maybe he's praying for our souls."

"He will need to pray if I see him," Dieter replied.

We joked as we drove up to Peter's house, each trying to outdo the other with innuendos about the "Frenchman."

Marianne was home when we arrived, and supper was waiting.

"Have a good trip?" she asked. "See any more lights, Dieter?"

Dieter started to take offense until he realized she was getting back at him for his comments the night before.

"Only you floating above Blanche Forte in a glowing white dress," he replied. "There were cherubs flitting about, cute little guys. Who are they anyway?"

"They were there to catch you when you fainted from my beauty," Marianne answered.

"Then I hope they are still around," Dieter responded. "We did find a cave, though"

Marianne's eyes lit up.

"It looked like a Templar cave," Peter said while opening a bottle of wine. "I'd never seen it before. I'm surprised it isn't marked on the map."

"There's a lot that isn't marked," Marianne said. "Our cave isn't."

"Yes, but that's a small one, this one isn't, and it's not far from the main path. It even has what appears to be a Templar cross."

"You'll have to take me," Marianne said.

We sat down for dinner, and Dieter raised his glass for a toast.

"To good company, good food, and good spirits."

"Amen," Peter said.

Marianne asked me, "So Bjorn, what do think of our little enclave? Are we crazy enough for you?"

"Not crazy," I replied. "But I am not sure if you are marked on any map."

She laughed, "That's a good thing, it keeps us safe."

"Speaking of which, we may have another guest tonight for dinner," Peter said.

Everyone turned to look at him. "A little Frenchman who's been following us around all day. He has taken an interest in Bjorn."

"What do you mean?" asked Marianne.

We explained what had happened, and while Marianne was concerned, she also did not seem overly surprised.

"This would not be the first time we have attracted attention in this valley," she said, though not explaining further.

"I have one question," I then asked. "The pentagram, the circle Dieter saw today, what is behind them?"

There was silence for a few moments as each of them delved into some common recess of mind.

"If we told you the story you might need a star chart rather than a map," Dieter finally said.

"Then you are Pleiadians," I commented.

They were taken aback, not knowing whether I was serious.

"Not exactly," Peter started to say cautiously.

"He was joking," Dieter injected, shaking his head.

"Still, it may have a relationship to this planet, the sun, and beyond," Peter said.

It quickly passed my mind, 'OK, here it comes.' I had enjoyed my time today, though what direction it had taken, I wasn't sure. I decided I was up for it,

"I'm listening," I replied.

What I heard was a complex tale that wove the sacred geometry of the ancient Greeks with Egyptian mystery schools, particularly related to the goddess Isis, and the ancient myth of Atlantis. Rennes le Chateau, and the places we visited today, were some key points that, when the dots were connected, formed a pentagram and other symbols that were once used to represent a divine order and purpose.

"There may be too many geometric coincidences just to be coincidences," Peter said. "And Rennes le Chateau seems to be a main point."

"So where does Mary Magdalene and the purported blood-line of Jesus fit in?" I asked, my credulity already swimming.

"This part of France was conquered Roman territory," Dieter explained. "It was a common trade route, only a few days travel by boat from Rome. It was close, but not too close, and even back then it was seen as something of a haven. The eastern shore is the French Riviera after all."

"Mary Magdalene came here not long after Jesus was crucified, fearing persecution. And remember, the mystery schools were still active then. They had certain knowledge, and understood this area as a safe place for the feminine. Mary is suspected of having been involved with them in some way prior to meeting Jesus."

"Well, if what you say is true about Mary needing to take cover, it does make some sense," I said. "I really had never thought about it."

"I should add, there is absolutely no record that backs any of this up," Peter said. "It is entirely speculation."

"But there is other evidence," Marianne remarked.

"It's still speculative," Peter said, with some softness in his voice, as if he had heard this before.

"Only if you are a man," she retorted. "There are certain things women would recognize that men don't see. It's not empirical, like forts or manuscripts, but in its own way equally valid. For instance, the Languedoc became a center for the healing arts, and women were welcomed equally with men, which was not generally the case elsewhere.

The troubadour tradition originated in Toulouse, with romance as its touchstone, an unlikely choice in those war-like times. Eleanor of Aquitaine, the mother of the kings of both France and England, helped spread that culture and was said to be sympathetic to the Cathars. The Cathar parfaits, something like ministers, were both men and women. Where the feminine is safe, culture thrives, which it did here for centuries.

None of this happens just by chance. It requires something

very specific and deliberate. It is apparent to me that a strong feminine influence was present here. It took nearly 40 years of a genocidal crusade by a patriarchal Church, followed by 300 years of the Inquisition, to repress that culture. It forced a lot of things into hiding."

There was silence in the room as Dieter, Peter, and I looked at our wine glasses. Finally, Dieter spoke.

"Well said, Marianne."

"There is one other thing," she added. "What also got lost was the wisdom of the oracle."

"You mean like at Delphi?" I asked, almost without thinking.

"There were oracles in other places, too, and they weren't only women," Marianne said. "Delphi is just the one most people have heard about."

"So this relates to your interest in caves?" I said.

Marianne's eyes brightened, but she said nothing.

"Not to change the subject," I said, "but I have something you might be interested in."

Maybe it was the wine, maybe it was because they had been so forthcoming with me that I felt I could trust them; but, I had decided to tell them about the manuscripts from the Lautrecs. I had a sense things were not going to go well when I returned to Toulouse, and feared the letters could wind up being suppressed, or worse. I also knew if I told them, these three could get swept into the investigation if I was charged for stealing the packet, but that possibility seemed remote.

"Now, this is very, very confidential." I began. "You could get into trouble for even hearing what I am about to tell you. So you need to be aware of that, and say you agree. It may involve something illegal, it wasn't, but some people might think so."

"What is it?" Peter asked.

"So, you agree?" I said.

"Give us a hint," Peter replied.

"What we were talking about last night, that I had come

across something." Then I added, "Dieter this goes beyond what I've told you."

They looked at each other, nodded, and in one voice said, "Yes!"

I relayed the story about visiting the Lautrec's, being handed the sealed packet, then accused of causing the aunt's stroke, and finally that no one but Juliette and I knew of the letters.

"So, what do they say?" Marianne asked.

I held my breath for a moment.

"One might be the earliest version of the Book of Revelation, possibly even in his own hand."

"Wow," Dieter said.

"There are three other letters," I went on. "I don't know who wrote them, but at least one is a kind of personal letter, signed with the same mark as I found in St. Sernin. It is the letter Y."

"Yeshua," Marianne said.

A chill ran through my chest as she said the word. I immediately thought, 'She knows.'

"It was addressed to a Mary," I added, and I thought Marianne was going to cry.

I began thinking of the peculiar paper that I couldn't read, but felt I understood. I didn't want to speak of it, however. Perhaps it was like the quantum theory when even looking at something can change it.

"Could we see these letters?" Peter asked.

"I hope at some point," I said. "If you tell anyone about this, I might get arrested."

"Your secret is safe with us," answered Peter, but then sounding concerned, "Are they in a safe place?"

"They are at Dieter's house," I replied, grinning a little as I looked over at him.

"So that's what they were," Dieter said enthusiastically, pumping a fist in the air in victory. "Yes, they are safe. I have them in my secret hiding place. It's protected."

"What are you going to do with them?" Peter asked. "If they are real, this is nothing to trifle with. A lot of people would do anything to get their hands on them. Anything."

"I'm getting that," I said with a sigh. "At some point, they need to be returned to the Lautrecs, hopefully without me going to jail. Yet at the same time, I want the right people to have a chance to look at them. The Lautrecs might welcome that, but given what I've seen so far, I wouldn't bet on it."

"If there is anything we can do," Peter said, "there are those who would be interested in helping."

"I might need a lawyer, or two," I said half-seriously.

"Just let us know," Peter replied.

While that was welcome reassurance, I still felt a sense of unease. There was a reason these letters had been kept secret for so long, and things have a way of taking very unexpected turns when powerful influences are at work. So while I felt good about the disclosure, I was aware I had also lost some control, and even cracked Pandora's box a little.

"Don't worry, Bjorn," Marianne said as if reading my thoughts. "It will be OK."

"Let's drink to that," said Dieter, uncorking another bottle of wine.

We spent the next while discussing various aspects of the letters, particularly their significance if they happened to be some writings of Jesus. Beyond circumstantial evidence, no historical artifact or corroborating record has come to light that definitively confirms what was said about him in the Gospels, or for that matter, that he even existed.

As the conversation continued, I began to feel drowsy and could hardly keep my eyes open. Perhaps it was the wine, or the hike, or just the events of the day. Though still relatively early, I apologized for my tiredness and was soon crawling into bed.

My dreams that night were not settled. I saw myself looking over the long valley containing Rennes le Chateau, and Dieter and I were debating the purpose of an old stone wall that sloped down toward a river separating some woods from a field.

I was distracted by a hawk cry above me, but I couldn't see it in the sky, and then I slowly realized the noise was a jay cawing outside the window, and I was startled awake. Dieter was still asleep in the other bed, and early morning sunshine was lighting the trees and yard as a cool breeze blew in through the curtains.

I still felt a little disoriented, as sometimes happens on a trip. I had the pieces, but something didn't quite fit. I began to wonder how long it would take me to reorient to the States when I returned because it happens both ways. Some call it culture shock, but it's place shock, too.

As I rolled over to catch a little more sleep, I noticed my painting bag on the floor behind my bed. It had apparently slipped down, and I had forgotten about it. I decided to get up and catch the early light. We were planning to leave today, and this might be my best chance to do a painting of the house. If it turned out, I would give it to Peter and Marianne as a thank you gift.

I quietly dressed and slipped out of the house, but not without disturbing Sophie, who followed me, wagging her tail. I sat down on a stone wall in the yard, and as I was about to paint, Sophie's ears perked up. She quickly started running on stiff legs down the hill alongside the house. I couldn't see what had aroused her but assumed it was a fox or another animal. She was soon out of sight.

I found myself painting a simplified, but realistic, picture of the home. Its white walls were tinted yellow and pink by the morning light, while the surrounding trees were dark green, almost black, in contrast. The painting sang brightly and certainly portrayed a pleasant place.

About this time, Sophie came trotting back, smiling with her tongue hanging out the side of her mouth. It was then that I noticed a cut on her side. It was not very large and looked like she had run into barbed wire or a sharp branch.

I got a little blood on my fingers as I examined her coat, and when I put my painting down to take her inside, I accidentally smudged a bit of it on the watercolor.

Marianne was already up and in the kitchen.

"I'm afraid Sophie suffered a cut," I explained.

"Oh, let's see," said Marianne with mild concern. "Hmm, that's unusual."

"What's that?" I asked.

"It's almost as if she was stabbed."

We examined the wound together, and I somehow knew that no vital organ had been pierced, but the object had entered the body cavity and would be causing internal bleeding. Sophie would be OK, but she needed care from a vet.

"I think you need to take her to a vet," I said.

"Do you think it's that serious?" Marianne asked. "It's not very big."

"It didn't hit anything vital, but it's deeper than it looks and is bleeding internally."

"Do you have some medical background?" Marianne asked, a little surprised.

"No," I said. "But do you have a regular vet?"

Marianne called the animal clinic, and while it was not open yet, an assistant had arrived early and said to bring in Sophie. By the time Marianne left, everyone was up.

I explained what had happened as Dieter and I began packing our things and putting them in the car. Peter was busy getting breakfast, and doing a few outside chores, when Marianne called. Sophie would be fine but needed some surgery, and she was going to stay while that was done. When she asked to speak with me, I thought it was to say goodbye.

"How did you know?" she asked unexpectedly.

"Know what?" I replied.

"How did you know?" she repeated. "You said just what the vet said."

"Just a hunch," I said weakly.

"No, you knew. What are you not telling me?" she

demanded.

I felt cornered. She was right, I had known, but I was afraid to admit it, almost as if I would be revealing a secret I didn't understand.

"Marianne, I can't explain it, somehow when I touched the dog, I just knew."

She was silent for a few moments, and then said quietly, "Thank you, you were right. I'm not sure I would have brought her in so soon, and the vet said if we had waited, she could have died from internal bleeding, even though no organs were damaged."

I was as surprised as Marianne. Where those perceptions had come from, I didn't know. Perhaps a kind of intuition, but it had felt very definitive. I had no medical training, and in fact, I was squeamish around the few surgical procedures I'd seen and had nearly passed out.

"I might not see you before you leave," Marianne said. "We really enjoyed meeting you, you are a special person. We must stay in touch, and I want to see those letters."

"You will," I promised. "Thank you for all your hospitality, you are special, too, both of you. I hope I can return soon, and I am sure Dieter feels the same. Do you want to talk to him?"

"Yes, but only if he's right there," she said. "I don't want to tie up their business phone."

Dieter and Marianne talked for a short while. After Dieter hung up, he turned to me and with a mischievous look said, "So, Bjorn, what else are you not telling me? "

Then turning to Peter, he said, "Let's eat!"

We had a leisurely breakfast, but it was different without Sophie lying nearby, hoping for scraps from the table. We discussed the letters a little more, and I assured Peter that I would keep him in the loop, at least through Dieter. Soon we were getting into the car to leave.

"Take care, Peter said. "Remember, we can help, but only if you ask."

I thanked him for his hospitality again, he and Dieter

hugged goodbye, and we headed back to the highway, going through Rennes le Chateau.

As we pulled out of the driveway and down the paved road, I noticed a white car parked on a dirt lane not far from the house. The vehicle was partially obscured by a hedge, but for some reason it caught my attention. As we drove into town, it came to me, it was similar to the car of the unpleasant Frenchman. I hadn't seen enough of it to be sure, but I wondered. Was he spying, and was that what Sophie had noticed, getting stabbed in the process? I then thought my imagination was getting away from me until Dieter said,

"I wonder where our French friend is today?"

"I thought I saw a car like his beneath Peter and Marianne's house when we left," I said.

"What!" Dieter exclaimed as he immediately turned the car around and started driving back. "If he's there, he's not going to get away this time."

The car was gone, however.

"Are you sure it was him?" Dieter asked.

'I didn't see anyone, and the car was partially obscured. It just caught my eye, so no, I can't be sure."

"Well, I am going to tell Peter anyway," Dieter said.

We drove back up to the house, and Peter came out, smiling and a little surprised.

"Forget something?" he asked.

"You may have a French friend snooping around," Dieter explained. "Bjorn thought he saw a car like his down below your home."

Peter looked at me as he chuckled a little.

"You sure you haven't mentioned those letters to anyone else?" he said, closing one eye and looking like a buccaneer. "I'll keep an eye out for him."

I suddenly remembered the watercolor I had made that morning. I reached into my things, and when I pulled out the painting, I noticed the reddish smudge from Sophie's blood. It was a small but permanent record, like a flake off a stone tool.

I handed the picture to Peter and pointed out the mark.

"I don't think I measure up to being the Picasso of la Pique," I added.

"Ahh, but you are," Peter said." Just as Picasso used his paintings to exorcise inner demons, this painting has transformed Sophie's wound. In a good way. It will have a special place on our walls."

Thoughts about my recent experiences were jumping around in my head as we drove through the valley, out of Rennes le Chateau, and onto the road leading back to Toulouse.

I was trying to make sense of it, find some common thread, when Dieter, looking querulous, asked me, "So Bjorn, how did you know about the dog?"

I had forgotten about Marianne's phone call. I didn't respond immediately but finally answered, "A lucky guess."

"That's was not Marianne's impression," he replied.

"It just came to me, and seemed to make sense. There wasn't anything mystical about it. I was as surprised as she that it was right." Then I added lightly, "I really don't know."

"But you did know," Dieter retorted quickly. "It may not seem like much to you, but not everyone can do that. I think you have a gift. You should pay attention to it."

It didn't feel like I had a gift, but as I gave it some thought, maybe I was influenced by the place. Obviously, its history captures most of the interest, but there was another magic residing just under the physical surface, magnetic and yet gentle. I could better understand how Dieter might see lights, and Marianne find oracles. Then again, perhaps that was all imagination, and then I remembered my dream, of the stone wall, and the cry of the bird I couldn't see. It was like a portent of what happened to Sophie.

I began to think I was imagining too much, but the beauty of the countryside didn't take any imagining. The rest of the ride was uneventful, and I agreed to show Dieter the letters when we got to his house.

CHAPTER FOURTEEN

As we approached Toulouse, it felt a little like coming home. We arrived at Dieter's about mid-afternoon, and as we were going in, Dieter paused by the front door as if searching for one of his little stones.

"Just checking," he said. "It's good."

He immediately went upstairs to his hiding place and brought down my briefcase.

I thought about calling Juliette to tell her I was going to show him the letters, but Dieter was eager to see them, and I didn't want to complicate the moment. I again said he couldn't mention it to anyone, and even seeing the letters might get him in trouble.

"I understand," he said respectfully.

I clicked the briefcase latches open and lifted the lid. The sweet scent of beeswax drifted into the room.

"What's that?" he asked, a little startled and as if it might be something mystical.

"The packet was sealed with wax," I answered. "It's a nice smell, isn't it?"

"Like ambrosia," he remarked.

I took the packet out of the plain envelope and was about to give it to him when I noticed his eyes were shut. So I waited until he opened them, and then he stared for a moment at what was in my hand.

"I don't want to touch it," he said.

I thought he wanted me to open it because of their age and fragility, but as I began to unfold the cover, he put out his hand to stop me.

"No," he said. "Don't."

"Don't you want to see?" I stated in surprise, and even with some disappointment. I had anticipated his response might be a little unusual, but not this.

"I see a glow around them," he replied hesitantly.

As I held the ancient packet in my hand, unsure whether I should put it back, I began to feel it getting warmer and thought of the power of suggestion.

"I already know what's inside," Dieter added, still looking a little startled. "It's as if I can read them."

Taken aback, I commented, "I had a similar experience."

"Yes," he stated with some wonder.

After a few moments, he gently touched my hand as if even that might be coming too close.

"You can put it away now," he said.

"You sure?" I asked, still a little incredulous.

"They are what you say, but they are not for me, at least not yet. They are for you," he said, "and Juliette."

I reluctantly placed the packet back in the plain envelope, returned it to the briefcase, and snapped the latches shut. We sat in silence for a while, each lost in our thoughts. The letters seemed to have enfolded us in their atmosphere, a sweet fragrance lingering in the air. I was pretty sure Dieter and I were having the same experience, but I didn't want to say anything, as if it would somehow break the connection. I didn't understand, but I was beginning to think at least one of the letters was capable of having a profound effect on just about anyone.

"Wow," Dieter finally said, his voice sounding different, "You really need to protect that."

"Yes," I replied, then suddenly feeling the need to bring something back to reality, "and, it's as I mentioned at Rennes, I need to return them to the Lautrecs."

"Why?" he remarked, now a little angrily. "You should put them out on the internet."

"And have the Count charge me with theft, just like he said I caused his aunt's stroke?"

"OK," he replied, nodding slowly. "But, I'd do it anyway."

101

"I can't, Dieter," I protested. "At any rate, not yet."

He then offered to keep them at his home, where they would be safe. While it was a good idea, I felt I should keep them with me for now. I wanted to retain some level of control. I again thought of calling Juliette and asking how the aunt was doing. My editor in New York would also be expecting a call, but it was still too early there to phone.

While we were in Rennes le Chateau, I picked up a bottle of the local wine Dieter had given to Peter. It was in my painting knapsack, which I had brought into the house.

"Here Dieter, a little present."

"You didn't need to do that," he objected but obviously pleased. "We have to talk about this, but right now, I must get ready to go to Holland to see my daughter. I leave tonight."

"So you were married?"

"Yeah, for 15 years. We still see each other, but I could never live with her again. She's OK with it, too."

It was a sudden change of subject, but Dieter was such a different character, and I began to imagine what his ex-wife was like.

"I'd better get going, too," I said. "The real world beckons."

We laughed, shook hands, and as I went out the door he clapped me heartily on the shoulder. As I was about to get into my car, I glanced over and thought I could see a glow around him as he stood in his doorway. I blinked my eyes, and when I looked again, it was gone. Dieter was simply waving goodbye. It was probably the afternoon light flickering through the leaves.

I appreciated how much Dieter had offered, and for what I had experienced over the past few days. I began to think Rennes le Chateau might make up for the loss of the Lautrec library angle in my article.

As I drove toward my hotel, I began thinking of the next steps. I first needed to find out what the situation was with the aunt. My fear was she had died, and the Count would start pressing for some kind of criminal charge. I was reasonably sure it wouldn't stick, but it was the French legal system, and I suspected it could be a nightmare. Then there was Juliette. Our connection seemed to only grow stronger while I was away. I was certainly thinking of her more, and I wasn't comfortable that it was a good thing. I also had to return the letters.

As I pulled into the small hotel parking lot, I needed to check for messages at the front desk, but first, I brought my bags to my room. I took the stairs from the parking area rather than the lobby elevator, feeling I could use the exercise after driving.

My room had a slightly stale, musty smell from being unused. As I flipped on the bathroom light, I noticed it had been cleaned in my absence, and new towels lined the racks. I checked to see if anything in the room had been moved, but it appeared as I had left it. I began to wonder whether I had been overly cautious in bringing the letters over to Dieters.

I took the elevator to the lobby, still with the briefcase. While perhaps unreasonable, I did not feel comfortable leaving it behind. As the doors opened, I saw two men at the front desk talking to the clerk. There was something familiar about one of them, and then I realized it was the 'Frenchman' who had been following us in Rennes le Château. He was wearing a blue police uniform. Dieter's suspicions had been right. The other man was older, dressed in a dark suit, and had an air of authority. The clerk was pointing in the direction of the mailbox with my room number on it, shaking his head.

I didn't get out of the elevator, and quickly reached over and pushed hard on the up button, but the doors remained open. I pushed on the button two more times, and after a long pause, the doors finally closed. The two men had not turned around, distracted by the usually observant clerk, who was still talking. The elevator gave a shudder, but it was going down, not up. Someone in the basement had pushed a button before me.

Thoughts scrambled through my mind as I slowly descended, but the first was how to get out of the building. When the elevator stopped, and the doors opened, a service worker was standing there behind a large white laundry cart. I pretended to look startled and confused, like I was on the wrong floor, and asked if there were some stairs I could take. He gave me a polite look and said, "No English," then motioned for me to stay on the elevator and go back up, and he would wait.

As the doors began to close, I suddenly reached over and held them open, waving him in as I stepped out. He looked flustered, but I insisted, saying, "Please, please," pulling his cart a little way into the elevator. He continued to protest, but the doors were now trying to shut and banging repeatedly on the front of the cart, a little bell ringing each time they hit. He finally shrugged, pushed the cart all the way in, and as the doors were closing, he pointed to the end of the dimly lit hall.

I went in the direction he indicated, hoping it led to a way out, not just back to the lobby. As I walked through the scruffy hallway, it occurred to me the service worker would tie up the elevator for a while and delay the two officers if they were planning to go to my room. At the end of the hall, there was a flight of stairs leading to a door. I took the steps two at a time, and reaching the top, took a moment and a deep breath before cautiously opening it. I found myself at the back of the hotel, not far from the parking lot with my car. It could not have worked out better if I had planned it.

I headed for my car, but as I came to the front of the hotel I peeked around the corner to see if the police were outside. I didn't see anyone. I quickly walked to my car, but when I reached for my keys they weren't there. I patted all my pockets until I realized I had left them in the room with my other things, thinking I'd only be gone a few minutes. Gratefully, I had the briefcase.

Still cursing myself about the keys, I started running through my options. I could call Dieter to pick me up, but he was at least a half-hour away, and I didn't want to get him more involved; besides, he may have already left for Holland. Juliette would certainly come, and might even know what was going on with the police; but, with a child and husband, that could take a while, in addition to being awkward.

I needed to get away immediately. Then I thought of Yoseph at the bookstore. His shop was within walking distance, and I might even be able to get there before it closed. And, perhaps, he could keep the briefcase for me.

As I walked away from the hotel, I kept looking over my shoulder as inconspicuously as I could, making sure I hadn't been spotted. It was evening rush hour, and I blended in with the pedestrians eager to get home. While the streets were crowded, I was able to make good time. I wasn't thinking of going into hiding, but I needed a little time to think. As I walked, I noticed the sun was getting low, and the city was taking on its characteristic pink glow.

Approaching the bookstore, I could see it was still open, and inside, Yoseph was talking to a customer. When he greeted me he, immediately sensed I was distressed.

"How are you doing," he said, looking concerned. "Is everything OK?"

"Well, yes and no," I told him. "Could I talk to you for a minute, privately? I might have a favor to ask."

"Sure, anything," he quickly replied. "But, can you give me a minute? I am about ready to close, and then I'll have all the time we need."

"I need to make a call," I said, looking for a quiet spot.

"Go in the back, it's private."

He then went to move the lingering customer along.

In his office was one of those old-style French phones, a heavy black model that you see in movies about World War Two. It made me feel like I was running from the German Gestapo, and about to make a desperate call.

As Juliette's cell phone rang, I hoped this would not be too much. I had disrupted her life, and maybe her husband was right about keeping away from me. I was reflecting on this when her answering service kicked in, "Bonjour. C'est Juliette…"

I had anticipated talking to her but noticed I enjoyed listening to her voice on the recording, with its gentle French accent. I also wondered why she hadn't picked up. Was she avoiding me?

"Hi, Juliette, this is Bjorn," I said after the message tone. "I just got back with Dieter, and I was wondering if you could give me a call. I'm at Yoseph's bookstore at the moment. It's kind of important. Take care."

As I ended the call, I began to relax. Yoseph was already locking the door and turning off the store lights. I sat down, grateful to be in the quiet atmosphere amid shelves stacked with friendly old books. However, it was old books that had put me in this mess. I looked at my briefcase and patted it. This was no time to be thinking ill thoughts about something so valuable.

As I waited, I noticed someone peering in the front door. He was backlit, so I couldn't see his face, but as he cupped his hands around his eyes to look inside, I could tell it was Karl.

I stood up, but Yoseph was already walking over to the door.

"Is it all right if he's here?" he asked. "I can tell him to come back later."

I thought about it for a second and then said, "No, it's fine."

I hadn't planned on telling Karl yet, but somehow it seemed OK. He had been helpful and very open with his family secret, and he certainly knew the ins and outs of this kind of business, perhaps even how I should deal with the police. Unfortunately, what little control I had tried to maintain was slipping away, and the water was quickly rising over my head.

Karl came in and greeted me warmly.

"How was your trip?" he asked. "Yoseph told me you went to Rennes le Chateau."

"It wasn't quite what I expected," I replied. "The place certainly has a history."

"I know the story. Abbe Sauniere was an unusual character, and during the war, the Nazis dug around there looking for things." He then added with a little bite, "They left empty-handed."

"My friends say its history goes back to Atlantis."

Karl and Yoseph smiled and shrugged.

"You said you needed a favor?" Yoseph asked.

"I think so. I am in a bit of a mess."

I told him the story of what happened at the hotel, and the Frenchman, who turned out to be a cop.

"I tried calling Juliette, but haven't heard back yet. I suspect the aunt died while I was away, and the Count has contacted the authorities."

Yoseph thought about it for a moment and then asked, "How can I help?"

"Well, if it's the aunt's death, I need to handle that myself, and will go to the police. But there is another part to the story. Before she had her stroke, the aunt gave me something."

I was suddenly uncertain how much to tell him. If he didn't know what was in the briefcase, and there was an investigation, he could honestly say he was unaware of what it contained. Yet, I knew he and Karl would be intensely interested in the letters. I was still hoping to hear from Juliette, which I thought might help in the decision.

"I was wondering if I might be able to leave my briefcase here until I get this thing cleared up a bit more."

Yoseph and Karl looked at each other. I had told them enough of the story that they could probably connect some of the dots.

"If you think that is best, of course," Yoseph said, his eyes brightening. "I have a safe where I keep my most valuable books and records. It would be very secure."

"That would be great," I said with a sigh of relief. "It won't be for very long, maybe a few days."

"However long you need it," Yoseph assured me.

"I will explain more at some point, but, for now..."

"Whatever you need to do," he interjected.

I handed him the briefcase, and we went into his backroom. In the corner was a substantial turn-of-century safe that stood about five feet tall. The manufacturer's name was painted in elegant gold letters across the door, bordered by filigree. Yoseph leaned over it with his back to us, and I could hear him dialing the combination on the lock. He twisted a silver handle and swung open a thick steel door. I could see several plastic sheaves containing individual books and manuscripts, all neatly arranged. A treasure trove, I was sure. He placed the briefcase on a shelf, then closed the ponderous door, clicked shut the lock handle, and gave the combination dial a few spins.

"There," he said. "I am the only one with the combination. Though Karl and my lawyer know where I have it hidden, in case something ever happened."

"I don't think that safe is going anywhere," I commented.

"Speaking of lawyers," Karl then injected. "The police can be difficult. You might need one."

"I hope not," I replied. "But if I do, I might be calling sooner than you think."

Yoseph's big black phone started ringing at that moment, and I added, "See?"

We laughed. When Yoseph answered, it was Juliette.

"I just got your call," she said, her voice anxious but also warm and close on the old phone. "Did you hear? The aunt passed away. I was worried about you because the Count has gone to the authorities. I left messages for you at the hotel."

"I just got back and didn't have a chance to pick them up. The police were at the front desk when I arrived."

She gasped a little. "So, are you with them now? How come you are calling from Yoseph's?"

"No, I left the hotel without them seeing me," and knowing Yoseph and Karl could hear, I hesitated before adding, "I came to Yoseph's with the packet."

There was brief silence at the other end of the line.

"Let me meet you there," she said. "This is too much over the phone."

I asked Yoseph if he would mind waiting until Juliette arrived, and he said it would not be a problem.

"How long will it take?" I asked her.

"About 20 minutes, I am in the car now. I have Artemisia with me. See you soon." She then added, "I am glad you are all right."

"I hope you are, too."

CHAPTER FIFTEEN

After hanging up, I turned to Karl and Yoseph, "I think I need to tell you something, but could we wait until Juliette is here?"

They both nodded. Karl said he wanted to step out for a few minutes to run home but that he would be right back. As he left, I turned to Yoseph and said, "I hope this is all OK."

"No problem," he replied with a smile. "It's not every day I am involved in a mystery."

"The real mystery is how to stay out of jail," I said.

"Don't worry. I am sure it will all work out."

He offered me some coffee, and while I was not much of a coffee drinker, I accepted simply to have something to do. The coffee was dark and strong, and the cream barely touched it. Surprisingly, though, I didn't feel the nervous punch of caffeine hitting my system.

"It's the way Americans make it," Yoseph explained. "They drown it, so too much caffeine is drawn in from the bean, while the flavor is diluted. Properly, it's about the experience."

I had to admit he made an interesting cup of coffee. At my urging, he told me about using the French press, the various ways beans are roasted and ground, and other intricacies. I found the conversation a pleasant distraction until a sharp knocking on the door interrupted us. Standing outside were Karl, Juliette, and Artemisia, who was pressing her face against the glass. We hadn't noticed their arrival, haloed in the pink glow of the sunlight on the brick building behind them.

We both stood up, and Yoseph went to let them in. Juliette looked surprisingly fresh, her face a little flushed. I walked over and hugged her.

"I'm glad you escaped their clutches," she quipped.

"It's good to see you, too," I responded.

We looked at each other for a moment, and I could sense a gentle longing. We all sat down, except Artemisia, who was busy running her fingers along the rows of books.

"Don't honey," Juliette said, shaking her head.

Artemisia looked at her, put her hand down, but continued walking among the shelves.

"I hope she's OK in here," she said to Yoseph.

"She's not the first to touch them," he replied.

I wasn't sure where to begin, but Karl helped by saying, "Our friend here seems to be in a bit of trouble."

Juliette then told me what had happened since I left. On Tuesday, the aunt had taken a turn for the worse and passed away during the night. This had sent the Count into a rage, and by morning he had been to the police, telling them I had brought about her condition. He was told they would need more evidence to bring charges, but it would be looked into. The Count has stature with the authorities, so it was being given priority. She had not yet been contacted out of respect for her husband, and the fact the Count had downplayed her involvement,

That would explain the Frenchman's appearance in Rennes le Chateau. I told Juliette the story. She said she had mentioned my leaving to her husband, and he must have spoken to the Count.

"William has been telling me what's been going on, but only because it's an embarrassment to him," Juliette said. "He even contacted a lawyer without asking me. I refused to meet with him."

"A lawyer might be good," I ventured.

"I know, but I didn't like the way it was done," she replied.

We sat for a moment taking in the situation. I was impressed the police hadn't simply arrested me. The pressure was not influencing someone, because if it had been up to the French cop I would already be in jail.

"You know," Juliette said, "I want to tell the police what happened. We were the only two in the room with the aunt. If you are guilty, so am I."

"How did this get so messed up?" I said, putting my head down.

"It's not your fault," she stated. "Besides, the aunt wanted you to have those letters."

I glanced up at her. She smiled a little, and I could tell she deliberately mentioned the letters. These were her friends, and we would eventually tell them anyway.

Her eyes laughing, she remarked, "See, I told you the whole world would soon be keeping your secret."

I decided this would be a good moment to confess.

"I should tell you, Dieter and his friends in Rennes know."

She made a "tch, tch" sound while pointing as if scolding, but she didn't seem surprised. I looked at Yoseph and Karl. Their faces showed little, though, for some reason, I felt a weight lifting.

"I'll get the briefcase," Yoseph said, always ahead of the game.

While he was in the other room, I wondered if it might have disappeared from the safe, like Houdini, but Yoseph was soon back with the briefcase in hand. As he gave it to me, it felt heavier than I remembered.

Karl had been quiet, but then in a voice that sounded deeper, as if coming from another time and place, he said, "I can't tell you what this might mean."

It was as if he knew.

The others noticed his change in tone, and even Artemisia stopped wandering and came over. Juliette put an arm over her daughter's shoulders. Everyone was attentive as I clicked open the silver latches.

I lifted the cover and was taken aback by what I saw. An orange stain the shape of the packet had discolored the white protective envelope. It hadn't been that way at Dieter's earlier. I realized the seemingly ageless packet was beginning to deteriorate, and quite rapidly from the looks of it. I hesitated for a moment before taking it out.

"We are going to have to be careful," I said. "These are becoming fragile with exposure."

Juliette gave me a concerned look.

"It was bound to happen," I said. "I'm surprised they held up this long."

Karl had come around and was looking over my shoulder. "Maybe you should let Yoseph handle them. He's experienced with this."

I quickly agreed and was about to hand him the envelope when he said, "Just a minute, let me wash my hands and get a few other things."

No one said anything; the silence was somber as we waited for him to come back. I had wondered why the letters seemed so fresh when we first removed them. I had started to almost believe they had mystical powers. The reality was, they were like any other material, and age had caught up.

When Yoseph returned, he took the briefcase, and we followed him into the room with the safe, where he had spread out some clean paper on a table. Then, picking up the envelope, he gently removed the waxed packet. There was still a faint scent of beeswax, but it was much less pronounced, and the packet had turned an orangeish brown.

I commented in dark humor to Juliette, "The fruit juice?"

"What's that?" Yoseph asked, suddenly concerned.

"He's making a bad joke," Juliette replied, looking perturbed.

"This could take a while," Yoseph commented as he placed the packet on the table.

Over the next few minutes, he gave it a close examination. While he did that, I told the story about the Lautrec's, and how it came into our hands.

Yoseph delicately removed the papyrus sheets and even more gently unfolded them onto the table. Surprisingly, they appeared unchanged, and he was amazed at their condition.

It was a relief that only the outside of the packet had deteriorated so far.

"This is somewhat out of my range," Yoseph stated. "These should be put in the care of a special conservator, and quickly."

Karl, meanwhile, had put on a pair of glasses, and was looking intently at the letters, mumbling as he went from one to another.

"This is Aramaic, not Hebrew," he said. "Probably first century."

I had not understood that Karl was that much of an expert, but then there was a lot I did not know about him.

"Can you read them?" Juliette asked.

"It would take time, though there is something about this one," he said, pointing to the same paper I had been so drawn to the first night.

He peered closer, and I noticed a slight shift in his posture.

"This," he said straightening up, entranced in thought, "is not what I expected."

"What is it?" Yoseph asked.

Karl didn't answer, obviously still in deep reflection.

"I'm sorry, what?" he said after a moment.

"What is it?" Yoseph asked again.

"I believe Bjorn has found something of great significance, and we should thank him."

Everyone turned, but all I could think to stammer lamely was, "It found me."

"Yes it did," Karl said.

Juliette drew close and held my arm, and then looked at Karl, "So what is it?"

"Let me see," he replied as he leaned over the table to study them further.

While we had been focused on the letters, Artemisia had found the coffee area and poured a glass of water. Almost as if she was being deliberate, she had come over and started to set the glass on the table with the letters. When Juliette spotted

114

her she quickly tried to grab the glass, but in her haste, she bumped it, and water splashed over the packet, which Yoseph had set apart from the other documents.

We stared as if in shock. I reached for the packet, but Yoseph stopped me, putting his hand on my arm.

"No," he said inexplicably. "Look."

The wax was returning to its original light color where water had touched the packet. A sweet, delicate scent began to fill the room. I looked in disbelief.

"Don't ask me how or why," Yoseph finally said, "but it appears that something in the wax is restored by moisture. I am guessing it is also what is causing the scent."

"Water into wine," I commented, mostly to myself.

"That might be more true than you think," I heard Karl say softly.

Juliette was still holding the glass when she looked at Yoseph, who looked back at her, and then as if some kind of invisible conversation was taking place, nodded. To my surprise, she poured a little more water on the packet, completing its transformation.

"I think that's enough," Yoseph stated with characteristic calm.

It had all happened so quickly I could only shake my head. Artemisia, meanwhile, had wandered over to the safe and was tracing the decorative scrollwork with her finger, and fiddling with the silver handle.

"I think that's enough for one day, honey," Juliette told her, but not scolding. "Perhaps it's time to go."

I knew how much Juliette wanted to know what the letters said, and that leaving was not easy. I offered to walk her to her car. Finally, I felt comfortable leaving for a few minutes. Yoseph was using a cloth to gently remove the excess water on the packet, after making sure none had splashed onto the letters. Karl was already getting back to translating.

"Let me know what they say," Juliette told Karl as she headed for the door. "I'll see you tomorrow."

Once we were outside, the city had turned a deeper red, the streetlights were on, and the air was warm. Juliette was holding Artemisia's hand as we went down the sidewalk.

"Don't worry about the police," I said, wanting to quickly address the subject. "At this point I think they only want to talk."

"I hope so," she stated with concern. "I couldn't stand the thought of you in jail. What do you think we should do?"

"I'm not sure, but for now I'll stick around here and see what Karl comes up with."

"Artemisia scared the daylights out of me," she remarked, still a little unsettled. "But I noticed the same thing as Yoseph."

"It was almost as if she set it up," I commented.

"What...", Juliette said, giving me a sharp, perplexed look.

"Artemisia has an uncanny sense," I explained.

She smiled. "I know what you mean, but she also needs to eat. I'd better get her home. "Then, her voice turned serious, "We should probably talk."

A lead weight dropped in my stomach, and I suddenly felt very alone. I had let my feelings go too far.

"I just want to spend some time with you," she went on. "You've been gone for three days."

The weight vanished as quickly as it had come; however, there still lingered a knot of uncertainty about what I was doing.

"Can I call you later?" I said.

"Of course," she replied with a grin, "even if from jail."

"Bad joke," I replied.

She gave me a quick kiss on both cheeks, European style. As she unlocked the passenger door for her daughter, Artemisia tugged on my shirtsleeve. When I looked at her, she smiled and waved goodbye. I began to feel much better.

Back at the bookstore, Yoseph and Karl were intently examining the letters. As part of his research into the Torah, Karl had studied Aramaic and other ancient texts. Aramaic was the language of the Aryan tribes who swept into the Middle East around 800 B.C., creating the Persian Empire. By 300 B.C. it was the common tongue throughout the region. That's also when it became the foundation for present-day Hebrew.

"Aramaic evolved and changed over time, so you can approximately date a document by the writing," Karl explained. "I'd say these are of the early Christian era."

"That's what my friend said, too."

Karl looked up, "So, you've shown this to many others?"

"Only a few. My friend is a conservator, who showed the photos to a professor, who dated the writing. But, the letters appeared in such good condition that they doubted their authenticity. All of this has been very confidential, by the way, remember I might be a criminal."

"You are not a criminal, and they are original," Karl said, looking me straight in the eye. "But, their condition is amazing. If I had not seen them myself, I would doubt it, too."

"What do they say?' I asked.

"I don't know yet. I can read a little, but it's going to take a few hours to get an initial translation."

He was quiet for a moment, then said, "There is something I am going to show you that I think will answer a lot of questions."

He had Yoseph turn three of the papers over onto their blank backs. I wasn't sure what he was doing. Papyrus has a woven appearance because it is made of fine strips of papyrus leaves pressed together. Karl pointed, and small red dots were almost hidden in the coarse textures. Yoseph turned the sheets over, and Karl pointed to the corresponding places on the front.

"It's the Aramaic letter 'Y,' and notice the red dots are directly behind them," Karl said. "This is Jesus' writing."

It was like someone struck a blow to my head, and my mind went as still as if I was back in Marianne's cave.

"Remember my family legend, the red dot and the letter' Y'? Part of the story I didn't tell you was a red dot in any proximity to the first letter of his name is a sign that it was written by him. It was to distinguish his writing from that of the scribes. It's not unlike his words being red-lettered in the Bible."

"I don't believe you," I said, breaking out of my stunned silence. "I mean, this can't be true. I didn't think Jesus could even write."

"Of course he could. It was not as uncommon back then as most people think. It was necessary for business," Karl said, chuckling. "Even the Pharisees, who were like lawyers, were impressed with Jesus' knowledge of the law and texts. He knew them thoroughly because he could read, and if you can read, you can write."

"But what…" I started to say.

"That's what you just found," he said, his eyes beaming. "His writing."

My mind was reeling, letters from Jesus. If it was true, not only did the packet contain the most valuable signature on earth, it would be the first physical evidence that he had existed, a missing link that has long plagued historians and ecclesiastics.

"Early on, the Church took the position that scribes wrote down what he said, as was the custom of the time, so he didn't need to write. This might have been convenient, because Jesus' actual writings would supersede all others, including the New Testament and what has been based upon it, even the Church. It could potentially upset the apple cart."

Karl had thought about this for a long time, and I was willing to listen.

"Do you actually believe someone with his understanding, his awareness, his vision, wouldn't write anything, not a note, not a letter, not a word? Do you know of anyone who could write, particularly of such stature, who wrote absolutely nothing? "

"They usually think they can't write enough," I said.

"Jesus did write, and these are the first letters ever to come to light." Then he said more quietly, "I never thought I'd see them."

I began to grasp the magnitude of what he was saying. He had been right to state that these letters could answer many questions and raise more.

Looking at Karl, I said, "I wanted to tell you about what happened at the St. Sernin Library."

I explained my inability to see the Book of Revelation I'd been shown the first day, the one containing the letter and the red dot. I told him of the apparent dismissal of the clerk, and the chill feeling I had upon leaving the building.

"These are not his only writings," Karl said pointedly. "It's amazing that no one, over all these centuries, figured out the sign."

"The Church apparently knows now," I said.

"Maybe, but I doubt it," Karl said. "You know how the packet was starting to deteriorate. It wouldn't have been long before the papyrus turned to dust."

"But that took almost a week of outside exposure," I argued. "If there are letters still hidden in the cover of that book, the Church will find them."

"I think they are already gone," Karl said. "The only thing left behind was the flake."

"You think so?" I asked a little incredulously.

"A long time ago, someone suspected something was in that book. It's a shame. Do you know why your packet started to deteriorate? Something in the wax is very sensitive to atmosphere, even breath, or the scent of your skin. Mankind has created so much pollution in various ways over the centuries, externally and internally, that certain delicate essences can be quickly destroyed. Whoever made that packet had knowledge of the natural arts, and how to make forms of protection that could either be a blessing or a curse. Why do you think the wax smells so sweet? That is the blessing. The curse is self-destruction under conditions of our own making."

"This might sound strange to you," he added, "but that includes the spirit of the person."

"Did the Cathars do this?" I then asked.

"They might have, I don't know," Karl answered.

I wanted to ask more, but I was already overwhelmed.

"There are other letters, of that I am certain, but for now, this is what we know," he concluded.

We all sat in silence for a few minutes, each lost in thought. I found myself looking at the paper that had caught my attention the first night. I was reminded of a sense of calm reflection, and my concerns softened. Perhaps things would work out, and if they didn't, that did not seem to matter. It was a strong, yet gentle, perception.

I noticed that Karl and Yoseph were looking at the same paper I was.

"What about this one," I finally asked, pointing to it.

"There is something different about it," Karl remarked, as if he, too, was pulling himself back from some other place.

Yoseph carefully drew it apart from the others.

"We have some work to do, "he said, looking at Karl.

"I have some business to attend to as well," I remarked, knowing now what I had to do. "I may be back in the morning, depending on how things go."

Yoseph gave me a concerned look but seemed to understand.

"Please do whatever you need to with the letters. They couldn't be in better hands," I told them.

There was so much I wanted to know, but there was little I could do here at the moment. It might take Karl all night long, if even then, to translate the writing. I just hoped he had enough time.

"You'll know what to say," Karl told me as he affectionately took me by the arm. "I know if you need anything, you'll give us a call."

"I will," I assured him, then more lightly, "Don't forget Juliette wants to know what they say."

We shook hands. Yoseph led me to the door, and as I was about to go out, he said, "This is a great day. Thanks for letting me be part of it."

I left in a different world than when I arrived.

CHAPTER SIXTEEN

As I headed back to the hotel, I had an unusual sense of calm. I wasn't sure if it was simply the quiet coming with the cool of the day, or something else. Night had descended, and strollers were taking full advantage of a summer evening. I felt confident walking back to an unknown situation with the police but wondered if I was being realistic.

I rounded the corner across from the hotel and saw three street performers under a light before a small crowd. It was The Actor and some of his troupe.

He was wearing a collarless white shirt with billowing sleeves, and the others were on either side of him. They must have been doing a more traditional act because the audience was clapping in time to their singing. I watched for a while, but it was not the time to engage. However, the Actor spotted me as I crossed the street and gave a discreet nod without stopping his performance. It was almost as if he knew.

I paused at the entrance to the hotel, looking to see if any gendarmes were waiting in the lobby, but it was empty. So I swung the door open and walked as calmly as I could to the front desk. The clerk had his head down, doing some paperwork.

"Bonjour," I said, causing him to look up. "I was wondering if there were any messages?"

"Bonjour, Messer Solberg," he replied courteously. "Welcome back. Yes, let me get them for you."

If there was anything unusual, he didn't show it. He reached into my room box and pulled out several envelopes, holding one apart.

"There is also this," he said. "They were here this afternoon."

"Merci," I replied, taking the envelope and turning a little aside to open it.

The letter was on legal paper and handwritten with black ink in a distinctive lettering style that looked almost calligraphic. There was an address and a phone number printed on top. It was in English.

Dear Messer Bjorn Solberg,

"Could you please visit me tomorrow, the 9th, at 11 AM, at the address noted above. I have some questions on a matter of concern. If you are unable to make the appointment, call me at the number above. Your cooperation is appreciated."

Respectfully,
Magistrat Robert Genseau (Judge d'instruction 'Judge of inquiry')

I gave a short sigh of relief because at least it was not a warrant, but it was odd the police were not being more aggressive. I knew, however, that an interview could turn into an interrogation, and I also took note that the day and time together came to 911, and hoped it wasn't an omen.

I thanked the clerk, gave him a tip, and took the elevator to my room. The clerk may have acted discreetly, but I was reasonably sure he had already mentioned the police to the hotel management.

Once in my room, the first thing I did was call Juliette, wondering if she had received a police visit by now. As soon as she answered, I knew something was wrong. She was formal and brief, and when she didn't use my name and said she would call back tomorrow, I assumed she was with her husband. I began to be worried. I then called Yoseph, who was very warm and welcoming.

"How is it going?" he asked with gentle concern.

"The police left a note requesting I visit them tomorrow, but it is not a warrant," I said.

"Let me have you talk with Karl. He knows more about this," Yoseph replied, and I could hear him explain to Karl what I'd said.

"What does the letter say?" Karl asked as soon as he came on, so I read it.

"That is generally a good thing," he commented after giving it some thought. "They would not hesitate to arrest you. But be very careful what you say. In France, unlike America, there is no right to have a lawyer present when you meet with him; and, a magistrate is both the chief investigator and the judge."

"It could take a bad turn, I know," I said.

"Don't worry, you'll be fine," Karl said reassuringly. "But I would wait to tell them about the letters, bring it up at the end after you have established yourself."

"That is a good plan. They may have already talked to Juliette, and if they have, I don't know what she told them. She couldn't talk when I called her just now. A bit odd, but…"

"Either way, be simple and straightforward. They have all the cards," Karl replied calmly. "But, you'll be OK."

I did not know where he was getting his reassurance, but I appreciated it.

"The letters will be here when you need them," Karl then said. "I should be finished by morning, and they are as interesting as we thought."

"What do they say?" I asked, almost forgetting the police.

"I am still working, so this is approximate. The first is like the Beatitudes in the Sermon on the Mount, but more of a rough draft, not quite the same. The short note is what your friend said. It is addressed to Mary, and given the era, may even be considered a kind of love letter.

"Mary Beloved, I come to you in the cool of the day, reminding you of the silent longing of your heart. In the secret place, where you are I AM. In Love Y"

"Which Mary?"

"I don't know," Karl said. "But it is Jesus."

"Really?"

I could almost see Karl smiling.

"It's not the Jesus I was taught about in Sunday school," I finally said.

"The third paper is also what your friend said," Karl continued. "The first lines of the Book of Revelation. It may even be a draft."

"By John?" I said, still not quite believing that there was something to all this.

"Possibly," Karl answered matter-of-factly. "There's no red dot on it, and it is written in a different hand than the other three. Remember, the packet was not organized by accident. Someone understood what they were putting in it."

I began to be concerned about what would happen to the letters after they were turned over to the police, and the Count. I could almost see the disintegration happening in that atmosphere, and presumed that's what happened to the packet with the near brush with the police earlier today.

"The last paper can be read many ways," and here Karl paused. "Which may make it the most important of all."

"What do you mean?" I asked.

"I can translate the words, but the meaning is not in the words. It's almost as if they were encrypted, with everyone given their own key."

"Like the Day of Pentecost, where each heard in their own tongue?" I asked, thinking to a childhood Bible class.

"Yes," Karl said. "It can be just like that."

We stayed silent for a few moments, and finally, I said, "We both understood the same thing, even though I couldn't read it at all."

"I think Yoseph is having that same experience right now," Karl chuckled.

My phone started ringing, another call was coming in, it

was Juliette. I knew what she was going to say before she said it, though the particulars I could not have guessed.

"The police came while I was away," Juliette said as soon as I answered. "William was here, and he is furious. He thought he had managed to get me out of the picture, you know, just a side issue, but now this magistrate shows up."

"What did he say?" I asked.

"The magistrate? He just wanted to set up a time talk. I'm supposed to call him tomorrow, at my convenience."

"No cop just wants to talk," I said. "What did William say?"

"He was on the phone to a lawyer when I came in – you'd think he would have been calling me," she said sarcastically. "He insists I do not meet without getting prepped, and then say as little as possible."

"That's not bad advice," I advised.

"He's just trying to protect his reputation, his business relationship with the Count it's not about helping me," Juliette retorted. "I know I have to be careful, but I am more concerned that what I say doesn't hurt you."

"Just tell him the truth, don't worry about me. There's nothing you can do about that," I said.

"Well, I'm not supposed to see you anymore," Juliette added. "William demands that there be no contact, no phone calls, no texts, no association, ever again, and if he has to, he will get a court order against you."

I could see my world shrinking, impermeable legal walls rising, and the doors closing.

"He can't do that," Juliette said, breaking the dark spell. "Because I would be the first one to violate the order."

Her feistiness was contagious, but I also knew that if criminal charges were filed, the court would prohibit us from any contact. She must have read my thoughts.

"You worry too much," she said. "Besides, I am not supposed to be talking to you, remember? I have to go. I am calling from the bathroom."

I could hear the toilette flush.

"I want to hear what the letters say," she said before she hung up.

I did not know whether to feel happy or sad, but there was a lingering ease, and unexpectedly, it reminded me of the bittersweet feeling I had holding the packet.

It was getting late, and I began turning my thoughts to the police interview; and how I was going to explain all this to my editor. I could see it would likely be too much to salvage. I lay back on the bed, but before I could even start to review what to do with the police, I began to fade and fell asleep without bothering to take my clothes off.

I was half awakened by a faint sound coming from my phone. I ignored it, but then it sounded again, and I realized it was daylight. Startled awake, I had no idea what time it was. I fumbled for the phone, which had become buried in the bedcovers.

I flipped it open and saw it was only 7:30. Relieved, I lay back and closed my eyes again. Then I remembered what woke me up and looked at the phone - it was a text from Wendy.

Falling asleep, I had completely forgotten I needed to call her, and the dread quickly returned in the pit of my stomach. This was not a call I wanted to make, but after giving it some thought, it was clear I needed to be upfront and not put it off until after the police interview.

Still, I procrastinated. Getting up, I took a shower, and then spent some time picking the clothes I would wear to the interview. I didn't want to look too casual and even be a little over-dressed. So, I put on a clean, pressed shirt, tie, sweater vest, brown slacks, and a tweed herringbone jacket. My shoes were a bit scruffy, but I had no better.

It was my standard reporter look, and good for almost any situation, at least in the States. While I was dressing, I also had some time to think about what I would say to Wendy, but I knew nothing was going to make it easy. I decided to text her back and see if she was still available, half hoping she wasn't.

"Thanks for your text, give me a call, lots to talk about," was the best I could manage. My phone rang almost immediately.

"Bjorn, how are you, how's it going, have you had any luck with the Lautrecs?" she asked in that non-stop New York way. "Tell me all about it."

"Hi Wendy, good to hear from you," I began. "I think the Lautrecs may be out of reach, at least for now."

There was a pause on the other end of the line.

"Well, keep trying, you never know. But if that's the case, I'm sure we can work with it, though I am a little disappointed," she said in a slower, more normal tone.

"I also have to tell you I am meeting with the police today," I said

There was an even longer pause on the other end.

"So, what's that about?" her tone very sober, and I knew the assignment was about to end.

I explained the circumstances and what steps I had taken, but I didn't mention the packet for some reason. I knew I should because it was inevitably going to come up. Yet, somehow that didn't seem to matter, it was as if it wasn't that important.

"I think we are going to have to re-examine this assignment," Wendy finally said. "Let me check, and I will get back to you. Sorry, Bjorn, I was hoping it was going to be something special."

"I understand," I said. "Let's see what happens today."

"OK, I'm not there, so I don't really know the situation. Why don't you call me, I can hold things for a little while, but you know my position."

"Thanks, Wendy, I appreciate that. I will give you a call," I said. "Though there is the time difference."

"Don't worry, if tomorrow is better, call me then," she replied, and I knew it was over.

After we hung up, I sat on the bed and laid back. There was emptiness hanging in the air that was silent and sad. I could feel Wendy's disappointment and even anger. This was going to put a hole in her editorial content, not to mention the considerable time, trust, and money that had gone into it. It was serious, and I had screwed up.

As I lay there, my thoughts drifted back to the police interview. I had decided to tell Genseau everything, including the packet, and what I did with it. I would explain how the aunt invited us in, how she pushed the packet into my hand, then her stroke, and the Count's fury when he came in. I needed to be careful not to say too much. I also wondered what Juliette might tell him, and was ashamed I had dragged her into this. I felt dirty.

Getting up, I looked for my car keys and phone and made sure I had my passport for identification. Who knows, they might want to take it, and I could be jailed. I also thought of calling Juliette, but that was out of the question. Then I remembered that Karl and Yoseph had been working all night translating the letters. Between my tiredness, loss of the article, and pending police interview, it had entirely gone out of my thoughts. I had time to call them, and I started to pull out of my fog.

When Yoseph answered the phone, his voice sounded tired but very present.

"How is it going?" I asked, hoping Karl had finished the translations.

"It is going well," Yoseph said. "However, he is still working on the longer text. It is presenting quite a challenge."

"You mean the enigmatic one?" I commented.

"Yes, that is the one," he replied, his voice softening a little. "I have to admit there is something about it that I can't quite explain."

"It's like you know what it says, even though you don't," I said with a chuckle.

"Would you like to talk with Karl?" he then asked.

"No, I do not want to interrupt. It's more important that he has the chance to do as much as he can. I have my police

129

interview at 11:00, and there is no telling what might happen. They could come for the letters."

I knew that I had pictures of them, but if the police asked for everything, I would have to give up my computer, phone, and camera. The fact I had also emailed them meant they might block my email account. I had no idea what my friend in the U.S. would say or do. It could become very complicated, but with the ultimate result losing any further access.

I also wondered what would happen to Karl's translation, but that was something I felt better left to Karl.

As usual, Yoseph had already anticipated my thinking.

"Don't worry, nothing will be lost," he said. "And you don't need to come in before you go. We already have plenty of coffee and croissants."

"Oh, that's good. I make a lousy cup of coffee anyway," I replied.

"Wait, just a second, Karl wants to speak with you."

"Hello, Bjorn, I'm glad you called," Karl said. "I want to thank you for what you've done. This is very important, and you should know that."

"I appreciate all you've done," I answered. "I just hope I haven't involved you in something that you do not deserve."

"Oh, this is a pleasure, and I would not have missed it for the world. Literally. It reminds me of my youth," he said, obviously thinking of his days as a runner for the French resistance. "I'm finding the translation has me pressed to the limit of my ability. I think we are on the way now, however. I have found a link."

I wasn't sure what he meant, but I could feel he had broken into something within the translation.

"Be careful with the Magistrate," he continued. "While he is an honorable man, as I understand, he has a legal duty and will not violate that. Just stay calm. No matter what he does, it's for a reason."

I was even more perplexed, but I figured I would find out what the reason was soon enough.

"Thanks, Karl, good advice. I have to go, but I will be in touch, I hope," I said. "And I hope the coffee is good."

"Yoseph is truly a master," Karl stated. "Let me get back to work. I will see you later."

With that, we hung up, and I was going out the door to what I did not know. Yet, I had a gentle feeling, almost like the enigmatic paper was following me, though I also thought my imagination was getting the better of me. As I turned the key, I pushed it too far, causing the starter motor to give a sharp grating noise. The sound startled me back into the real world, and I headed over to the court building.

CHAPTER SEVENTEEN

"Why didn't you just take the book? You wanted it!" he said harshly as if it was an incontrovertible fact. "That's what you came for."

I had been in Magistrate Genseau's office for about half an hour, telling him everything that had happened, and I was stunned by this sudden change of tone.

The magistrate was in his early 60's, attentive, at ease, but formal. There was an assurance about him that engendered trust. He was taking notes while I spoke, even though it was also being recorded. I noticed he was using a fountain pen with a gold nib and a rosewood barrel. It brought to mind medieval scribes. Observing his lettering, I realized this must have been the pen he used to write my summons.

I had explained what I did with the letters after leaving the Lautrec's, and where they were now. I also told him that Juliette and I had visited the aunt at the hospital because Juliette was concerned about her.

I further said the allegations about my wanting to take anything, much less assault the aunt, were untrue. I went there to get a story, as it was a remarkable opportunity, and the stroke was entirely unexpected.

When I had finished, Genseau had asked a few clarifying questions. He seemed particularly interested in who was present. I said the only people in the room were the aunt, Juliette, her young daughter Artemisia, and myself. And, as far as I knew, there was no one nearby. I told him the Count was already on his way to meet us when he, and a staff member who was with him, heard the commotion and came running. I commented they had not seen her go into the seizure.

Genseau had then asked about my relationship with

Juliette. I wasn't expecting the question, and perhaps a bit un-convincingly, said she was a new acquaintance, and we were just getting to know each other. I added we shared some common interests.

"I see," he said, looking at me over the top of his glasses.

That is when his tone changed.

"Why didn't you?" he continued to demand. "Why did you assault her? She was an invalid in a wheelchair!"

"I never assaulted her," I said as calmly as I could, and as Karl had advised. "And I didn't know about the book, it was a Bible."

"You knew the Bible was valuable, and that there were priceless things in the room," he continued accusingly. "Why didn't you just take them and leave?"

After a moment's pause, I said, "Because they were valuable?"

"Don't play with me," he snapped.

Then he started shuffling some papers on his desk, breaking off the interrogation as suddenly as he started it. I wondered if he had pushed as far as he had planned. It was uncomfortable, but also reassuring in some way.

"OK," he said, nodding as if to indicate a change. "It seems like there are some gaps in your story, but we can fill those in later. Would you care for some more coffee?"

I looked down at my cup and noticed my hands were shaking slightly. I hadn't touched a drop.

Before leaving the magistrate's office, he told me that I was not under any charges, but the investigation was ongoing. He also advised me I was free to travel and could keep my passport, but I was to notify him if I changed my address, and finally, to not leave the country.

That last part I had been half-expecting, and more dreading. However, on him saying it, the reality sunk in. I was officially under a criminal review. Then I had the thought, 'At least I wasn't in jail.'

He would not give a time frame on my in-country restriction and suggested I might want to contact the U.S. Consulate, as he would be notifying them of my status. I asked if I should get an attorney, and while he didn't discourage it, he said that would be up to me. I had the feeling he was hinting perhaps to wait. I didn't know whether that was to make things easier for him, or in some way, for both of us. It seemed like an unusual intimation coming from a judge, but then again, I was in a different legal system than in the U.S., one with which I was very unfamiliar. It felt risky having a judge be both investigator and jury, but there was a human feel to it, which I liked. It was a different system of fairness. I'd have to wait and see about that.

One other thing perplexed me. He didn't ask for the letters or indicate he wanted them. Karl had cautioned me to not say too much, so while I told the magistrate about them, I only said they appeared very old. Because the Count was unaware of them, I thought they would be an important piece of new information, but it was as if they were insignificant. Still, I assumed Genseau would retrieve them after the interview. In the meantime, however, he had no idea what I, or anyone else, might do with them. It left the impression he was lax and not taking any precautions.

He formally thanked me for my time and said not to contact him, but he would stay in touch with me. I left the office more worried, yet somehow more reassured, than when I went in. Maybe Karl having said he was honorable was influencing my perception. I didn't know.

As I was leaving the building, Juliette, her husband, and I presumed an attorney, were getting out of a car in the parking area beside the courthouse. So, as unobtrusively as I could, I went the other direction.

My car was also in the parking lot, so I walked around the courthouse to give them time to go into the building. It was a warm, hazy day, and when I reached the back of the courthouse, I looked up at the third floor, and out of curiosity, tried to determine which office was Genseau's. The pale red sun was reflecting off the windows, so that was all I could see. Then one opened, and it was Genseau. I couldn't tell if he noticed me, but I moved closer to the building to be less visible. He looked deep in thought, and after a moment, he turned away, closing the window.

When I came back around to the parking lot, the coast was clear, but I wasted no time in leaving. I drove to the hotel, rehashing the interview and what I'd said. Did I do the right thing not telling him what the letters were, should I have said less, why did I bumble the question about Juliette, and what was she going to say to him? Lurking in the back of my mind was having to contact the U.S. Consulate Office, and what would they think; and, related to that calling Wendy.

However, the first order of business was to get in touch with Yoseph and Karl.

I parked my car at the hotel, grabbed my art backpack, and started walking to the front of the hotel to get better cell service. The sun was reflecting its pale red face on the windows across the street, just like at the court building.

Then, suddenly, I had a change in perception unlike anything I had ever known or even conceived. I became conscious of being conscious.

I looked around and said to myself, 'This is one the best places in the world to live, and yet even here, the buildings, trees, everything, looks slightly grey. Then I thought, 'If this is as good as one can reasonably expect in life, it isn't worth it.' Right on the heels of that came an almost paralyzing sense of innocence and vulnerability.

Wanting to resolve the unexpected impressions, an answer came as from an outside voice; "There's always joy." I said to myself, 'That's right, joy is independent of outer circumstance.' I then considered the feeling of knee bending vulnerably. Again, like another voice, I heard that was something that would have to be resolved later. Through it all, I felt deep compassion. What I didn't know was my life had just changed.

CHAPTER EIGHTEEN

The experience outside the hotel had passed as suddenly as it started, and I continued walking to the area with good cell phone reception and called the bookstore.

Yoseph answered, but this time the tiredness was gone from his voice.

"How did it go?" he asked.

"About as I expected. The magistrate was very polite, though he did grill me a bit. It was strange, he never asked anything about the letters."

"That is curious, what did you tell him?"

"Not much, just that they were old, but nothing about what they might be. However, one piece of bad news is while I am allowed to travel, I cannot leave the country, at least while it is under investigation. He said no charges have been filed."

"Let me have you talk with Karl."

"How are the translations?" I injected.

"Talk with Karl," he said and went to get him.

I began to wonder if there had been a problem. Finally, Karl came on the phone.

"Hello, how did it go?" he asked, with a gentle tone of concern.

"It wasn't bad, though I cannot leave the country," I replied.

"Did they take your passport?"

"No, and I am free to travel within France. All he wanted was to be informed if I changed my address, and suggested I contact the U.S. Consulate Office here and tell them my situation, which he was going to do, too."

"Well, that's too bad, but I wouldn't worry about it. That is standard procedure. How are you doing?"

"I'm OK, I have some things to do. I may, no, I will, lose my writing assignment, and that's going to be a financial strain."

"That's hard," he said, and then changed the subject. "Well, I've finished the first part of the translation, though it is very preliminary. Can you come down, I think it would be good for you to see."

"Yes, I'm on my way," I said while noting he had said "the first part" as if there was some other part.

"We will see you in a few minutes then. And, by the way, the paper that you noticed is all you thought it was. I think you will find there's even more that's interesting. I will show you when you get here."

When we hung up, I didn't feel like he was ignoring my plight, but more as if things were righting themselves. I had less apprehension about how it was going to work out, even though in a way everything was the same.

I briefly thought about calling Wendy, but it was the middle of the night in New York, and I wasn't in a rush. It took me a few minutes to walk to the bookstore, during which time I simply let the day take me. As I entered the bookstore the gentle creak of its old door made me think how much buildings are imbued with their past, and take us there, a reminder of a longer type of time. Yoseph came to greet me, and with an unusual display of affection, he gave me a hug.

"Come, see what we've done," he said, leading me to the back room.

I wasn't sure what to expect, but before we even got to the room I could smell the faint aroma of beeswax. If anything it was getting sweeter. And then I saw the letters on the desk. Karl had them spread out in a row, and they seemed to glow with a wonderful pale yellow light, subtly tinged with rose. I stopped, and almost didn't want to enter, out of respect for something I could only describe as powerful gentleness, perhaps it was even holy.

"You can call it holy, it's OK," Yoseph remarked with a little laugh, even though I hadn't said anything.

Karl was at one end of the table, bent over it with a magnifying glass.

"Come, look at this," he said gesturing to me. "I've never seen anything like it."

I put my backpack down as he handed me the glass, pointing at the beeswax envelope the letters had been in. The envelope was completely unfolded, exposing the inside faces. There were two larger sides, which had been the front and back, and several smaller ones, that were the flaps used to close it. How they had managed to open it without any damage I could not imagine.

"Look closely, and tell me what you see," Karl instructed.

I held the glass near one of the larger sections, and as I moved it in and out to focus, I could faintly see writing. The letters were a very pale pinkish color, and blended in so subtly with the waxed vellum it would have never been detected without a magnifier.

"Wow," was all I could think to say, and shook my head a little as I looked inquiringly at Karl.

"Amazing, huh?" he said with a little smile. "It is three other sections of writing, which I have yet to translate."

Now I could understand why he had not mentioned finishing.

"That's unexpected," I said. "Why would they do that?"

"I've been thinking about it," he replied. "I suspect they wanted to make full use of everything without making the packet larger. Whoever did this was also very careful that this part was concealed. If someone had found the envelope, they would not have seen this."

"So how did you find it then?" I asked.

"Totally by accident, and by that I mean Artemisia's accident if that's what it was. I was checking if any water had seeped inside the envelope, and it had. As I was wiping it dry I noticed some hydrophobic differences in the way it spread on the wax."

"Hydrophobic?" I queried.

"Wax naturally repels water, but it seemed to cling in some

places. Upon closer examination, I saw it wasn't only in that one area."

"Pretty observant," I said.

"Perhaps," he responded. "That's when I got the magnifying glass and realized what it was. It was very exciting."

"Do you have any idea what it might say?" I asked.

"Not yet. It seems to be written in Occitan and Aramaic. Occitan has never been codified, so some of the same words are pronounced and spelled differently. And this is likely old Occitan, which makes it even more difficult," he explained.

"That aside, I am thinking it may be the most important part of the packet," he continued. "Whoever put this together went to great lengths to double, even triple, hide this. They did not want it to ever fall into the wrong hands."

"What do you mean triple hide?"

"They hid it in a Bible, first off. Second, I would not have found it but for the water stains. Even more, I wouldn't have been able to see it without the magnifier," he said, scratching his head. "On the other hand, they did not have lenses like this back then. Or did they?"

"I remember reading that crystals, or maybe gemstones, were used in Roman times as magnifiers, though they were very small," I said.

"Hmmm," Karl murmured.

The mention of wrong hands reminded me of my predicament, and I became even more concerned the police might show up at any moment to confiscate the letters.

"Karl we may not have much time. The magistrate knows about the envelope now, and he knows where it is. I expect he will send someone to get it, today."

"Well, we'll see," he replied philosophically. "Tell me about your interview."

I was perplexed he did not show more concern, but perhaps he was getting tired.

"Shouldn't we wait on that?" I commented. "It seems the translation is more important."

"Perhaps it is," he said, sitting down at the table. "I still want to know about the interview. Tell me, I can listen and work."

So, I told him what I had said to Genseau, and also that Juliette was being interviewed right after me. At that, Karl stopped looking at the letters and turned to me.

"That's good," he said.

"Why?" I stuttered.

"Well, it means we have more time, for one thing."

"Maybe a little," I replied.

"I do not think they will come today. Genseau will want to talk with Yoseph and me personally, and not leave it to an assistant. He also has a busy schedule. As a judge magistrate, he holds court. You are not his only case, you know," he said a little teasingly. "So, I don't think we will see him, at least for now."

I couldn't deny his assessment. I also had the impression that Genseau did not fully believe the allegations, and was acting on them partly because of the Count's position. He might not be in such a big hurry. I relaxed a little, but not so much as to forget he had ordered me not to leave the country.

"So, let me show you what I've translated, and then I need to get back to the envelope," Karl said, returning to the table.

During this time Yoseph had been busy with customers, but he came in with two cups of coffee.

"You might need this," he said putting the cups on a side table. "I made it a little stronger for you, more American style."

Karl then motioned me over to the paper that had influenced me so much.

"It is very much like the Day of Pentecost, as you said. If my assessment is correct that this was Jesus, it is as if he had written down various thoughts, perhaps about what he wanted to say given an opportunity."

"Why is it that I seem to understand it even though I can't read it?" I asked.

"Well, that's the interesting part," he answered. "As I said, the particular words he used can have several meanings, it is the way Aramaic works as a language. There are only consonants, just like Hebrew. Anyway, not to get too detailed, it is hard to know which meaning is the one he meant, and maybe he did that deliberately. He was a master with language, it twisted the scribes and Pharisees in knots."

"So…?" I inquired.

"Well, it was hard, or seemed hard, to know. But then I noticed there was a rhythm to the way he wrote, almost like music, a certain pulse. I think when we look at the writing, which is very unique in its style and even spacing, it connects with something deep within ourselves. It is more tonal than verbal."

I stared at the paper, and his having said that made it come alive, almost dance on the page. I didn't know if I was just being influenced by what he said, or if it was true, but if it was accurate it opened another realm to sacred texts.

"What's more," Karl continued. "If my theory is correct, something like that also happened on the day of Pentecost, where not everyone listening knew Aramaic, but they could still understand. The tone of voice, the words, and rhythm, can create an effect that carries meaning beyond the words themselves. They called it speaking in tongues, in this case, it might be writing in tongues."

"I suppose that's possible," I said, not quite ready to accept it, but part of me knew he had hit a key.

It also reminded me of the experience I'd just had in front of the hotel. We both sat in silence for a while, sipping our coffee. Karl turned back to study the writing on the envelope, and I got up and went out to talk to Yoseph.

"How's it going?" he asked with a look that told me he already knew what Karl had discovered.

"That's pretty amazing stuff," I said. "Did you know that's what he was doing?"

"No, not at first, but he is a remarkable man, very percep-

141

tive. It is almost scary."

"I'm a little worried about the police coming anytime. Karl doesn't think they will, and that the magistrate, Genseau, will come in person," I said. "So it may not be for a while, even days, I guess."

"He's usually right," Yoseph said. "But I still think we should have a game plan because he will come eventually."

"I'm afraid of what will happen to those letters," I then said.

"I think they will take care with them. This kind of thing is not as uncommon here as it might be in America. We have more very old documents, and people experienced with handling them."

"I was thinking about the quality of the atmosphere," I remarked. "You saw what happened, they began to disintegrate."

"That part concerns me, too," he said.

I began to consider what the Count might do when he finds out a packet was also involved, which he would know now that I had told Genseau. Then, when he finds out what they might be it would lead to even more serious accusations.

But, I couldn't do anything about that at the moment, I needed to think about what I was going to do while waiting to hear back from Genseau. It might be days or even weeks. I decided I'd go back and watch Karl work, and maybe reflect on it while around that special letter. I hoped I wasn't becoming a relic worshipper.

When I came in Karl was peering intently through the magnifying glass, working incredibly fast. It wasn't only the time pressure, but he was simply extremely knowledgeable. I wondered who even knows about old Occitan, much less being able to decipher it as if it was your first language? I had little time to wonder, however.

"I know what you are thinking," Karl said without looking up. "This is a language that has fascinated me and my family as far back as I can remember. We still speak it. It's important not to lose your language, which some feel would be like losing your identity."

"You are really good at it," I said.

"Thank you. I don't believe that losing a language means losing identity. More it means losing a connection with the world the language captured long ago, things that we may have lost touch with, or no longer know. It's like walking into an old building, it carries the memory, or impressions, of all that has happened there, particularly if they were very strong things, such as in a church, like St. Sernin."

"Yeah, I've felt that," I said, but thinking of my experience walking into the bookstore this afternoon.

"You have to be careful, though," Karl added. "Some things do not need to be carried forward. They had their time and should be allowed to fade, it can be a trap, too."

"And here we are doing this," I remarked.

"There are also things that need to be called to remembrance," Karl responded.

"Can you tell me what you have found?"

Before he could answer my phone rang. It was Juliette, but I did not even have a chance to say hello.

"Meet me at the café tonight," she said, and then hung up.

Still not looking up from his work, Karl said, "Juliette?"

CHAPTER NINETEEN

The transcription of the envelope went quickly, and even though it was written in old Occitan and Aramaic, he was done by mid-afternoon. I suggested taking a break, but first, he wanted to talk about what he had found.

He said there were two parts. One related to the Book of Revelation, and the other to the Song of Solomon. Then on the flap that sealed the envelope, there was a quote from Jesus, underneath a pyramid symbol and a red dot. He believed the pyramid might have a relationship to the Knights Templar or some secret meaning known only by a few. The presence of the red dot made him think it related to Jesus.

"You might not know this," Karl said. "But the Cathars saw a close link between John the Beloved and Mary of Bethany. They believed she was the Beloved, not John. If the letters are related to the Cathars, and I think they may well be, then it would not be unexpected they included the letter to Mary."

"I'm no Bible scholar," I said.

"You don't have to be," he replied. "In fact, it might help, because these writings could go counter to a lot of what is taught about the Book of Revelation, as well as Mary, particularly in the Orthodox Church."

"Could you explain?" I asked.

"Well, the Cathars also apparently believed Mary of Bethany was the same person as Mary Magdalene. There's room for some legitimate Biblical debate on that point, and it is still unclear from these letters. What is clear, however, is that whatever Mary it is, she is being quoted here."

"So, is that the red dot?" I asked, a little confused.

"I don't think so, but she was the author," he said with a smile. "The envelope is a transcription of her words."

"I'd like to see," I said, my interest rising in pitch.

"Let's go eat first," he said, laughing. "I thought you were hungry."

The analysis was unlike anything I had ever read, but it was good we took a break first. My thoughts were swirling between the mystery of the letters, the weight of the interview with the magistrate, Juliette's phone call, and the need to call Wendy and sort out what was next. On top of all that, I couldn't leave the country.

"Eat. It will help settle your mind," Karl said, looking at me listlessly stabbing my food.

"I'm not sure I should be drinking," I said, taking a sip of the wine he had ordered us, and then another.

"It's probably just what you need," he commented.

"Do you think we should get back in case the police arrive?" I said, still feeling worried.

"No, the letters will be there."

"I think you're doing amazing work. I am very impressed."

"This is more important than you know, but let's not think about that now. How's Juliette?"

"She was very brief on the phone. She just said let's meet at the café tonight, and then hung up."

"Mmmm," Karl looked at me supportively. "She's a nice girl."

"Yes, and I've gotten her involved in something I never should have."

"I think she needed something to get involved in," he remarked.

"But not the police. I mean, we're being investigated for killing someone, at least I am."

"That's serious, yes," he said simply. "So you have to contact the Consulate here?"

"That's what he suggested," I said. "I don't even know where it is."

"It's not very far," he said, then after a pause. "Have you considered taking a trip while you are waiting?"

"He could call for me anytime," I replied, surprised at his risky suggestion. "I don't think I can."

145

"You liked your last visit, why not go back?" he said, continuing to encourage it. "I'm sure there's more you want to see."

"I'd like to," was all I could think to say. "You know I can't leave France."

"It's a big country," he remarked. "I'll pay this, and do not even think of protesting."

"But…" I began, but he was already heading toward the cashier.

Karl was right. The letters were still there when we returned, and no sign of the police. Yoseph was looking over what had been transcribed from the envelope and got up as we came in.

"Are you sure that's what they say?" he asked Karl with a look of concern and wonderment.

"Yes, it's pretty clear," Karl answered. "I have to admit it's very unorthodox. The church is not going to like it, I'm afraid."

"They will challenge it," Yoseph said. "I don't think some of the rabbis are going to like it either."

This was new, as up until now, only Christianity had been involved.

"I know," Karl said, and reaching over to the transcription of the envelope, he handed it to me. "Bjorn, why don't you read it and tell us what you think."

I paused and took a deep breath before diving in. Here apparently were the writings of someone who was actually with Jesus and the Apostles, who lived among them, ate with them, and knew them as people. There was no intercessory church or orthodoxy, and they were coming to light for the first time in how long, a thousand years, maybe two thousand? I was reminded of Karl saying language can carry the lost meaning of the past.

"These are my words, of Mary Magdalene, and they are right and true. He loved me, and I loved him. I was with him

146

from the beginning, and in the beginning was the Word, and nothing was in the beginning without the Spirit, the Word."

Then followed words from the Book of John.

"In the beginning was the Word, and the Word was with God, and the Word was God. The same was in the beginning with God. All things were made by him, and without him was not anything made that was made."

The similarity was beyond striking, though one was more personal.

Then another quote from Mary, followed by one from The Song of Solomon.

"The voice of my beloved, behold His right hand is under my head, and the left embraces me. The Spirit looks through my heart, leaving nothing covered. My soul longs for union, and is not denied, as a bride adorned for the new Heaven and the new Earth."

Then this passage from the Song of Solomon.

"The voice of my beloved! behold, he cometh leaping upon the mountains, skipping upon the hills.

My beloved is like a roe or a young hart: behold, he standeth behind our wall, he looketh forth at the windows, shewing himself through the lattice.

My beloved spake, and said unto me, Rise up, my love, my fair one, and come away."

"I don't know," I said when I had finished reading. "It seems like a love story."

"That was my impression, too," said Yoseph.

"And yet it goes deeper than that," I commented without thinking about what I was saying. "It touches on what you said about that other letter, the one that can be read in so many ways."

"What do you mean?" Karl said, his interest perked. "Explain that a little more."

"It's hard to put into words…" I began.

I was thinking of my experience outside the hotel, where I had thoughts and feelings that raised questions, and the answers came as if from some outside source, like another voice. But I was beginning to realize that voice was also mine, it wasn't separate. I'd just never recognized it as such, like a forgotten language.

"I think the whole packet is trying to get us to remember something, in a voice that sounds very much like our own, but it is calling from far away, it's very faint."

Karl and Yoseph looked at each other.

"Perhaps that's enough for now," Karl said. "Though there is one other thing."

With that, he handed me another translation sheet.

"The words are from the cover flap, the one that sealed the envelope, and that is where the symbol is, too," he explained.

"Neither shall they say, Lo here! or, lo there! for behold the kingdom of God is within you."

Above the words was a pyramid symbol divided into seven layers, with a red dot in the center.

"What do you make of it?" I asked.

"Well, a pyramid can have many meanings. The number seven can indicate completion, of something finished. There are seven days in the week, for example, or the seven spirits of God mentioned in Revelation. Jesus is said to have exorcised seven demons from Mary Magdalene. Perhaps it was put there as seal of completion for what was in the envelope."

It did feel like something was finished, the translations certainly. However, it wasn't the completion of my journey, I hoped. I was interested to hear more, but I had suddenly become very tired, and the thought of going back to the hotel before meeting Juliette seemed too much.

"Yoseph, do you have any place I could lie down for a few

minutes?" I asked despite feeling it was rude not to pursue the conversation further.

"There is a couch in the back hallway," he said. "It's quiet, no one will disturb you. I may even use it after you."

It felt like jet lag, where a heavy sack of sand is pressing down on your chest, and there is an irresistible urge to give in. Some people ignore it, hoping to catch the rhythm of a new place. I'd rather lie down, and blame the airlines for seeming to arrive in the morning rather than the evening. It usually passes in a few minutes.

My body sunk into the cushions. The transition to sleep was so immediate my dreaming blended with wakefulness. Soon I was emerging from closing my eyes into a full-color scene. I was in the room talking to Karl and Yoseph, when there was a light through a window. As I looked out, I could see branches and I was on the sidewalk. The band of troubadours was performing down the street, with a crowd around. As I walked towards them, the crowd parted, and a man emerged holding wooden boxes in his arms. It made me uncomfortable the closer he came. I tried my best to get out of his way, but I couldn't, there was no place to escape, and my feet were as lead. Finally, the dream was disturbing enough that I forced myself to wake up.

Sighing, I did not try to go back to sleep. Obviously, whatever was troubling me was close on my mind and heart. Why the dream had those elements, and what they meant, I didn't know. I didn't want to spend time figuring it out. I had been on the couch for only about 15 minutes, and I continued to lie there. It was getting on toward 6:00, and Yoseph would be closing the shop. I got up, and after a peek into the bookstore area, I went back to see Karl.

I was surprised the letters and envelope were no longer laid out on the table. Instead, the packet had been reassembled, appearing just as it had when I first brought it in. There was no one in the room, and I realized I hadn't seen Yoseph in the front of the store either.

I returned front, thinking I may simply have missed seeing them, but the bookstore was empty. Then, while I felt I was being overly cautious, I went back to the office and looked around for someplace to move the packet out of sight.

At the end of the table was the black briefcase I used to bring the packet, and then I saw my pack. I had archival watercolor paper in the backpack, which would safely protect it, so I took several sheets and placed the packet between them. I thought the briefcase would be too obvious a hiding place, so I put the packet into my backpack, and hid it behind a chair so at least it wouldn't be seen at first glance.

Wondering if they had just stepped outside, I went to the front door to look. I half opened it and noticed a crowd a short way down the street. The troubadour troop was performing. However, I didn't think Karl and Yoseph would leave the store unattended for that. As I pushed the door open further, I saw Karl and Yoseph talking to a man, whose back was to me, through the mottled glass pane. Something about the man was familiar when I recognized the French cop! So, they had come, I thought. But Genseau did not appear to be with them.

I paused and noticed Karl making a subtle motion of his head as if to ward me off. I wasn't sure, but a moment later, he did it again, this time looking right at me. The French cop still hadn't seen me.

I stepped back into the store, closing the door slowly so it wouldn't creak. It was clear Karl was warning me, and I further took it to mean I should get out of the shop. I could use the back door. It also appeared that Karl and Yoseph were deliberately keeping the interchange outside, but I couldn't be sure. Perhaps it was to protect me, but it might also have been to protect the letters. It felt odd that it was only the French cop because, as Karl had said, Genseau would not leave the packet retrieval to others.

Passing the office as I went toward the back door, I decided to take the backpack. If the French cop was after the letters, then I was the only one responsible, and I didn't want him to be the one I gave them to.

Swinging the pack to my shoulder, I quickly went down the hall to the door. I figured Karl and Yoseph would know what I had done, and I would be waiting in the alley. But, as I closed the door behind me, I heard a solid metallic click, I was locked out. I had no choice but to wait.

As is common in Europe, the alley was under repair. The work was extensive and had been going on for a long while. The paving stones were torn up, and the ditch was at least 15 feet deep, the sides almost like a cliff. There was no way to get out except going down the steep bank to the planks on the bottom, and back up by temporary wooden steps at the end of the alleyway.

I kept listening for Yoseph and Karl to come back into the store, but I couldn't hear anything through the thick security door. After a while, my curiosity got the better of me, and I decided to go through the alley, and around to take a look.

As I slid down the bank, rocks and dirt came along with me. I laughed a little as I remembered the Cathar men had smuggled their treasure out by scaling down sheer cliffs, perhaps even carrying these same letters.

When I got to the bottom of the trench, I clambered up the steps and walked around to the corner. The performers and crowd were still there. While I was making my through the periphery, Stephane spotted me, and as if it was part of the performance, he waved a banner emblazoned with the rooster, a national symbol of France. I just nodded back, not wanting to draw any attention.

When I came to where I could see the front of the store, I saw the French cop walking toward me. It was like my dream, although he carried leather books in his arms rather than wooden boxes. When he came closer, he looked right in my direction, but lost in thought, didn't immediately recognize me. He was so close that he would see me if I moved, and if I didn't move, he would also see me. I was as trapped as in my dream.

At that moment, Stephane shouted "Cocorico!" and leaped in my direction, waving the rooster banner. The crowd surged back to give him room, pushing the French cop away and out of sight. I hurried back around the corner, but not before I saw Stephane still waving the banner as if it was for me. I walked past the deep trench in the alley and to the block's back. I didn't think the French cop would come that way, though I wasn't sure.

There was a row of shops on the street, and a brightly lit patisserie caught my attention. I thought about ducking in but decided against it. Across the way was a small wooded park, and I figured that would be a better option. I found a bench behind a row of bushes where I could be obscured but still observe the street.

It had been a close call, and while the backpack was secure, I touched it anyway for reassurance. I couldn't help but think how prescient my dream was. The similarities were too many to dismiss.

But now, I needed to find out what happened at the book-store and let them know what I'd done. It had been a risk to take the letters away like that, and I was worried Yoseph and Karl might be in real trouble if the police had found them missing. Yet, I had noticed the French cop didn't seem agitated; in fact, he looked sort of happy. I couldn't understand how that could be if he had come for the letters.

It was then that I saw the French cop coming around the corner, still carrying the books, though I didn't think he was following me. I cautiously waited to see what he would do. Instead, he walked down the street and into the patisserie. He came out with a paper bag dangling under the books a short while later. Despite his bitter demeanor, I guessed he had a sweet tooth.

He then started crossing the street toward the park. I quickly turned my back, praying he wouldn't pass by. However, I could feel him getting closer and then heard him sit down on the bench on the other side of the bushes, with his back to me. I cursed myself for not leaving when I had the chance.

I tried to make myself as inconspicuous as possible when a loud group came carousing around the street corner. It was the troubadours, and they also went into the patisserie. They were still boisterous and making quite a ruckus when they came out.

Suddenly the French cop shouted something, I assumed telling them to quiet down. The troubadours went silent for a moment, then one started waving the rooster banner as the others began crowing, "Cocorico!"

The French cop got up, grabbed his books, and stormed over. There was a loud conversation, but the exchange was brief, and soon the troubadours headed one way and the French cop the other. Walking away from each other, there was the sound of a rooster crow, causing both sides to look back at the other. However, this time, it was a real rooster calling from somewhere, and they continued their separate ways.

How odd, I thought. It reminded me of the story where the cock crowed three times after Peter denied just as Jesus predicted. But in this case, who was Peter, and what was denied? I began to think I had been around the Bible too much.

As I waited to ensure the French cop was not coming back, my phone rang. It was Wendy. I hesitated but answered.

"Hi Wendy," I said.

"Hi, Bjorn," she replied. "How's it going?"

"It's going, but it appears the situation is still working out," I said. "I have not heard back from the magistrate, and until I do, I won't know anymore."

"How long do you think that might be?"

"I don't know. He said he'd call me, and not to call him. It could be days or weeks. I just don't know."

"Well, I've been thinking," she said. "We can't do the article, I'm sorry about that. But I've spoken with my boss and explained the situation. She agreed to honor your return ticket, as we have already paid for it. We will need you to turn in the camera, computer, and company phone, and we're canceling your hotel and car. We can give you a few days leeway, but that's about it. Also, there will be no more per diem, but we are not going to ask for any money back. We'll just write it off.

"Thank you, and I understand," I said, as my stomach sunk. "I'm really sorry."

"It happens," she said, in a matter-of-fact way. "There may be some legal things down the road. You were working under our auspices, even as a freelancer, but we'll cross that bridge if we have to."

"And just so you know," she continued and her tone shifting, "I'm concerned about you."

This was an unexpected change, and I felt a genuine extension of friendship. With that, I decided I should tell her about the packet. While it was a very long shot, it would be a blockbuster story if the letters proved out.

"You know, Wendy, thank you, and again..." I began.

"No, I really am concerned," she interrupted. "And if there's anything I can do offline, I would like to help. I do feel responsible for you."

"I will stay in touch then," I said, realizing that mentioning anything about the letters at this point would be too much. "There is one thing that I'd like to tell you about all this, but maybe now is not the time."

"Yeah, it probably isn't," she responded. "But perhaps when this is all over, we can get together. I hope it does not turn out to be serious."

"I hope so, too," I replied.

"So, what are you going to do?" she asked.

"Well, I've made some friends, and they have offered to help," I said. "I also need to contact the Consulate, and they might have some suggestions, though I don't think that is going to be much of an answer."

"At least you've made some friends," she said. "And you always manage to land on your feet."

It was an astute observation coming from someone I didn't think knew me very well. Also, I had never thought about my life that way, and I didn't know what to say. We agreed to stay in touch, and I sat for a few minutes afterward, absorbing it all.

While the assignment, and the sense of purpose it brought, was over, at the same time, losing it was freeing. I no longer had to worry about the article and all the commitments that came with it. I was now able to handle things independently, and in some sense, I came away from the call feeling better.

CHAPTER TWENTY

The roller coaster ride of the last hour had only heightened the need to talk to Yoseph and Karl, but returning to the bookstore seemed too risky. I had no idea what had transpired with the French cop, or if leaving had been what Karl meant. So I called instead.

"Hello, Yoseph, this is Bjorn," I said when Yoseph answered.

"Bjorn, I'm glad you called," he said with relief in his voice. "We were worried about you. Where are you, what happened, do you have the packet?"

I was leery of giving my exact whereabouts, as protection for them and me.

"I'm fine, though a little shaken. And yes, I do have the packet," I said. "What happened? What did the police want?"

"Don't worry, everything is fine," Yoseph said, in which also I detected a little mirth. "Wherever you are, I would stay away from here for tonight. And, we are glad you have the packet. We assumed you took it."

"Should I return it to you, isn't that what the police wanted?"

"It was very strange," Yoseph replied. "The packet of letters never came up. All he wanted was to buy some books."

"What?"

"Yeah, he only wanted some books. He flashed a badge when he came in, saying it was official business. So, of course, we thought it was about the letters, or maybe you. But it wasn't. He wanted language and history books on the Languedoc."

I couldn't believe it, though I was glad he didn't see me. I was also beginning to think the magistrate must not have told him about the letters. It was curious, though, that he would have come to this bookstore,

"He was officious and obnoxious at first. But Karl was very good, and by the end, he laughed with old stories about the city. I must admit I sold him some expensive books," Yoseph chuckled. "But they might relate to your case, and are probably for the magistrate. Obviously, we didn't ask."

I smiled hearing about the sale. But, if Genseau hadn't told him about the letters, I wondered who else he hadn't told, and why.

"So, I guess it was still a good idea I left, thank Karl for warning me. I had fallen asleep and had no idea what was going on. I would have walked right into it. That would not have been good," I said. "As it was, I almost ran into him on the street, three times in fact."

"It's probably best you didn't. We managed to get him outside, thinking of you, as well as the letters," Yoseph said, confirming my understanding of Karl's nod.

"Speaking of that, I should bring the packet back, I have it in my backpack."

"We think you should keep them," Yoseph then said. "They are yours, and Karl has finished what he needed to do."

The suggestion was completely unexpected.

"Wouldn't they be better in your care, and in a safe place?" I replied. "And, also, that's where I told the magistrate they would be."

"From what I've seen, you give them the right kind of care," Yoseph said. "And if the magistrate inquires, I will just tell him you have them now."

I wasn't sure I could give them the proper care and preferred they stayed with Yoseph. But, on the other hand, it wasn't right for me to expect him to keep something that the police believed was stolen. As I'd come to expect, Yoseph could almost read my mind.

"Have you considered that maybe those letters belong to you?"

"What do you mean?" I said, again taken aback. "I don't own

them."

"Well, the aunt gave them to you. As the head of the family, she had every right to do so. Legally they are yours, a gift from the aunt, and you can do with them what you want."

I wasn't sure his legal analysis was correct, but that they would be mine never occurred to me.

"That isn't what the Count would think," I remarked. "Nor the police."

"Well, the Count will be the new heir, and as such, of course, he can try to contest it. But, it was done before his time, and you have a witness to the transaction, Juliette," he explained. "As far as the investigation, I personally think it's not going anywhere. They are just accommodating the Count out of respect for his position."

"So accommodating I can't leave the country," I commented.

"You can think that way," Yoseph replied. "Anyway, we think you should keep the letters."

"What I'd really like is to see Karl's final translation of the letters," I then said.

"Karl would love you to. He's gone home to get some sleep, but he'd like you to have it," Yoseph said. "It is an amazing thing you have done, and much more important than either you or I know. I'm glad I've been able to be part of it, thank you."

He made it sound as though everything was resolved and OK, but I knew it wasn't, or at least I couldn't see it that way. I appreciated his perspective, however.

"Your thanks may be premature, but anyway, you're welcome. And please let Karl know that I'm OK. I'm going to see Juliette in a little while," I said. "And oh, by the way, I lost the writing assignment. They did not want to get involved. I never told them about the letters."

"I'm sorry to hear that, but maybe it's for the best. I think you have better things to do now."

"I'm not sure what you mean, because as of now, I can't see

much light."

"You'll land on your feet," Yoseph stated.

"Funny you should say that. My now 'x-editor' said the same thing when she told me she was ending the assignment."

"Hmmm, she was right," Yoseph said. "I'll tell Karl you want to get together. Maybe here tomorrow."

"OK. I have some stories to tell you," I said in closing.

"Until tomorrow," Yoseph said as we hung up.

I could not quite believe how things had played out, but I was off to meet Juliette. It was getting toward evening, and the city was taking on its pinkish glow. But, first, I wanted to stop by the hotel.

I kept my eye out for the French cop as I walked back, but I was reasonably sure he had left. So I went in the front door, and the always observant but detached clerk did not look up. That was a relief, as I had anticipated the police might have returned.

Going up the elevator, I contemplated what had happened and began to think maybe I wasn't in so much trouble after all. Then I thought of going to the Consulate, and my restrictions, and the feeling faded. Still, I did have the letters back, and I was free to travel, so it could be worse.

I took a shower and changed clothes, but not before hiding the backpack behind the bed. I wished now I had taken the briefcase as well, but maybe I could get that tomorrow.

I retrieved the backpack, and while I didn't want to be carrying the letters around, I did not trust leaving them in the room. Outside the hotel, I noted the pinkish glow of the city was fading into a deeper red. It was pretty lovely, and I thought of making a quick painting. Simply having the thought felt good, but I also wanted to get to the café. I wondered how Juliette's interview had gone, hoping Genseau didn't grill her the way he did me.

It took about 15 minutes to walk to the café. Along the way, I continued to admire the city's beauty, which by design or default had managed to keep many of its older districts intact. Then, thinking of what Karl said about buildings holding memory, I began imagining what they had seen.

Through my reading, I knew Toulouse had suffered sieges over the centuries, as well as celebrations. Kings had walked where I was walking, as well as people fleeing for their lives. All of this, the worn cobblestones remembered. I could hear the wooden wheels of horse carts rumbling over the pavements as if I were there.

Baby carriages were the rumblings now, and I wondered how infants felt about the bumpy ride. They probably liked it. The cobbles also curtailed easy bicycle travel, though the riders seemed used to it also. I wished there were more streets like this in America, but we are too addicted to smooth roads and speed.

Juliette had not yet arrived when I got to the café. She hadn't given a time, and as I looked around, I recognized Madeline, with her pale complexion and dark eyes, at a table with Robert, the accountant, and his wife, Jeanette. I went over and re-introduced myself, which was unnecessary as they remembered me.

"Please sit down," Robert said. "How have you been? How's the article coming?"

It was an embarrassing question, and one I wanted to avoid.

"I'm fine," I said. "I came to meet Juliette here."

"Oh, you just missed her," Jeanette said.

I was shocked. I thought I was early and berated myself for first going to the hotel. I gathered she had not told them about my coming either.

"Did she say where she was going?" I asked.

"She had to take Artemisia back home to put her to bed," Jeanette answered.

I obviously looked disappointed, so Robert said, "Sit down, have a drink."

I needed to talk with Juliette, and while reluctant to join

them, I sat down, not quite knowing what else to do.

"So, tell us about your article," Jeanette asked.

"Umm, I'm afraid I lost the contract," I replied.

"Oh, what happened? I'm sorry," Jeanette said apologetically. "Maybe you don't want to talk about it."

"It's OK," I replied. "These things happen. I will spare you the details, but it was my fault."

Unintentionally, that effectively closed off the conversation.

"I don't mean to be rude, but I think I need to go for a little walk. It just happened, and I'm still...well, it's a bit difficult," I said.

I choked up a little as I said it. I hadn't realized how much it meant to me.

"We understand," said Robert, while Madeline looked at me with her dark eyes like clear, deep pools.

I left feeling even more embarrassed, and as I walked away, I had the idea of going over to the park with the old fountain where Juliette and I first talked. On my way, however, a strange feeling came over me. I couldn't quite put my finger on it, but it was as if the unusual paper in the packet, the moment of clarity outside the hotel, and my experience in Marianne's cave, converged into one thought. I needed to have some time apart.

CHAPTER TWENTY-ONE

By the time I arrived at the Park it was getting dark, and I thought it was not a good idea to be going to a poorly lit place with what I had in my backpack. So I decided to return to the hotel. The sky had turned a deep purple, and the buildings were now a dark red.

As I came in through the hotel door, I noticed the desk clerk nod over toward the lobby area as if pointing. Juliette was sitting in the lobby. She got up, and without saying a word, put her arms around me and her head on my shoulder. We were silent for a few moments, then she let go, took my hand, and led me to the elevator.

After the door closed, she grabbed me and kissed me hard and passionately. I responded in kind, and we stayed embraced even after the doors opened on my floor. I was glad no one was in the hallway, not that I would not have cared. We still hadn't said a word.

When we got to my room, we kissed again, only now we were removing clothes, and the only words she said were, "Kiss me all over."

The day's tension, and all that was happening, was concentrated and then released as we fell onto the bed. No holds were barred, and every crevice, root, and soft lip explored, gently at first, and then harder, until as one we came together. Time became one thing, minutes were hours, and hours were minutes. We finally fell asleep, still not having said an intelligible word. That would have to wait until morning.

Juliette arose before I did, and going over to where we had strewn our clothes, she began dressing, still not saying anything. I enjoyed watching as her bright nakedness slowly vanished beneath layers of silk, cotton, and wool until she looked as she had in the lobby. It felt like she was ready for war, or maybe love.

She sat down at the table, and finding a sheet of paper and a pen, wrote for a minute and then got up to leave.

"It's all in the note," she said, and then left much more gracefully than we had arrived.

It was an unusual exit, not at all what I had expected. But, then again, she was an unusual person. I lay there for a few minutes, fearful that this was her way of saying goodbye. I couldn't blame her. I got up and went over to the note.

"I have no words for what I felt.

The Café – tonight (don't be late)."

I had to laugh.

After showering, dressing, and making sure the backpack was where I had put it as our passion ignited, I sat down to organize my day. I needed to pack my things as I only had another day or two here unless I paid for extra time. The magazine had treated me well, and while the hotel was not expensive for the area, it was outside my price range, and even more so now. I needed to find another place, and for who knows for how long.

I also had to get together with Karl. I was burning to see the final transcription. And while it was a burden to have the letters, I was beginning to feel comfortable having them, and their being close.

I also needed to check in with the U.S. Consulate. I was reasonably sure they would try to be helpful, while displeased with the situation. I did not know what Genseau told them, but whatever it was, it wasn't good. And then there was the Café tonight.

While those things would help fill the day, I was feeling at sea. In a way, I had lost my purpose to be here, yet I could not leave. Perhaps Karl was right in suggesting I take a trip. Even though we had just met, Peter and Marianne had extended a sincere invitation to return, and they would be keen to see the letters. I felt a peculiar draw to go back to the cave. While the famous Neolithic paintings at Lascaux were nearby, they were off-limits except to archeologists and sponsored researchers. While they had made a facsimile nearby, I wanted to see the real thing.

I also originally intended to visit the village of Gosol just across the border in Spain. It was where Picasso had an early breakthrough leading into cubism, but that was out of the question now.

The time with Juliette was still ringing in my body, and I felt refreshed, which was unusual. My typical experience was closer to a line in an old Cowboy movie where an older dance hall lady shared her wisdom with a younger one, "Every man feels depressed after sex."

It was still too early to call Yoseph, and as I wooled thoughts around, I decided to go to the cafe across from the bookstore. I could wait there and perhaps do another painting. So, picking up the backpack, I took the elevator down to the lobby. The usually expressionless clerk was by the desk, but I thought I saw a smile flicker across his face.

The pink blush of the city was fading as the sun continued its inexorable rise over the morning. Though it was still early, the traffic was becoming heavy, and as I crossed the street, I noticed a lightness to my step.

Sitting by the window in the cafe, the book store was still in shadow. I decided to just drink coffee and watch the street rather than paint. A man was sweeping the sidewalk, and a vendor had his cart, where the evening before the Troubadours had performed. It was a peaceful scene until I noticed a little sign on the bookstore door. I went to look.

It was written in French, and I immediately thought the police had come and taken Yoseph to the station for questioning. I wondered if they had picked up Karl as well. They would have called me if something less pressing had happened. I then thought maybe the store was being watched. While I was looking around, an elderly woman walking by asked, in accented English, if I was lost.

"No, I was just surprised the shop is closed today," I said, pointing at the sign.

"Don't worry," she replied. "It says he will be back in 15 minutes. About now."

Even as she was speaking, Yoseph and Karl came walking up the street, and Yoseph gave me a wave.

"See?" the woman said. "No worries."

I admonished myself for being overly suspicious and wondered if Karl's suggestion of taking a trip wasn't a bit of genius. In my haste, I had left the backpack in the cafe, and was relieved to find it still there. Along with everything else, I was becoming careless.

Yoseph had opened the shop, and Karl came to greet me at the door. However, rather than inviting me in, he said, "Come, I want to show you something."

He took me to where the ally was being dug up. There were no workmen yet, and we went down the wooden steps into the deep ditch.

"I didn't want to say this in front of Yoseph," he began. "But are you OK?"

"I am," I said, wondering what he was getting at. "I'm a little scattered, but other than that, I'm excited about what we've found, and would really like to see your translations. Thanks for doing that."

"OK," he said. "I want you to see something. I've shown it to Yoseph, and he agrees it's very curious."

With that, he pulled aside a tarp that had been put over some shoring beams. Initially, it just looked like a small hole had been dug in the side of the dirt bank. As I peered in, however, I could see some exposed stone, apparently the old foundations of the building. After my eyes adjusted to the dark, I saw the same symbol carved into the stone that Dieter had found in the cave. It was a Templar cross.

"Wow," I said. "Is it real?"

"I would imagine so," Karl said. "Toulouse is an ancient city, and the region was a home base for the Templars. The city has

165

been built, and rebuilt, and rebuilt."

"So this was once a Templar fort?"

"Not necessarily, but it would be interesting to look into the history of this location. I would guess when the workers found this, they reported it to the antiquities department, and work was stopped until it could be studied. I just thought I'd show you."

Pausing, he then added, "Perhaps it's a sign."

"A sign of...?"

"Maybe we'll find out," he replied enigmatically.

"Can I take a picture?"

"Of course."

I turned on the phone camera flash because of the lack of light, and when it went off, I was temporarily blinded. Blinking my eyes, I could envision a host of knights in armor wearing white tunics emblazoned with a red cross. They were standing around us, holding their swords downward, with the tips of their long blades touching the ground.

I shook my head a little, and the image faded as my eyes readjusted.

"That was weird," I muttered.

"What's that?" Karl asked

"I could see knights standing here. It was as if they were real. I think I need that vacation."

Karl nodded and cocked his head a little.

"Your perception, it's a gift," he commented. "Let's go back, and I will show you the translations."

Still in a bit of a fog, I followed Karl back out of the ditch, reminded of yesterday's dream, and sliding down the bank with a backpack like the Cathars with their treasure. I was beginning to wonder if it was the place or me. However, one thing I was sure about, last night with Juliette was not in my imagination.

I briefly considered getting something at the patisserie, but I didn't want to delay seeing the translations. When we entered the bookstore, I could smell something sweet, but it wasn't the delicate fragrance of beeswax. Karl and Yoseph had closed the store to get some rolls from the patisserie. Yoseph was already enjoying one and motioned us into the office. The coffee was brewing.

As we sat down, I was a little saddened that the letters were no longer spread across the table. They had become almost like old friends. Karl then opened my briefcase.

"I think you should put the packet back in here. It might be safer than your pack."

I couldn't have agreed more. I opened the backpack, and carefully pulled out the packet, still safely lodged between the protective sheets of paper. I was not surprised to see the paper had become faintly discolored, the stain looking like a pale red dot. Fortunately, the packet itself had not deteriorated or been damaged and appeared very much like when I put it in, as far I could tell.

"Let me see that," Karl said, and taking the packet, he handed it to Yoseph.

Yoseph looked a little concerned, but I saw a change come over his eyes. It was like he was taken somewhere that perhaps only he could see. After a few moments, he handed the packet back to Karl, who handed it back to me. Yoseph then turned, and without saying anything, left the room.

"I think he wanted to hold it one more time," Karl said quietly.

I noticed Karl, too, had a different look in his eyes. They seemed softer and deeper, as if something dormant in him had been revived. As I placed the packet between new watercolor sheets, I, too, had a strange sensation, a memory that felt ancient and yet seamlessly connected with the present. The atmosphere in the room took on another character. Whether it was my eyes or imagination, the light seemed to flow like a subtle, soft flame I didn't want to end.

I am not sure how long we sat there, but gradually it passed, the light returned to normal, and I finished placing the packet in the briefcase. I looked at Karl, and Yoseph came back into

167

the room, and for a while, we were each in our own worlds, saying nothing, as if basking in the memory of something that couldn't be explained, or needed to be.

"Good roll," Karl said.

I looked over, and he had taken a bite as if nothing had happened. He sipped his coffee, and Yoseph went back into the bookstore. I wondered if I had imagined it all. But I hadn't, and Karl and Yoseph hadn't either.

We spent the next several hours reviewing and discussing the translations, though I was still in that other world in some ways.

"You have to understand how different Aramaic is," Karl said, explaining why translations can be more art than science.

"Words in Aramaic do not always draw a separation between place, time, and inner and outer experiences, unlike Greek and Western languages, which are much more literal and specific. In Aramaic, the meaning flows the same way we experience life. A word can combine tone, color, rhythm, feeling, and even magic as if they are happening simultaneously. It is a perfect language to convey spirit. It was made to order for someone like Jesus."

I could feel what he was saying and was envious of such a language. I wondered why it had been lost.

"Aramaic, Hebrew, and Arabic all share a similar root," Karl went on. "The range and depth of many of the words do not have a counterpart, or even a substitute, in Western languages. Add to that the nature of what was being conveyed, which even today challenges comprehension…well, you get the picture.

"It sounds impossible," I said.

"Maybe it is, but we do the best we can," he said, laughing. "Let me show you."

He then brought out a copy of his translation of the letter that may have been the precursor to the Beatitudes in Jesus's Sermon on the Mount.

"This is the phonetic Aramaic translation," he said.

"Toowayhon laylein dadkeyn b'lebhon d'hinnon nehzun l'Alaha."

"Now translated into English."

"The Pure in heart shall see God."

"The word 'nehzun' literally means 'see.' But the English word 'see,' even though technically correct, is inadequate because 'nehzun' also means a sudden insight, a flash of light, the light of understanding. It changes what it means to 'see' God.

A little light went on in me with that description, and it also reminded me of my experience in St. Sernin.

"Remember when I found that little flake in the Cathar Bible? When I first saw it, it was like a flash of light."

"Nehzun," Karl commented.

"I don't know if I could say I saw God."

"It led you to all of this. Who knows how a flash of light should work?"

I couldn't deny that. I was beginning to see things that could be compared to a sudden insight. While I didn't automatically attribute it to seeing the little flake, who knows?

"Let me show you another. Here we have the letter to Mary. I'll read it in English."

"Mary, the Truth, though not gained by logic and reason alone, never violates logic and reason. Your heart is true, where you are I Am."

"At the close Jesus says, 'I Am' or 'Ena Na' in Aramaic. Now, this is very interesting, because normally in Aramaic, a person would simply say 'Ena,' or 'I,' because the 'na,' or 'am,' is implied or not needed. Furthermore, no one says the full 'Ena Na' because that would indicate something far greater, something eternal, without beginning or end. Essentially it is a reference to God."

"So he was saying he is God?"

"It could be taken that way. But it could also mean 'of God' or 'of the spirit of God'. It's still quite a statement however you take it."

"Or that he loved her that much," I said.

Karl laughed, "Perhaps."

I began to think of Juliette, and how much she would want to be here for this. Maybe there would be an opportunity.

"Let me show you one other thing, it has to do with the word 'Word.' In the writing on the envelope, this passage essentially follows the opening of the Book of John. Let me read it in Aramaic."

"Brisit itauhi hwa milta."

"And in English."

"In the Beginning was the Word…"

"Now 'milta' is Aramaic for 'word,' but this has always been a mind-bender for theologians and translators because, once again, there is no counterpart in a Western language. 'Milta' has a meaning more like in Genesis when God spoke and said, let there be light, and there was light. 'Milta' means that kind of Word. It has the power of manifestation."

"Ena nehzun," I said.

"You're getting it," he said, tapping me on the shoulder

I was glad Karl was doing the translating, even though I knew he felt it was deeply inadequate. I was also beginning to have an idea that the magazine assignment had just been a door to the real reason for coming here, one that I could never have foreseen. Maybe Karl had been right, "Who knows what a flash of light means?"

Insights were coming in unexpected ways. Questions I didn't even know I had were being asked and answered. Windows were opening to things I'd only vaguely felt or perceived. I could only hope they would clarify enough to understand them.

The time was going by, and I began to be concerned about making it to the Consulate. It was important that I at least contact them. I didn't know the consequences of not doing so, but I didn't want to find out either. If I had broken a French law, particularly a serious one, there was likely not much they could do, but anything might help. I also wanted to make the visit short and get back to Karl as quickly as possible.

"I hate to break this off, but I think I need to go," I finally said. "Though I would really like you to tell me more about the pyramid symbol if you know."

"Ahh, we have more to discuss," Karl said. "The transcription is nearly complete. I just need to clean up some details. We will have time."

"I hope so."

As I was leaving, I found myself surprisingly less troubled about the letters being taken by the police. Perhaps it had to do with finishing the translations, or maybe I was becoming like Karl and Yoseph, who seemed content to let things work out. I hoped my lessening worry was warranted. I knew the letters would likely be returned to the Count, restrictions could be put on everything Karl had done, and even my saying anything about them might be prohibited.

Furthermore, it was unrealistic that they were legally mine. In the unlikely prospect they were, they would likely fall under some antiquities act, and be kept in the country. I had no idea how that worked in France and dismissed any thought about keeping them.

On the other hand, I couldn't help wonder how much they might be worth if they turned out to be genuine. But money felt like it would violate the spirit of the letters. Subtle as that might be, I would want to honor it. However, I also questioned whether I could resist such a lucrative prospect. Money has a force field, and practical people would think I was crazy not to take it. I would probably agree no matter what I did.

It was getting too complicated, and I needed to quickly get to the Consulate. The reality was I was under investigation for theft and possibly murder, and then there was Juliette. I couldn't believe I still did not know what Juliette said to Genseau.

CHAPTER TWENTY-TWO

Karl had persuaded me to keep the letters, though how I did not know. At any rate, I found myself walking to the Consulate, briefcase in hand. The building was in the same vicinity as the café where I was to meet Juliette, should there be a time crunch.

As I was admiring the old buildings, some cantilevered far over the street. The city's wonderful morning glow had passed when an idea suddenly popped into my head. What if the letters, and the red dots, were like marks on a treasure map? Not a map of a physical place, but the mind and heart, a treasure map to ourselves. Then I felt the grey weight of the Consulate visit creep back in.

The Consulate was in an older three-story building, and there was little to distinguish it from other buildings on the block. I walked through the arched entrance and to the front desk. The young woman behind the counter was dressed in a blue blazer, with a little American flag on the pocket.

"Yes, can I help you?" she asked with a welcoming smile.

I had to admit it was good to hear an American accent again. I hadn't realized how accustomed I had become to the French.

"Yes. Thank you. I'm not sure who I need to speak with, but perhaps the person in charge."

"Well, have you lost your passport?" she asked. "Or is it something else?"

"No, I haven't lost my passport," I said. "Well, not exactly."

She looked at me quizzically.

"It has more to do with a legal matter. I may be in some trouble with the law."

Hearing that, her face turned serious, though I had the impression she had listened to this kind of thing before, which surprised me a little. However, given the number of Americans who visit Toulouse every year, run-ins with the law were probably not uncommon.

"I will have you talk with our consulate representative. Let me get some information, and then please have a seat. Would you like a cup of coffee or some water?"

"Not right now, thank you. But if it's any help, I believe a court magistrate has already called, and someone may be expecting to hear from me."

She nodded and asked for my passport, which I gave to her with a little trepidation. She took it to a back room where I could hear a scanning machine. She wrote down where I was staying, my phone number, and my e-mail address. I felt some relief when she handed my passport back and appreciated she didn't ask any more questions.

It was good to feel a little like I was on home turf, but there was also a governmental air that made it impersonal. I was entering into 'the system,' and the trap was closing. While I waited, I began to review the day, everything Karl had said concerning the translation, and the experience when we first took the letters from the briefcase. It seemed like that was days or weeks ago, rather than only a few hours.

A couple of people came and went, but it was not a busy place. I looked at my watch, and an hour had passed. Then, sensing my growing impatience, the clerk told me it would just be a little longer. There had been some mix-up with affairs in Paris, the home office for the Consulate in Toulouse. I hoped it hadn't concerned me.

"I'll accept that coffee," I finally said, just to pass the time.

"It's French roast," the clerk teased.

"Just put a lot of cream in it," I teased back.

She was pleasant and kept herself occupied with paperwork between visitors. Then, handing me the coffee, she sat down beside me.

"So, what are you doing in Toulouse? Have you been here

before?"

"No, this is my first visit. I came to write an article on art," I said, not wanting to add that was no longer the case.

We chatted casually about where we were from and what I had seen. I was careful not to say too much, as I couldn't tell if she was friendly or surreptitiously trying to gather information. I wondered whether I was overly suspicious, but my years as a journalist had conditioned me to be a little cautious. After a while, the phone rang, and she went to answer it. I hoped it was the representative, but apparently, it wasn't, and she went back to her paperwork.

I continued to wait until I became concerned the office would close before I could meet with the official, and I would have to come back the next day, or the meeting would stretch out, and I would miss Karl and even Juliette.

I looked at every potted plant, leather and stainless steel piece of contemporary furniture, the documents framed on the wall, the United States Great Seals behind the clerk's desk, and the color and texture of the rug until I was totally bored. That was when I took notice of the pyramid on the Great Seal's reverse face.

"Do you mind if I take a closer look?" I asked.

"No, please," she said, moving her chair over a little so I could step behind the desk.

I had heard stories about the symbolism in the seals. The 13 arrows in the eagle's left talon represent the 13 original states and times of war. The olive branch in the left talon was the peace side, and it had 13 leaves and berries. There are also 13 stars in the crest above the eagle and 13 stripes in the shield. I thought it was a lot of 13's.

Then I examined the pyramid on the reverse seal, and it had 13 rows of building blocks. However, there was no capstone, just like the Great Pyramid in Egypt. The radiant "Eye of Providence" was in its place.

I was beginning to think how it might relate to the pyramid symbol Karl found in the letters when my musings were interrupted by the ringing of the clerk's phone. After a brief conversation, she said the consulate representative was coming down to see me. I had been there nearly three hours, and it was a little past 5:00. I was not getting back to Karl.

"Hello Mr. Solberg, I'm Randy Chamberlain, the consulate representative for Toulouse."

I nodded hello, and we shook hands.

"I'm sorry you had to wait, but I needed to check on a few things before we talked. Why don't we step into my office?"

As we went in, I reminded myself of what Native American humorist Will Rogers said, "Never miss a good opportunity to shut up."

"Would you like some coffee or water?" Randy said as we sat down at his desk.

It was much more accommodating than the magistrate's office, and there was no tape recorder, as far as I could see.

"No, thank you though," I replied, hoping to keep the meeting short.

We began with small talk, and I noticed he knew things about me that I had just talked about with the clerk. So I listened to what he had to say, and what Genseau had told him, noting there was no mention of the letters. However, what was mentioned were 'items of great value' as the motive for the assault. So Genseau was still on that, I thought.

"What items did he say?" I asked in my most wrongfully accused tone.

"He mentioned the Bible."

"Was that all?"

"Yes, I think so. Why? Were there other things?"

"There were a lot of extremely valuable things in that library," I said, evading mention of the letters.

"Please, tell me your side of the story," Randy then asked.

I explained what had happened but debated whether to mention the letters. Unable to decide, I said nothing, even though they were right beside me in the briefcase. I figured it was enough that I was accused of trying to steal a Bible and

176

causing the aunt's death. Perhaps it was only an illusion, but it was as if the packet was a kind of protection, even influencing what I said. At any rate, I could feel its presence and wondered if he could, too.

"The woman who was with me can corroborate my side," I said in concluding my story. "I didn't go there to steal anything, and it wasn't to talk to the aunt, but the Count."

I now regretted not having pressed Juliette about her meeting with Genseau. Maybe pressed was the wrong choice of words, I thought, smiling to myself.

"Yes, what is her name? I don't believe it has been mentioned," Randy asked. "So, she is not supporting the Count's story? Have you had any further contact?"

It seemed Genseau had been judicious in his comments and only gave them information about me.

"Yes, we've stayed in touch. Her husband does business with the Count, and he wants to keep her out of this as much as possible, but she supports my version."

"Well, that's helpful," he said. "What's her name again?"

He paused, not having anticipated my reluctance.

"I need to explain something to you, let's sit over here," he said, motioning to a sofa and chairs in the corner of the room. He poured each of us a glass of water.

"You are not aware of this, but your situation is becoming a diplomatic incident, and we are trying to diffuse it. The Count is a very influential person, as you may know. So the more we know about what happened is helpful. There have been too many curveballs already."

"What do you mean curveballs?"

"I'm not at liberty to discuss that, but let's just say it involves matters not related to you."

I had been so worried about the letters and criminal charges that I never considered anything beyond them. However, this other matter was likely at the level of the main office in Paris, maybe the State Department in Washington, and perhaps even the Secretary of State. I assumed it caused

Randy's delay in meeting with me.

I understood he was offering to help, but then again, maybe not. Accepting it would mean high-level assistance around the charges. On the other hand, it could mean sacrificing me to the Count to save this other "matter." My curiosity was aroused as to what it was.

"I will only say that at this point, the Count doesn't care whether the charges he is leveling against you are true or not. He just wants to get you," Randy continued with some candor. "In his mind, you've violated the family name, and he is determined not to let it go. This is the Lautrec's home province, they see it as theirs."

"We also believe the Count is reluctant to go to the press, because he does not want any publicity, not yet anyway. He is threatening to make it a major incident if we don't do something about it. While we are prohibited from getting involved in criminal matters, the Count wants you prosecuted. He does not want you to leave until you are."

"So that's why my passport has been restricted?"

"It could be. All we know is the magistrate notified us of your passport classification, the possible charges, and that you are not permitted to leave the country. That he allowed you to keep your passport, and to travel within France, is unusual. But he has the authority to do that. More often people are held pending a hearing or trial. In that respect, you are fortunate."

"Do I need to get a lawyer?"

"We would like you to and are recommending several we've worked with before. They understand the complexities of international law. Because of other sensitivities, we will be monitoring this, even though we cannot get directly involved with the French criminal courts."

I couldn't have agreed with him more about having a lawyer, except the magistrate seemed to prefer I didn't. And, so far anyway, that had proved to be the best advice. I didn't understand what was going on, except the Count was behind it. It was also apparent, at least from what I was hearing, that the magistrate had not mentioned the letters to anyone, which was perplexing. Perhaps I was still making too much of them.

"Yes, if you could provide me with a list of lawyers, I would like to have that," I said, but thinking I would still hold off.

"While we can make recommendations, we cannot pay for your legal expenses," Randy explained. "However, we can help you with funds on a short-term basis if you need them. Also, if you should be put in jail, I will visit you regularly, and provide you with things like extra clothing, food, and other items, if you are not being adequately cared for. It's a French jail, and that can happen."

I didn't like his talk about jail. It made it sound like a foregone conclusion.

"We will make sure you are being treated under the standards that the United States expects for all of its citizens," he added.

"I appreciate that, but could we wait until after that happens, and maybe keep it to things as they are now?"

He seemed to take a little bit of offense, but I also had the impression he had momentarily slipped into a rote speech. I could also appreciate that he was trying to please the Paris Embassy, and was likely under considerable pressure. I further assumed the Count was impatient with the magistrate, and trying to push him into action. However, from what I knew of Genseau, that was only going to go so far.

Even though I was a pawn in a bigger game and didn't like it, I felt an almost disassociated calm that was in contrast to the situation. Hearing of the still mysterious "matter" made me wonder even more if my coming to the Languedoc was never about the article. However, I had come to the Consulate because Genseau advised me to, and now that I had done that, it was time to leave.

"I appreciate all the advice and help. You've given me a lot to think about, and I'm sorry this has happened. I hoped the

Count would change, but I guess not."

"We are working with it," Randy said, sensing he might have fallen short of bringing me on board.

"Thank you. I know you'd rather be dealing with more pleasant things," I said.

"Helping US citizens, and those who are in trouble with French law, is one of our primary functions," he said, reverting to his official line. "It is not pleasant for you either."

He gave me the list of attorneys, his private phone number, and some brochures on the French legal system.

"This is my direct line. Please stay in touch, and call me - day or night- if you need anything. We want to help," Randy said.

He meant it sincerely, but I knew what he wanted was for this to go away. I did too.

The secretary had left by the time we returned to the front door, but she had put a message for him on the desk. As he picked it up, I noticed the word 'Depeche.' It means 'dispatch' in French, but I knew it as the name of a Toulouse newspaper. We looked at each other.

"This is routine," he said somewhat unconvincingly, and I wanted more than ever to get out of town.

CHAPTER TWENTY-THREE

Upon leaving the Consulate, I looked at my watch, and it was almost 7:00. The rose glow of the city was beginning to fade, and I had missed Juliette. The café was only a short distance away, but it might as well have been a hundred miles. I had expected my unaccountable ease to begin fading like the rose light, but somehow it hadn't.

When I arrived at the café, I saw dark-eyed Madeline and Dieter. I was surprised he was already back. Then I saw Juliette. My relief was palpable, though I anticipated she would be furious. Instead, Juliette threw her arms around me.

"You're right on time," she whispered in my ear.

As it turned out, she had been delayed as well. Her husband had worked late, and she couldn't leave Artemisia until he came home. Dieter then called out hello, and he and Madeline joined us.

"So, the criminal returns," Dieter joked while giving me a bear hug. "We were wondering what bars you were behind."

"Not yet."

"These bars are better."

Madeline hugged me, too, and we all sat down.

"What are you drinking?" Dieter asked. "I think it should be strong medicine."

I hesitated.

"You sit, I will get you just the thing," he said as he headed over to the bar.

"I thought I'd missed you," I said to Juliette. "I'm sorry. I got hung up at the US Consulate."

"I wasn't worried. I knew something was going on," she replied, looking me straight in the eye.

She looked wonderful, though there was a tinge of sadness

and wear on her face. Then she cut right to the point.

"I am leaving William."

She had told the others, but before I could respond, Dieter was back.

"Here," he said, putting a very small bottle in front of me, and then the others.

"What is this?" I asked, never having seen it before.

"It's Underberg. Let me show you how to drink it."

He unscrewed the cap, put the bottle in his mouth, and holding it only in his lips, he tipped his head back and drank it all in one go.

"Ahhh," he said, shaking his head a little when it was gone. "Now you do the same."

We all did, looking like circus seals balancing little bottles, and then plunking our empties on the table, laughing. It was good medicine.

"So, Dieter, I thought you were in Holland?"

"I had to come back. She was making me too nervous, my ex-wife. She's beautiful, and she takes good care of our daughter, but I just had to leave."

I wasn't going to analyze his family situation, but I had noticed he was drawn to women and they to him.

"What about you?" he asked.

I wasn't sure how much to say in front of Madeline, but I decided not to hold back.

"I'm in limbo. I just came from the Consulate, and they want to be helpful, in a way. The investigation is ongoing. I told the magistrate of the letters, but he hasn't done anything about them yet, and he didn't ask for them. However, I am restricted. I can travel within France but can't leave the country. And for some reason, he didn't take my passport."

"I told them about my interview, too," Juliette said,

"What happened?" I asked.

"It wasn't pleasant, but he was confident that I would not be involved."

I was a little surprised he had made a decision so soon. But he had probably heard enough by now that he was quite sure about what happened in that room, and it wasn't the Count's version.

"Did you tell him about the letters?" I asked.

She looked at me with a directness I had come to appreciate and said, "I told him exactly what happened."

"Did he ask you what the letters were?" I queried again, still surprised at his seeming lack of interest.

"Just what I thought they might be."

"Did you tell him?"

"Only that they were old," she said. "I know what they are, and I knew you, Karl, and Yoseph needed time to translate them."

"I didn't tell him what they were either," I said. "Just that they were old."

We were on the same page, and I felt a little ashamed that I thought she wouldn't understand the situation as well as I did. But, I was the one who needed to up my game, and it was a good feeling.

"Just so you know, I have them right here," I said, patting the briefcase on my lap.

There were startled looks around the table.

"You what?" exclaimed Juliette.

"They are right here."

The ensuing conversation was lively but hushed.

"What are you going to do with them? They need to be protected," Juliette said in a whisper. "Why didn't you leave them with Yoseph? They were safe."

"Not really. Genseau knew where they were, so he could have taken them at any time. But that isn't the reason. Yoseph and Karl thought they would be best with me. Yoseph even thinks they are mine, that the aunt gave them to me, and they were legally hers to do with as she pleased, not the Count."

"I think they are yours," Juliette said.

"In a strange way, I think so, too," I said. "I don't believe the courts would agree, however, and certainly the Count wouldn't if he even knows about them."

"What?" Juliette said in surprise again.

"I don't think Genseau has told him, for what reason I don't know, but it is the only way he would find out. No one else knows but us."

"That's not true," Juliette said. "My lawyer was there when Genseau was interviewing me."

That threw a wrench into my theory.

"However, he is not supposed to speak to anyone, attorney-client privilege, but you never know," she said. "But, he told me that the Count is the complaining party, and he brought the accusation to Genseau, not the police. A person can do that in France, unlike the US. That means he can see the transcripts of all the interviews, but only after the magistrate brings charges, or drops them."

I knew it would come out eventually, but at least for now, it seemed the letters were safe. That led me to doubt whether they should be here at the café if they were sensitive to people and places.

"I think we should go somewhere else," Dieter said, as though picking up on my thoughts.

"Yes," Juliette said. "Let's go to the park. It's still light."

In the meantime, Madeline had been listening quietly, but not fully understanding what we were talking about.

"Can I see them?" she asked innocently.

"Not here," I said.

As we began to get up, Dieter grabbed my arm.

"Don't turn around, but look over at the end of the bar, slowly."

I did as he said and saw the French cop pretending to nurse a drink and look nonchalant. So, he was following me, or maybe Juliette.

"The little bastard," Dieter hissed.

"What should we do?" I asked Dieter.

He thought about it and then said, "You, Juliette, and Madeline head to the park. I am going to go over to him."

As he began to get up, I grabbed him by the arm.

"I'm going with you."

He nodded, and I discreetly slid the briefcase to Juliette.

"See you there," I told her.

After they left, Dieter and I got up and began walking straight toward the French cop. When he saw us, he looked startled and hastily made as if he was going to the lavatory. When we got there, however, he was gone.

"Piss off," Dieter said.

I had no idea what I would have done if he hadn't left. I had acted on impulse, and it was not the smartest thing to do. I now knew, however, that I was under surveillance. I did not know the law around meeting with potential witnesses, but I was worried it might mean no contact with Juliette.

Juliette and Madeline, meanwhile, had only gone a short distance and stopped to watch.

"I don't like it," Juliette said when we caught up with them. "What were you thinking?"

"I have no idea, but he's gone for now."

"What does he want?"

"It might be he's watching where I go, making sure I don't slip the country. It could also mean if I'm charged, and you are a potential witness, it could be taken as witness tampering or something."

"I still don't like it," she said.

"He better not get too close," Dieter interjected. "I will tamper with him."

"Don't worry, I'm not leaving France," I said, trying to defuse his anger. "He's wasting his time."

By the time we reached the Park, Dieter had calmed down, and we were laughing about the incident. It felt good to be going there with Juliette, almost like it was becoming our place.

The fountain was bubbling away, and the water had that reflective pinkish glow. We found a table away from the street, and I put the briefcase on top. As I removed the packet,

I intended to hand it to Juliette but found myself giving it to Dieter instead. He did not object this time.

"I don't want to open it, it's too fragile," I said.

"You don't need to," Dieter commented.

His mood changed, and I could feel his respect and care radiating around it as if it was a holy relic. My concern about the atmosphere dissipated, and if any damage had been done, I had the feeling Dieter was healing it.

We were all quiet. He then handed it to Juliette, who gently took some time before giving it to Madeline, who held it so lightly I thought she was going to drop it. When it made it around to me, I put it in the briefcase and snapped the clasps shut. As I did, there was a sputtering sound, and all the lights along the street lit up. It was getting dark.

"Good timing," Dieter remarked.

"What do they say?" Juliette asked in anticipation.

"Karl is cleaning up the final transcript, but he seems certain it is what we thought, and there was more. He found writing on the inside of the envelope.

"What do they say?" Juliette asked again, pointedly.

I conveyed what I had learned, describing each of the letters, and when I said they might be originals of Jesus's and Saint John's writings, Madeline gave a little start.

"You can't say anything to anyone," Juliette told her. "Really."

"Besides," I said, "this is all speculation, though there seems to be reason to believe it's true. However, whatever they are, apparently the letter that can be read in so many ways is the key. Everyone has had some kind of experience with it. I don't know what it is."

"It's like sunlight. You can't see the light itself, but without it, you can't see the world," Juliette said, then adding, "except under lesser light."

Her analogy reminded me of Aramaic, and its ability to convey so much in a single word.

"So, what are you going to do with them?" Juliette asked.

"That's a good question. I could return them to the bookstore, but somehow I'd like to keep them, though that may not be realistic, or the best. The magazine has canceled the article, they don't want to get involved. I am going to be losing my hotel room, and car, and I don't know how long I'm going to be detained in France. I need to find a place to stay."

"What?" Juliette said.

"We didn't have a chance to talk the other night," I said, looking at her as if peering over the top of glasses.

"Why not stay with me?" Dieter said.

Then there was a splash, and we all looked toward the pond. As we were talking, Madeline had quietly slipped away and jumped in. We found her swimming around and giggling.

"No, I didn't drink that much," she said as she climbed out dripping wet. "I couldn't resist. I know it's silly, but I think that packet, or whatever it is, made me want to do it. Maybe I've been baptized."

Juliette and Dieter were a little surprised at her, but she was young and a little impulsive. And who was I to judge about acting on impulse?

The pond was still rippling and rhythmically reflecting pink as the waves pulsed against the sides. I remembered my dream of Artemisia eating the little flake with the red dot, and wondered if Madeline had seen anything under the water. She needed to be taken home, and Dieter offered her a ride.

While walking back to the café, Dieter again took up the invitation for me to stay with him.

"Yes, you can come to my house. We have many things to talk about. We can go back to Rennes le Chateau."

It would be a solution, and if I stayed any longer at the hotel, I would have to cover the expense. I also needed to start paying for the rental car, but I wanted to keep that for now.

"I would appreciate that, it's a generous offer. Are you sure?"

"Of course, my house would love to have you."

I had to laugh, "Of course, I love your house, too."

"I have to get home, Artemisia has school tomorrow," Juliette said.

I had assumed we would be together tonight, and wondered if something had changed.

"I will drive you to the hotel," she said, taking my arm and drawing close. "I want to tell you some things."

There was a glimmer of hope.

"I will have a room ready tomorrow," Dieter said when we reached his car. "And I am going to Rennes le Chateau the next day. I hope you will come, I've already told them you would."

"What?"

"Yes. You want to go, don't you?"

"Well, yes, but…"

"Then it's done."

Juliette had been listening, and after a moment, said, "Dieter, would there be room for two more?"

"We will make room."

This unexpected turn left me watching and listening. I could not have hoped for anything more, but it was happening so fast.

"Are you sure?" I asked her. "What about Artemisia, and your husband?"

"Artemisia is the second one, and she loves excursions. I do, too," she said with a pert smile, not mentioning anything about her husband. "Dieter, I will call you about times and arrangements."

"I wish I could go, but I have to work," Madeline said a little despondently as she was starting to shiver.

"This is only the beginning," Dieter told her as they climbed into his car. "I have more to tell you, too."

Turning to me, "I expect you for dinner. Maybe we will cook the lamb."

I wasn't sure if he meant in a biblical sense, but I welcomed a hearty meal.

"I hope you don't mind me inviting myself, and Artemisia," Juliette said as we walked to her car.

"No, it will be fun. It just happened so quickly."

Juliette just smiled, "Get used to it."

CHAPTER TWENTY-FOUR

She told me what she meant about the divorce as we drove to the hotel. William had become even more distant after the meeting with Genseau. It exacerbated an already untenable situation. Despite his feelings for her, they had begun discussing divorce. She saw the trip as a way to mark a break.

"This does not involve you," she then said.

"Are you sure?" I asked.

"It is going to happen anyway," she replied. "I hope you don't think I am trying to pressure you, but I would like to be with you."

This was pressing the edge of what I was comfortable with, and my habit was to withdraw. Then I thought maybe I needed to control that impulse. There was something different going on here, even why we met, which I still didn't understand.

"I'd like to be with you, too," I said, surprising myself.

"I really loved last night," she said very quietly.

"I did, too," I said even more quietly.

We drove in silence, and then we both burst out laughing. As we pulled up to the hotel, she leaned over and kissed me.

"Don't call. I'll see you at Dieter's," she said.

I watched her drive away, feeling connected even to the red taillights of her car as it disappeared down the street. My feelings were in contrast to the trouble I could see ahead. I felt reckless even thinking about such a relationship, particularly now. I enjoyed her definitiveness, however, and hoped I wasn't becoming too trusting and unrealistic about it.

The evening air was still, and softness emanated from the old buildings. It was as if they were listening and had heard and seen this many times before. Even the rumbling sound of tires on the cobbles was familiar. I imagined how the rain would reflect the light from windows and streetlamps in the pattern of ancient stones. It would be a wonderful painting.

When I entered the lobby, I looked at the front desk, and the clerk wasn't there as usual. A little perplexed, I peeked through the office door. He was sitting at his desk, head down, pen in hand. He saw me and gave a brief acknowledgment.

"Bonjour. No messages."

At least that was a relief, and I thought how I was going to miss his discreet manner. It was as much a part of the city as the ancient buildings.

Going up to my room in the elevator, I remembered last night with Juliette. The elevator felt empty, and the dimly lit hallway even more so. When I unlocked the door, I was surprised to see clean towels and the bed had been remade. I could only wonder what the housekeepers thought, as I had left the sheets as a display of our passion. I was also glad I had taken my briefcase.

Partly closing the curtains so I could still see the quaint street, I sat down to reflect on what I would do tomorrow before going to Dieter's. I wanted to talk to Karl and Yoseph, hopefully in the morning, and I needed to inform the magistrate of my change of address.

As I looked over at my watercolor backpack, I realized this might be my last time in this part of the city, and I could do some final paintings. I also needed to pack my things and check out.

I had a feeling I was free from the investigation for a few days, but I needed to tell Genseau that I was moving. I had become less concerned about him coming for the packet. Nonetheless, I didn't want to draw unnecessary attention to it either. As I closed my eyes sitting in the chair, I could envision the packet in my briefcase, with its warm golden glow, even in the dark. The Aramaic words started coming back to me.

I thought of 'Milta,' meaning 'Word,' but so much more. I imagined it floating off the page, drifting into space. Each letter was like a musical note combined with the others to make a chord. As it moved, I followed it without trying to direct where it went.

I was beginning to dream and decided to drift with it. Soon other words came that related to 'Milta,' which became a symphony. It was a journey with color, sound, and feeling, all rolled into one, just as Karl described.

I imagined a whole gathering of people moving with one accord in one place with radiance emanating around their heads like tongues of blue flame. I could understand everyone who spoke, even though it seemed unlikely they would know English, and then I woke up.

I was too tired to take off my clothes, so I just lay down on the bed, pulled the covers over me, and fell asleep. In the morning, I remembered the 'Milta' dream, and I was beginning to understand how much meaning a single word can have. I looked over at the black briefcase and wondered whether it was only a dream.

As I gathered my things to leave the hotel, I assumed the dream would fade, but it lingered. However, I didn't want to dwell on it, as looking too closely might change it.

In saying farewell to the room, I took one more look out the window, half expecting to see the French cop standing on the street corner, watching. But there were only old buildings leaning over the street, and the warm cobblestones reflecting the morning sun's pink light.

I went down to the front desk and told the clerk of my departure. He dropped his detached demeanor for a moment and said it had been a pleasure to have me stay. I'm sure he had said it before, but I hoped I had given him a few memorable moments. It took two trips to bring everything to my car. As it turned out, Wendy had arranged to cover the expense, so I left a generous tip.

"Merci," the clerk said as I put the franc notes on the counter, nodding his head lower than usual. It was the old saying, "Don't give thanks, give money."

"And thank the housekeepers for cleaning, particularly yesterday."

He nodded again, but with a quizzical look as if thanking the cleaning staff was unusual. I waved to him, feeling free but also stepping into the unknown.

I doubted anyone would mind if I left my car parked at the hotel while I walked to the bookstore, hoping Karl would be there, too. I had my painting backpack, along with the briefcase, wanting to make a day of it.

Yoseph was in when I arrived, and he greeted me with a hearty, 'Bonjour!"

He wanted to know how the meeting at the Consulate had gone and then said Karl was in the back room finalizing his transcripts. Then, hearing my voice, Karl came out and greeted me warmly, taking my elbow as he shook my hand.

"How has it been going?" he asked. "Are you settled into your new place yet?"

How he knew I was moving was a mystery.

"Ahh, it feels like you are on the move," he said, picking up on my question.

His keen observation, and natural intuitive sense, was impressive. He was rarely wrong.

"Come, you wanted to know about the pyramid," he said, leading me to the backroom, with Yoseph following behind. "How did your Consulate visit go, and where are you moving?

"It's a friend of Juliette's, Dieter. I don't think you know him. It was quite an offer, and we will be taking that trip you suggested, he was who I went with before. Juliette and Artemisia will be coming along, too."

"That's good," Karl said.

"The Consulate was somewhat helpful, but there is some other matter with the Count they are worried about upsetting. I am a pawn in their chess game, but I would like to know what that other thing is."

"Let's look at this pyramid," Karl said, apparently satisfied with the brief explanation.

Yoseph, meanwhile, had opened his great safe and pulled out a folder containing several diagrams.

"Now, this may sound a little strange to you, but I think you'll understand after I explain," Karl began, spreading out the first diagram.

It was the Great Pyramid, but this one had features I had not seen before.

"There are many ideas about the Great Pyramid, some too mundane, others quite unbelievable. However, everyone recognizes it as a significant structure, the last of the Seven Wonders of the Ancient World. That is no accident," Karl said.

"You may have noticed there is no capstone," he went on. "Some believe it was stolen or lost. Others believe it was never there because it represents invisible Spirit coming down from above. It is represented as the 'Eye of Providence', or the 'Eye of God', on your dollar bill."

"Yeah, I just saw that in the Consulate Building, the Great Seal of the United States," I said. "So, is that how this relates to the letters?"

"It does, or at least the principles do. There is a theory that the capstone was deliberately removed during some remote time because it was made of seven layers of valuable materials such as gold and silver, with gemstones at the very tip. Those, too, could represent Spirit. For instance, gold can symbolize love, silver truth, and the precious gems as lenses to focus the light, or Spirit, coming down."

I didn't know how Karl knew all this, but I suspected I was just touching the tip of the iceberg, or pyramid in this case.

"If these letters were known by the Cathars, was that part of their heresy?" I asked.

"It could be. Some of these beliefs, or knowledge, go far back, way before Christianity. They crop up in the Old Testament and Gnostic teachings, and have been mentioned in the Dead Sea Scrolls hidden by the Essenes. Jesus and the Disciples knew of them. A few scholars even discern references in the New Testament."

"You have to remember, when most of these letters were written, the Great Pyramid was in its original state, covered in polished white casing stones. It was magnificent, like a temple, the highest building on earth. The casing started being stripped off in the Middle Ages after an earthquake loosened them. What we see now is only the outer core, but inside still has the most important parts."

I wanted to know more, but I was beginning to think this could be an endless rabbit hole as well. However, I pressed on.

"What do you mean, most important parts?"

Sensing my beginning skepticism, Karl took a step back.

"Maybe that's for another time. But, I will tell you this, the Great Pyramid contains many secrets you may have to see for yourself to understand.

I can tell you, but you have to promise not to take my word for it."

I smiled at his honesty.

"OK," I said. "What about these seven lines in the pyramid?"

"One way to look at it is this. We have a body, a mind, and a heart, represented by the first three levels, or lines, starting at the base. They are the physical aspects of a person if you will. In the next three levels or lines above those, there's life for the body, truth for the mind, and love for the heart, which activate all the levels below. You might call them the higher aspects. The seventh level is Spirit, which flows down and through all the other six. It is the capstone of the pyramid," Karl said.

"I hear the words…" I started to say.

"I told you that you have to see for yourself to understand," Karl commented.

"Maybe you should have told me in Aramaic," I replied.

We both laughed.

During this time, Yoseph had been attending to customers in the shop. It had been a busy morning, but he had sweet rolls from the patisserie. I tried making the coffee, but with only limited success. It was becoming clear my frequent visits to the shop were coming to an end.

"So, what are you going to do with the translations?" I asked Karl.

"I think that is up to you," he replied. "The letters found you."

"This is not my field of expertise," I said. "I've never considered being responsible for that part."

"Take your time. It will come," Karl said. "Think about it on your trip."

"That sounds like a good place to start," I replied.

I was touched by the gentle wisdom in his words, which reminded me of my 'word' dream last night. Karl and I shook hands when I finally left, and Yoseph gave me a brief hug.

"I'll let you know what I come up with," I said at the door. "I'll be back in a few days.

"We'll be here," Yoseph answered.

I had a bittersweet feeling walking away. I might be in jail the next time they see me.

I had the rest of the day free until I had to go to Dieter's, except I still needed to contact Genseau to inform him of my address change. I debated whether to go to his office at the Court building and risk running into the French cop, so I decided an email would suffice. I didn't want to expose the letters to that atmosphere anyway. I could feel them in my briefcase, and there was lightness combined with a weighty sense of protection. I knew their value.

Karl's comment that I should determine what to do with them was also on my mind. His suggestion that it would 'come to me' felt right, and so I put it out of my mind and found myself walking toward the Park. I thought it would be a good place to paint and see what the 'spirit of the place' might look like. I had no idea of its history.

I passed by the Café, which was just beginning to open. The waiters were still setting up the tables, opening umbrellas, and arranging chairs. I admire that the French do not generally tip the servers as the job is considered a profession, and they are paid a commensurate wage. I also noticed the restroom, remembering how the French cop had faked going there as a way to escape. I wondered where he was and if he might show up again at Rennes le Chateau.

A few people were lounging in the Park when I arrived, and I sat down at the table where the four of us had been the night before. It was a good view of the pond and fountain. I pulled out my painting supplies, taped a sheet of watercolor paper onto a backboard, and picked my favorite sable brush. Then I went to the pond to fill my water cup. I liked using local water, imagining it might imbue the painting with something of the location. As I dipped the cup into the pond, the ripples in the water reflected a pink tinge.

I hadn't thought much about making art over the last few days, and it was good to be doing it again. I took a moment to relax and ease into the flow, then I wet my brush, swirled it in one of the shades of green, and dove in, a little like Madeline in the pond.

It took about half an hour to complete, and what emerged had a surprisingly different look than the Park on the surface. I had started with the lush green trees, but that had changed to a deep red, which wasn't there. The grass, too, took on a darker hue, accented with light patches beneath the trees. I wondered what had happened here. I saw figures and crowds of people in the distance. All this went into the painting.

When I was finished, it looked like a historical scene, though in a very abstract way. The colors were densely local, though contrasting with the light summer day. I am fascinated with what Spirit was captured and whether I should portray it.

In Native American culture, many refused to have their picture taken because it would trap their Spirit or soul. Even today, it is not permitted to photograph certain ceremonies; and, if someone does, they risk losing their camera or phone.

It is taken seriously. I thought, perhaps disingenuously, that whatever was here only showed what it wanted of itself. In any event, I liked the painting, and it would have made a good one for the article.

I sometimes paint several at a given location, but because the first is usually the best, I packed up my things to go, I didn't want to leave my car at the hotel too long, and I also planned to paint the street in front. Manmade places don't feel violated; it is almost as if they want to be painted, and it is congruent with their purpose.

It was a pleasant walk back, though I avoided going near the courthouse just a few blocks away, and I still hadn't emailed Genseau.

As I was unlocking my car, I noticed a flash drive on the ground, which must have dropped out of my computer case. I was cautious, however. If it wasn't mine, there was no telling what was on it. Free flash drives were a ploy used by hackers to infect computers with malware. However, it looked like one of my own, and I put it back in my computer case, taking note I needed to be more careful.

From where I was parked, I could see the street, and it was a good angle, so I went ahead and painted the scene while sitting in my car. The feel of the painting was quite different than in the Park, even though it was still in the old area of the city. There was a timeworn quality broken up by small patches of color from the stained glass panes in some of the windows. The sky was a beautiful blue, though I was a little surprised the pink color of Toulouse was not a dominant feature.

I then emailed my change of address to Genseau. I kept it brief and mentioned I now had the letters. I didn't want him, or the French cop, poking around the bookstore. I didn't mention my trip, assuming he had my phone number. I hit send and felt a sense of relief; it was one less thing I had to worry about.

I still had an hour or so to kill before going to Dieter's, and

I went to pick up some things at the patisserie. I wasn't planning to go back to the bookstore, just yet anyway. So I parked near the patisserie, but I went to the alley out of curiosity before going in. The workers had returned, and one of them came up the steps and lit a cigarette.

"American?" he asked.

"Yes, and my French is not good."

"Neither is my English. Big, eh?" he said, looking at the ditch.

"Quite a hole."

"Where in America?"

"Wyoming."

"I love Wyoming. Buffalo, cowboys, and Grand Tetons," he said, chuckling at that last item, which means Big Breasts in French. "We should still be there, we got along with the Indians."

"Have you been?"

"No, would love to go, maybe someday."

"So, why so deep?"

"Ahhh, we found some things, come see."

"Is it alright?"

"Yes, you're with me."

I didn't want to say I knew about the Templar mark, and feigned surprise when he showed it to me."

"And there's more," he said, pulling back another canvas tarp.

Underneath, there was a cut stone in the shape of a pyramid. I couldn't believe it. It was polished red stone, about 12 inches square at the base, and the precision was remarkable.

"What do you think it is?" I asked.

"The archeologists say maybe Roman, maybe something else. But the marble is ours."

I could detect a kind of pride as he spoke. Red Languedoc marble has been quarried in the region for millennia.

He stamped out his cigarette and said he had to get back to work. I thanked him for the discovery. It was clear this location held some special significance; but, then again, maybe it was like that all over the city. I wanted to tell Yoseph, but first, I went to the patisserie and bought some pyramid-shaped petit fours to mark the occasion.

"Back so soon?" Yoseph said when I entered the store.

"I know, I was just stopping at the patisserie, and one of the workmen in the alley invited me down to see something. You know what they found? A stone pyramid, about a foot square. They don't know what it is, maybe Roman."

"I know," Yoseph said, suddenly smiling. "I saw it this morning. Karl did, too."

"What is it?"

"Karl thinks it might be a pyramidion, the capstone of a pyramid."

"He seems to know a lot about pyramids," I said.

"Let me have you talk with him, he is still here."

Karl was surprised to see me, too, but when I explained what had happened, he said maybe it was time to continue our earlier discussion.

"First, pyramids were used as markers, and more common than most people know. There may have been one here at one time."

"Really?"

"Yes. Not all pyramids were like the Great Pyramid. This one was not large, the capstone gives a clue about its size. However, it might be why the foundation of this building is deeper than they expected."

"I have been doing some research," he continued. "There was once a Templar library at this location. Before that, it is believed to have been a Roman shrine to the 'spirit of the place", which I think you know about."

"So what do you think the 'spirit of the place' is here?" I asked.

"I believe it somehow relates to records, maybe sacred records. It is appropriate that it is now a bookstore, and that you found those letters and brought them here."

"What about libraries like at St. Sernin Cathedral, wouldn't they be on an even more significant site? And if the letters are that significant, why not there?"

"Where did you find that first little flake?" Karl asked rhetorically. "This one is more personal, like it's your place. Not everything has to be dramatic, or even public."

I liked the sound of that. I had always felt at ease in the shop but assumed it was because it was a quiet bookstore.

"Those who have been on this site have maintained a quality of atmosphere, knowingly or unknowingly. The influence of these locations is real, it's not just imagination as some would believe. Many cathedrals, however, have been the focus of major disturbances, and as we know, the letters cannot survive for long in that."

As Karl spoke, I could feel something that went deep into the earth. It was like a marker on a map, a red dot, or a red pyramid. It also reminded me of Dieter's fixation on specific locations around Rennes le Chateau.

"You should note that when you first came here, you had a sense of trust," Karl said.

"That's true."

"And that when you left the letters here they were safe."

"That's true, too."

"But now you have them, and you are moving around."

"Yesss...?"

"This is the starting point of a journey, a marker on a map, just like you thought."

How did he know? I didn't wait to find out.

"And the journey is?"

"That is for you to discover."

He was continually throwing it back to me, but I knew he was not talking only about physical places.

"Are you talking about a map of the soul?"

Karl said nothing, but I had hit a key. I was beginning to be more comfortable discussing what I typically dismissed as too esoteric, but Karl had been something of a guide through my skepticism,

"I like the thought," I finally said. "Maybe it'll come on my trip."

"Take your time," he replied.

Yoseph entered the office as if on cue, and we shared pyramid-shaped petit fours. Before we parted company again, Yoseph handed me a hard leather case lined with a soft cloth used by conservators for preservation. The packet fit perfectly.

"You never know where you will be taking them," Yoseph said. "At least they will be safe."

"Thanks. I guess I should have been more careful."

"You've had a lot on your mind, and I think they are fine."

Karl then handed me a copy of his translations.

'You already know what they say, but others might not," he said with a twinkle in his eye.

As the smooth golden latch on the case clicked shut, I felt a slight tug at my heart. It was almost as if I was leaving for good.

CHAPTER TWENTY-FIVE

It was getting close to 5:00, and I dreaded being stuck in rush hour traffic. The lights, however, seemed timed as if by magic, and I found myself at Dieters earlier than I anticipated. As I got out of the car, I could smell something cooking on the grill. Dieter was indeed good to his word. Going into the yard, I found him standing at a red brick fireplace.

"Lamb?" I asked.

"Roasted to perfection," he replied, waving a barbeque fork. "You're right on time."

He had saved the bottle of sparkling wine I gave him from Rennes le Chateau, and as we sat down for supper, Madeline came out of the house. I wasn't aware they had been seeing each other, but somehow I wasn't too surprised. It seemed like a good match, at least for now.

"So, do you have the packet?" Dieter asked.

"It's in the car, along with my other things. Are you sure this is OK, my staying here, I mean?" I asked, thinking two's company, and three might be a crowd in the house.

"Of course, your room is ready, and stay as long as you like."

Madeline was quiet, but the dark circles around her eyes seemed less noticeable, and she looked more at ease than I'd seen her before.

"I think we'll bring the letters with us this time. I'm sure Marianne and Peter would like to see them. I'd take them out here, but they are fragile. Do you mind if we wait and do it there?"

"That's fine," Dieter said. "I understand, though I would like to see them. Before it was too strong."

"They do have a presence," I noted.

Dieter had called about the addition of Juliette and Artemisia, and Madeline had been able to arrange work so she could go, too. Juliette had called and would be coming in the morning. It was going to be crowded in Peter and Marianne's house, so Dieter had a tent for himself and Madeline, and one for me.

"I hope you don't mind being outdoors, or you could always sleep on the couch. The weather should be good though, and the stars are wonderful," he said, looking over at Madeline.

"No, I don't mind. It will be good to be outside. I just need to make sure the letters are safe."

"We'll have Sophie guard them," Dieter joked. "You saved her life, she'll save your letters."

After supper, we all went up into Dieter's special room with its array of swords and staffs. He picked up one of the staffs, and went through a series of moves, gracefully parrying and warding off invisible assailants. He was a student of Aikido and other martial arts.

"It's not about hurting or killing the other person," he explained while making a series of elegant moves, ending with the staff pointing at someone on the ground. "It is about controlling them. Come here, I'll show you."

"Don't hit me," I said as I got up. "I'm unarmed."

He put down the staff and told me to grab him by the collar. As I reached, he took me by the wrist, and in a moment I was on my back looking at him standing over me.

"See?" he said.

"I believe you," I replied as he pulled me to my feet.

"Now you try," he said, grabbing me by the front of the shirt.

I took his wrist, and the next thing I knew I was on the ground again.

"I'll show you," he said, explaining how he stepped into my space, causing me to lose my power, and then threw me off balance using my backward momentum against me.

"It is the art of the other person defeating himself," he said.

"I don't need anyone's help to do that," I remarked as he

pulled me up.

He then had Madeline step into the center, and after a few minutes of instruction, she had him down to the floor. It was impressive to watch such a petite person doing that to someone so much larger. She seemed to be enjoying herself. I then wondered what might happen in a confrontation between Dieter and the French cop.

Anticipating a long day tomorrow, we all headed off to bed, but not before Dieter pulled me aside and asked whether I had heard from the magistrate.

"No," I said. "I've given him your address because I left the hotel. He has my phone number, but I haven't heard anything."

"Good," Dieter said. "I have a plan."

"A plan for what?" I said, a little confused.

"To get you out of the country."

"Dieter, I'm not leaving. I can't do that."

"It's always good to have a plan."

"Thanks, but...."

"No, it's OK. You're not going to take "French leave" as they say in the military. But we will show you a way if you need it."

I appreciated the offer, but that was the last thing on my mind. I never anticipated that he, and apparently others, had been considering ways they could get me out. I went to bed feeling I might have made some friends.

The morning sun woke me from a sound sleep. I had not had very much wine, but apparently enough to slip into a dreamless night. I felt refreshed and looking forward to getting into the countryside. Nature is the best medicine.

Dieter and Madeline were already in the kitchen preparing breakfast, and I could smell the French coffee before I was halfway down the stairs.

"Bonjour Bjorn," Dieter said as I came in. "The car is packed, and Juliette will be here in a few minutes. Why don't you sit, we are eating on the patio. Here's some coffee."

"Thanks. Is there anything I can do?"

"You can wash the dishes when we're done," Madeline said over her shoulder.

"No," Dieter said. "He's a guest."

"You cook, I wash, fair trade," I commented.

Outside, the air was still a little cool, and sunlight was dappling through the leaves. I was attracted to the light flickering on the grey bark. I put my hand on the trunk and was absorbed into the show. Turning my palm toward the sun, as if to receive it, I felt its gentleness.

As I lingered in the feeling the kitchen door opened, and Juliette and Artemisia came out of the house. I had not heard them drive up. Juliette stood by the door as Artemisia went scampering to the tree and touched it.

"Hi Bjorn," Juliette said. "Miss me?"

As it turned out, Juliette needed to take her car, and I would be riding with her. I had wanted all of us to be together, but this would give Juliette and me time to talk. We would be following Dieter, and on the way, visit Montsegur.

"It is where the Cathars had their last stand," Dieter said, reciting the story of the four men who escaped with the reputed treasure. "I think your letters were in their backpacks."

"I do, too," said Juliette.

"Maybe they will light up at their return," Dieter added smiling.

"Or disintegrate, given what happened there," I replied half-seriously

In my thoughts, however, I wondered what Dieter might see, real or not.

The drive to Montsegur took a little over an hour, with the Pyrenees rising in front of us as we traveled into the increasingly rugged country dotted with farmhouses and small villages. I could feel the weight of the last few days lifting, along with the ghosts of history that seemed to be in every rock outcrop and river along the way.

Artemisia had brought a little backpack and kept herself occupied in the back seat by laying out the contents and arranging and rearranging the items. She was also wearing a new pair of hiking boots, which she kept admiring. Juliette and I were free to talk, if discreetly.

"I'm glad I could come," she said. "William was not in favor of it, and didn't want Artemisia to go."

"What did you say?"

"I told him this wasn't going to be his decision."

"Does he think you are with me?"

"Yes, I think he does."

I was looking forward to finally spending time together, but I could see how much she was involved with the marriage. I trusted, however, that she was doing what she needed to in coming on this trip, and hoped it wasn't a mistake.

I noticed it had become quiet in the back seat, and I saw Artemisia staring at me. She then put her finger to her lips and shook her head as if to say, "Don't talk."

When I looked over at Juliette, she was crying softly.

We traveled in silence, letting the green countryside roll by until Juliette finally spoke, wiping the still drying tears from her face.

"I really want to go on this trip, and I really want to be with you," she said with the beginning of a smile and a little laugh. "But what I really want is to sleep with you."

The sadness broke. She explained the stress had been building with the tension around a divorce, the police investigation, and caring for Artemisia.

"You haven't had an easy time either. How are you doing?" she asked.

"I don't know. But I'm looking forward to being with you, too."

"Have you heard anything yet?"

"About the investigation? No. Staying with Dieter is a big help though. I have no idea what to do with the letters. Karl says they came to me, so it's up to me to decide the next steps. I told him I don't know about these things, and he said, 'It'll come.' I hope so, that's part of the trip."

Juliette thought about it for a minute.

"Well, they came to me, too, and I do know a little about these things. Though I think Karl's right, it'll come, but let's do it together," she said with a twinkle in her eye.

"So, what do you think we should do?" I asked.

"You said Genseau didn't seem concerned about them, so if he doesn't ask, then keep them."

"I can't. I would give them to Karl, but he doesn't seem to want that. I think Genseau will ask for them at some point. But it was curious he sent his little henchman cop to get some books on Hebrew and Aramaic, but not the letters."

"What?"

"Yeah, the French cop came to the bookstore and bought some books, apparently for Genseau. At first, Yoseph thought he was coming for the letters, but it seems he didn't know about them."

"That is curious. What's Genseau up to?"

"I don't know. But Yoseph sold him some very expensive books."

Juliette just chuckled.

I then told her about the Templar symbol and the red pyramid in the alley.

"It seems the site was a Roman shrine, and later a special Templar library, and now Yoseph's bookstore. Karl thinks it is a marker of some kind."

"I wouldn't be surprised, Toulouse is full of them," she commented.

So, it wasn't very unusual. But I still liked the idea that it was my spot, though perhaps Karl only said that to make me feel better.

As we drove, I could sense a change in the air as we went higher into the mountains, and closer to Montsegur. I began to look around for possible hiding places for treasure, but also wondered if it was already in the car.

Dieter pulled off the road and into the village of Montsegur. Looming over the little community was a large, sheer-walled,

500 hundred foot high limestone projection called a pog, or peak. I could see why the Church's first assault had failed, and in the second attempt, how 100 mercenaries held off 10,000 Catholic troops for nine months.

"This is it," Dieter said as we got out of the car.

"Wow, I didn't realize it was that massive."

"Yeah, the Catholics had some inside help, otherwise the Cathars could still be up there. By the way, what you see isn't the original fort, that was razed after it was captured."

We wandered around the village, which had become something of a tourist spot. I learned that in the time of the Cathars, the community of Montesegur was considered their spiritual center, and where they kept their most sacred books and writings. It was their library. I gripped the handle on my briefcase just a little bit harder.

The Cathars did not have churches or official services. Instead, their meetings were more informal and likely held in people's homes, where the writings were used as source material.

That some documents had been smuggled out seemed even more likely, as they would have already been here when the Crusade began. The Cathars did not treasure worldly goods or relics, as their wealth lay in their teachings, which were more valuable than gold.

Following the Albigensian Crusade, the Church prohibited laymen from reading the Bible in the Languedoc area, making it a crime punishable by death.

A path had been made to the top of Montsegur, which made it a relatively easy hike. Juliette said Artemisia would not have any trouble, and though she seemed decidedly uninterested in the mountain, she really wanted to use her little backpack and new boots.

There was a 360-degree view from the summit, which gave a feeling of being above it all. I could also see the four men's difficulty going down the sheer cliffs that protected most of the peak. However, I suspected they knew a way, and had planned it all.

I felt something special about the letters returning to their home, and Juliette did, too. Before the climb, I had moved the leather case from the briefcase to my backpack, thinking if the letters left in a backpack, they should return in one.

After looking around, we went behind some boulders, and I pulled out the leather case and removed the packet, raising it a little in the air like an offering. I didn't know what to expect, if anything. I found myself thinking about the mercenaries who went into the bonfire with the Cathars. They had a free pass under the terms of the surrender, and I wondered what moved them to do that. Maybe the Church had cause to worry.

Juliette touched me on the shoulder as I was pondering and pointed to Artemisia. She was sitting down and drawing on the ground with a stick.

"Is she writing?" I asked.

"Could be, I don't know," Juliette said.

I leaned over to see, and it appeared to be letters. Dieter was also looking, and then he made a 'whooshing" sound, waving his hands in the air as if magically erasing all the marks. Artemisia giggled and, imitating Dieter, gleefully swept away what she had written. Her joy, and innocence, was infectious.

"I wish I had a picture of that," Juliette said. "But maybe it's best as a memory."

I took note that Artemisia was writing in a place for sacred writings. It even reminded me of the story where Jesus wrote on the ground to distract people about to stone a woman accused of adultery, saving her life by exposing the crowd's hypocrisy. Perhaps pointing out the truth was part of the spirit of the place.

Wanting to see what I might come up with if I painted, I took a sheet of watercolor paper out of the backpack, and my hand brushed against the leather case. It felt warm.

The colors flowed onto the paper as I painted, and soon there emerged a dark mass surrounded by a fluid pale blue sky. It was not a pretty picture, but a red spot toward the middle of the mountain helped offset the heaviness.

Dieter came by, and looking at the painting, said, "You've found the cave."

"What do you mean?"

"There are caves in this mountain, where The White Lady is said to have died."

"What?"

"She was a Cathar parfait, or holy person, who had renounced the world. The Cathars didn't have priests, and the parfaits were those who carried the teachings. The only difference was men wore black robes, and the women white. That's how she got her name. There are many legends about her, and she helped restore the fort on Montsegur just before the Crusade started. The Church chased her for 30 years, but she was never caught. Supposedly she passed away in one of the caves here, but no one knows. Her body was never found."

"Wow, can we go there?"

"Maybe on our way back. We need to get going."

I was a little disappointed, but he was right. That was for another time.

"Maybe I could hide there, you know, 'French leave,'" I said jokingly.

"Then you could become part of the legend," Dieter kidded back. "But you'd have to die."

I knew Dieter felt something unique about the area. However, it was not a key point in the sacred pentagram configuration he explored on our earlier trip, and in which he had the greater interest. Nevertheless, he picked up a small rock and touched it to his lips before hurling it over the side. A tour guide scolded him, but Dieter was already walking away.

"What was that about?" I asked him on the hike down. "You knew the rules against throwing things over the cliff."

"The stone wanted to be free," he replied. "It was tired of being stepped on."

CHAPTER TWENTY-SIX

When we left, I could see Montsegur in the rearview mirror for a long while. Juliette had been moved by the visit, and I could feel her begin to relax.

"I loved it up there," she said. "I didn't like looking at the field where they burned them. I don't know why anyone would want to go to that spot."

"I don't either. I wonder if the Cathars ever had a ceremony to sanctify it. I guess there are no more to do it."

"I know some who say they are," Juliette said.

"Really? Have you talked to them?"

"Not specifically, but they are around. The Church didn't get them all. A few went to Spain, others to Switzerland. But they kept it secret."

I was curious to meet them but wondered how much had been retained. It sometimes seems like pretend when people pick up religions from the distant past; however, I did like the spirit of the sect.

The drive seemed to fly by until we came into the long valley with Rennes Les Chateau below us. Dieter stopped, and after getting out of the car, he raised his hand, said a few words, and sprinkled what looked like cedar flakes in four directions. We watched from the car, and I thought maybe he was performing his own kind of Cathar blessing.

Artemisia looked on in fascination. She was leaning forward between the front seats, and when Dieter was done, she kissed her mother on the cheek. Then she sat back down and resumed playing with the things in her pack, which now included the stick she had used to draw on Montsegur.

Dieter stopped in Rennes le Chateau and went into a wine shop to get some of Peter's favorite vintage. The community has only about 90 residents and is called a commune, rather than a town or village. The Church of Sauniere fame was not far, and I asked Juliette if she wanted to take a quick look. Artemisia didn't get out of the car as we started to go. Instead, she waved her little stick out the window and shook her head.

"What do you think that's about?" I asked Juliette.

"I don't know, but the church can wait."

Dieter came out with a case of wine, and as he was placing it in the trunk, he looked toward the church and then slammed the door shut. Coming to our car, he poked his head in.

"Over there, it's that white Renault," he said with anger in his voice.

It was the same car we had seen the French cop driving before.

"When we left Toulouse he probably thought we would take the main road, and he has been waiting," he said. "He's not in it now, otherwise I would confront him."

I didn't know what to say. I wasn't completely surprised, but it brought back everything I had left behind.

"Let's just go to Peter's," I said. "We can deal with this later. I don't think he's going anywhere."

Dieter walked back to his car, looking over his shoulder.

"The French cop? He's really following you?" Juliette asked with some concern.

"I think so. I just don't understand. Genseau doesn't seem like the kind of person to order something like this."

"Maybe it's not Genseau," Juliette said.

"What do you mean?"

"You know the Count is known for being unscrupulous. If he's that way in business, why wouldn't he be that way that here? And to think, William is working for him."

"But he is a cop, he's not a private detective."

"So?" Juliette said in a way that made me think maybe I was being a little naive.

"You mean he's moonlighting, or corrupt?"

"I wouldn't put it past him."

"Well, maybe. Anyway, let's go. We can't do anything about it now."

Driving up the winding road to Peter and Marianne's, I noticed my painting on the dashboard where I had put it to dry. Absently I picked it up, and Juliette asked to see it.

"It's very dark," she commented.

"Well, that's how it came out."

"What's the red dot?"

"Dieter says it's a cave. Did you know there are caves at Montsegur?"

"No," she said. "I would love to go into a cave."

"You might get that chance," I commented.

When we pulled into the driveway, Peter and Marianne came out to greet us, with Sophie not far behind, wagging her tail.

"Welcome back, Bjorn," Marianne said as she hugged me. "And this must be your friend Juliette. Hello, I'm Marianne, and this is my husband, Peter. Welcome to our humble home."

"Thank you," Juliette said. "Dieter has spoken about you often, it's a pleasure to finally meet you."

"And who do we have here? You must be Artemisia," Marianne said, extending her hand. "We have a wonderful little room for you."

Artemisia had been holding on to her mother's hand, which she let go to shake Marianne's.

"She's a little hard of hearing," Juliette explained. "But she can read lips."

"Ahh, a special child," Marianne said as she turned to Artemisia. "It's a gift, you know."

Sophie, meanwhile, had gone up to Artemisia and nuzzled her, pushing a little with her nose. Artemisia smiled, and patting Sophie on the head, she looked up at her mother.

"Yes, you can go play," she said as Artemisia went running off with Sophie.

Dieter had already begun to pull things out of the car, including the wine, which he handed to Madeline.

"Hi, I'm Madeline," she said as she handed Peter the case.

"Beware the stranger bearing gifts," Peter said smiling. "I'm Peter, and this is Marianne. It seems Dieter is a little light on formalities these days."

"No, I'm not. I know you like presents, and I thought I'd give you two at once."

"Well, if that's the case, let me give you one in return. I've made the arrangements to go to Gosol."

The name Gosol rang in my ears.

"Shhh," Dieter said. "I haven't told him."

"Ohhh," Peter said a little sheepishly.

"So what's this about Gosol?" I asked.

"We can talk about that later," Dieter said.

"You know I can't go."

"Who said you were?" Dieter replied with a wink.

Marianne and Juliette had started walking toward the house arm in arm while Madeline continued helping Dieter unpack.

"Let me show you where you and Artemisia will be staying. The boys will be sleeping outside, they can take care of themselves, though it looks like they need Madeline's help."

It was a beautiful evening, and I could again feel the magnetic pull from the earth as I had on my earlier visit. Peter showed us where to set up our tents. There were two areas separated by a trellis flush with grape vines, and under the shade of some apple trees.

"It won't be too long now. That is if someone else doesn't get them first," Peter said, looking over at Artemisia, who was throwing Sophie the stick she found at Montsegur.

"Do you make your own wine?" I asked.

"Sometimes, but these are table grapes. I have others down below that are the same as the wine Dieter gave me. But, I usually sell those to a vineyard in Limoux, it's a little side business."

"I'd like to see them."

"Maybe after dinner, you need to get set up."

Dieter took the spot farthest from the house for privacy, I assumed.

"So, Dieter, what's this about Gosol?" I asked.

"I need to talk to Peter first and find out what he's done. It's going to be your escape route."

"What?"

"You don't have to do it, of course, but then you will never be Picasso of the Pyrenees."

I let it drop. There was no way I could leave the country, and I was no Picasso of the Pyrenees or anywhere else. Though I would have really liked to visit Gosol.

The tent Dieter provided was roomy. I assumed Juliette would sleep with Artemisia, but I noticed the ground pad and sleeping bag were big enough for two. I lay back to test it for comfort and rest for a moment. I shut my eyes, and immediately colors were dancing around as if I was still looking at the flickering dapples on the tree in Dieter's yard. The same feeling came over me, and although I was wide-awake, it felt like a dream.

"Bjorn, you can come out now," Dieter called, pulling me back from my vision.

"Sorry, I was having a dream."

"I can imagine," Dieter said with a sly look. "Let's eat."

Marianne had been cooking in preparation for our arrival, and the house smelled of sweet basil and olives, along with the distinctive smoky fragrance I remembered from before. The well-worn boots and jackets still lined the entryway.

Juliette and Madeline had set the table, and Artemisia was poking the now partially chewed stick in the ashes of the fireplace. She had worn Sophie out.

"Don't do that honey, you'll just make a mess," Juliette told her.

Artemisia slowly stopped swirling the ashes and got up to go into her room. As she did, Sophie struggled to her feet and began following her, trying to get the stick and making her laugh.

"It is a wonder meal," Dieter said as he sat down at the table on the patio. "Can you come cook for me?"

"You can't afford me, dear," Marianne replied. "But you can be my dishwasher, meals included."

"Deal," Dieter replied.

Peter, meanwhile, was opening one of the bottles of wine, letting the cork out with a small pop. As he did, Sophie began barking and headed for the door.

"It's only a cork, Sophie," Peter said, laughing as Sophie continued to bark.

Peter then began explaining the origin of the wine.

"This is from Limoux, just down the road, and made with the Muszac grape, which is unique to this area. Did you know that sparkling wine was invented here? Yes, by a monk in 1531, several years before Champaign, and this was the grape he used. It's first aged in barrels, not bottles, that comes later. It's called the Methode Ancestrale. It's sweeter than Cham paign, and that's why I like it so much."

"Are you going to serve it or talk about it?" Marianne said as she placed two large quiche Lorraine pies on a table already brimming with plates of salad, salami, cheese, and olives.

"To our guests," Peter said, raising his glass. "And may their futures be the sweet wine."

Juliette had poured a small glass for Artemisia, who wrin kled her nose.

"Give it to Sophie, for some reason she likes it, which is unusual for a dog," Marianne told her. "I'll get you some apple juice, it's from our trees."

Artemisia lowered her glass toward Sophie, spilling a little on the floor. I grabbed my napkin and bent down to wipe it up. Artemisia was still leaning over, and her head was close to mine. I looked up just as she was reaching to touch my hair.

"Hi," I said.

"Hi," she said back in one of the first words I had heard her speak.

After we had cleaned up the spot, Juliette looked at me. "Tonight," she said softly.

CHAPTER TWENTY-SEVEN

After dinner, Dieter washed the dishes, while Peter and Marianne were keen to know how my article was coming and the latest on the letters.

"I understand your fears have come upon you," Peter said politely.

"I'm afraid so. The Count has brought charges that I caused his aunt's death, and a magistrate has started an investigation. I can keep my passport, but I can't leave the country until it's done. Because of the controversy, the magazine canceled the article."

"I'm sorry. They don't know what they're losing," Peter said. "It's odd, though, that you can keep your passport."

"There's a couple of odd things," I continued. "For instance, driving into Rennes we saw the car of that French cop."

"Really, again?" Peter said in surprise.

"Yeah, I'm glad he wasn't in it or Dieter would have made sure he wasn't."

"He has no business here," Dieter chimed in.

"Anyway, I've met with the magistrate who seems very astute and capable. That he would send a spy to follow me around doesn't seem to be in character. Juliette thinks the French cop might be freelancing for the Count."

"That would be illegal," Peter said. "Maybe you should report it."

"I have no evidence, and the magistrate said not to call him, that he'll call me. I haven't heard any more from him, though he apparently sent the French cop to buy some books on Aramaic and the Languedoc from my friend's bookstore, which was also where I told him I was keeping the letters."

"That is odd," Peter said.

"The letters?" Marianne said with anticipation.

"Yes, I told the magistrate I had them, although he doesn't know what they are, just that they're very old. Anyway, he has never asked for them, which is another odd fact. I would think they would be important in the investigation. The Count only claimed I was trying to steal a Bible, and I have the impression the magistrate hasn't told him about them."

"He'll find out," I continued. "As the complainant, the Count will get the report when charges are filed, or the investigation is completed."

"Where are they now?" Marianne asked, her eyes bright.

"They are here," I said.

"Ohhh, can we see them?"

"Of course."

Juliette came with me as I went to get the briefcase from the car, with Sophie eager to trail along.

"This is exciting," Juliette said.

Sophie had trotted ahead and was sniffing the car, but then curiously backed away. As I began to open the trunk, I noticed some scuff marks around the keyhole.

"Did you do this?" I asked Juliette, not having seen them before.

"Do what?"

"These scratches here."

She looked over and then at me.

"Someone has been tampering with my trunk."

When I opened it, the briefcase was gone.

"I can't believe it."

"The French cop," Juliette said with vengeance.

In a panic, I immediately started rummaging through the trunk.

"The French cop came while we were eating," Juliette said. "That's why Sophie was barking, it wasn't the cork."

"I don't know, maybe it was taken while we were at Montsegur. There are thieves all over," I said, knowing that didn't make sense as my computer and cameras were still there.

Then it dawned on me. I couldn't remember taking the leather case with the letters out of my backpack after leaving Montsegur. So the only thing in the briefcase was the translation.

"Hold it," I shouted as I dashed over to my tent, now worried he might have gone in there as well.

The backpack was in the corner where I left it, and the leather case was still inside. Juliette had followed me, and as I held it up, we hugged spontaneously.

"That's way too close for comfort," I muttered.

Now, I also knew it was the French cop who had stabbed Sophie when I was here before. She had sniffed him out. As we headed back to the house, I told Juliette not to say anything.

"Don't tell, not yet anyway, Dieter will kill the guy."

They had cleared the table and put a beautiful cloth over it like an altar. Taking the case out of the backpack, my hands were still shaking slightly from the close call. I hoped they'd think it was just anticipation. I opened the case, took the packet out, and the sweet aroma of scented beeswax filled the air. I set it down on the cloth.

"I can feel them," Dieter said.

"So can I," said Marianne, to murmurs from the others.

Madeline knelt by the table and was joined by Marianne and Juliette. I carefully opened the envelope and pulled the letters out one at a time. I laid each on the table, and the silence continued as if they were witnessing a sacred act.

"This one is from the Book of Revelation," I said, pointing. "This one has something to do with the Sermon on the Mount, kind of like notes. This one we think is a love letter, addressed to Mary, which Mary we don't know."

Upon saying that, Marianne caught her breath.

"Can I touch it?" she asked.

"Please," I said.

She reached out as if someone was putting a ring on her finger and touched the letter. Then her eyes closed.

"What a gift," she finally said. "I don't know how to thank

you."

Juliette and Madeline followed.

"This last one is an enigma. Everyone who has tried to translate it has said it can be read in so many ways that it's almost impossible. It's written in Aramaic, where the meaning of words can be so different there may not be one way."

Dieter watched with interest, and then he pointed at the last letter.

"That's it," he said. "That's the one I've been feeling."

He put his hand over it, said a few words in that strange language of his, and then withdrew his hand. When he was done, I continued.

"There's writing on the inside of the envelope as well, but I don't want to unfold it. I don't know how my friends managed to do it in the first place."

The briefcase had contained my copy of the translations, so I had to improvise what the letters said.

"They are real," Peter stated when I was finished. "What are you going to do with them?"

His practical question broke the spell, and people started to take a deep breath and relax.

"I don't know yet. They will probably wind up with the Count. My friend in Toulouse, who's been translating them, says that they came to me, so I should be the one to determine what should happen."

"That's right," Juliette said.

"But I'm not experienced with this kind of thing."

"That's as it should be," Peter said. "As soon as the experts get a hold of these, everything is going to change."

He was right. I knew that whatever the true meaning of the writings was, it would become dissipated by debate among theologians, financiers, historians, pundits, and last but not least, the internet. The letters might even disintegrate and end up as a footnote in some obscure book. However, there could be some who would actually catch the spirit, and maybe that would be enough.

"I'm afraid you're right, and nothing less than secreting them away for another thousand years would save them from that."

As I said those words, I realized that I needed to let the chips fall where they may. While I had to be wise about it, I also had to trust that whatever was working out around them would be the right thing. They had survived this long, and it was almost as if there was a plan.

I started to put the letters back in the envelope, and as I did, Juliette began handing them to me, our fingers touching. The gentleness was almost too much to bear.

That night, Juliet and I made the kind of love the Troubadours once sang about. It was not surprising those wandering minstrels originated around Toulouse, as the Cathars did not believe sex was just for procreation. So it was fertile ground for the songs they spread throughout Europe.

I could hear Dieter and Madeline laughing.

"Don't mind them," Juliet whispered in my ear. "They are doing the same thing."

CHAPTER TWENTY-EIGHT

Before sunrise, I heard Peter banging around and loading things into his large four-wheel-drive vehicle. I listened for a while and then became curious. Juliette had gone back to her room to be with Artemisia, so I slowly crawled out of the jumble of the sleeping bag to see what he was doing.

"Bonjour, Peter," I said, approaching his Land Rover, which was still in the dim pre-dawn light.

"Bonjour, Bjorn. So you're coming?"

I did not know where, but I took it as an invitation.

"Sure, I'd love to," I said.

"Well, get your things, and you might want to put on some clothes," he said smiling.

I had on a sweatshirt but hadn't noticed that it didn't fully cover below the waist.

"If you have boots you should wear them, too."

"By the way, where are we going?"

"Andorra."

I had heard of it.

"So, another high point, eh?" I commented.

"It's going to take us a while to get to the trailhead."

As we were talking, Dieter came out of the house whistling and carrying a food basket.

"Morning, Bjorn. You coming?"

"Yeah, why not?" I said. "But I didn't mean to invite myself."

"No, not at all. It's just us. Juliette, Madeline, and Marianne will have a girls' day. You might want to put on different clothes."

I went into the tent and quickly dressed, grabbing my painting knapsack. After taking the letters out last night, Juliette and I decided they would be safer in the house, and she would keep them in her room. We still hadn't told anyone about the theft of the briefcase, not wanting to set Dieter off and thinking it could wait.

Juliette was sleeping when I went to tell her what I was doing. I shook her a little, and she rolled over looking like an impressionist painting of intimate family life.

"Ummm," she said, still half asleep. "You leaving?"

"Yeah, Dieter and Peter are going to one of the special points."

"OK, have a good time," she said as she leaned up to kiss me. "It was wonderful."

Then she rolled over to go back to sleep. Artemisia was curled up next to her, having come over from her bed when Juliette returned. As we pulled out of the driveway, we turned left rather than right and into Rennes.

"So, we're headed the other way," I commented.

"It's a shortcut. Very few people take it. You'll see why," Peter said.

Within a half-mile, the paved road turned to gravel, and as we started to climb it became rough dirt. Approaching a blind bend, Peter stopped the car and got out to look at what was ahead. There was a steep drop on the driver's side, and a sheer cliff rising on the other.

"This is going to be rough, fasten your seatbelt and hold on," he said, getting back in.

He slowly wheeled the car around the corner when suddenly it dropped into a ditch gushing with water, and everything in the back of the car hit the roof. Then we struck the opposite side of the ditch, and once again, everything was thrown in the air. Peter gunned the engine as the front wheels clawed into the dirt, pulling us out of the hole. Finally, the car climbed up the other side and back onto level road.

"You OK?" he asked.

"I didn't think you could make that," I said.

"Now you know why not many go this way. The tricky part is you can't see it from around the bend. If you don't know it's

225

there, you can wreck your car, or worse."

The road descended the side of the ridge, and after a few more switchbacks, we came to the main highway leading to Andorra. We had gone over the mountain rather than around it. The rest of the ride took about an hour, and on the way, Peter and Dieter discussed the esoteric origins of the Pentagram.

It was related to the creation story in the gnostic Book of Enoch. According to the Book, a Divine order of beings called the Elohim was asked to come to Earth and oversee the advancement of human beings. The Elohim had attributes almost of gods; for instance, they could create living things. The Elohim, in turn, delegated responsibilities to a group called the Watchers to assist human beings in their development, while being warned not to bring them along too quickly. However, the Watchers secretly violated that trust when they found sex with humans a very desirable experience, even though it was prohibited. The offspring were essentially giants and other abnormal creatures, but with abilities far beyond regular people because of the mixed parentage. As a result, the situation on Earth went out of control.

By the time deviation was discovered, it was too late to stop the destruction that was occurring. So the Biblical Flood was created to wipe the Earth clean and start over again. According to the Book, this was the story of the Fall of Man, and eating the forbidden fruit.

According to legend, the Pentagram was left as a symbolic representation of the true state, and composed of land features, so it was too large to be destroyed. All it would take is for someone to again reach a level of understanding where it could be deciphered. It was quite a story, but at least I better understood why Dieter was intrigued.

As we passed a little town named El Pas de la Cassa, a main junction to the Pyrenees, I became concerned about our proximity to the border.

"Isn't that a Spanish name?" I asked Dieter.

"Don't worry, we are still in France."

We turned off the main highway onto a dirt road leading into a mountain valley just after the town. After a few miles, Peter pulled into a drive that led through a blind ravine. On the other side was a cabin nestled against the mountainside.

"Here we are," Peter said. "Now the journey begins."

A lean, grizzled, older man came around the house to greet us. I was a little surprised to see him wearing cowboy boots, a cowboy hat, leather vest, chaps, and blue scarf as if he was out of the American West. But then I remembered the original cowboys were the Spanish vaqueros from Mexico, and Americans were the ones who had copied.

Peter and Dieter went over to talk to him as I stretched my legs, admiring the rising peaks and deep, resonant quietness. The man was talking in a distinctive dialect that was quite different, although it sounded like Spanish. I later learned it was Catalan. After a few minutes, Dieter waved me over.

"This is Josep, our guide," Dieter said. "He doesn't speak much English."

As we shook, his hand was calloused as tree bark and firm to the point of pain. I nodded, and he pointed to one of the horses.

His manner was so direct I just did as he indicated. He hadn't asked if I could ride, which I assumed was the vaquero way, "Just do it."

Dieter had taken my backpack out of the car and handed it to me as he went to his horse. Peter and Josep were already mounted, and without pause, we were on our way.

The trail veered along the side of the mountain, and while our pace was not rapid, it was steady, the metal horseshoes clattering on the rocks and leaving a wispy cloud of dust. Josep was in the lead, followed by Dieter, then me, with Peter bringing up the rear. I was not a very experienced rider, and I wondered if they thought I was expendable because all the horses except mine seemed to know the way.

As we climbed, I could see the valley we'd driven into

stretching out far below and the mountains rising high before us. I could imagine myself a thousand years ago, watching out for pursuing soldiers.

Riding in single file limited our conversation, and the
silence was so clear it felt like a violation to raise your voice.
The rhythm of the horses, even though somewhat uneven
over the rough trail, became the only thing. We went up
and then further up for about two hours, with many side
paths along the way, leading where only someone who had
grown up in these mountains would know. Josep knew them
instinctively.

I was getting tired, and the horses were beginning to show
wear, notably mine. We had left the steep climb behind and
were on a high mountain meadow. When we finally crested
the ridgeline, it seemed the whole of the Pyrenees was
stretched out before us.

"Here we are," Dieter said. "Gosol is that way."

"Gosol!" I said, jerked out of my rhythmic reverie. "But
that's in…"

Dieter, Peter, and Josep had stopped, and they were looking
at me. They then turned to look at each other and burst out
laughing.

"We crossed the border a while back, didn't you see it?"
Dieter said in mock surprise.

I glanced behind me, and there was only the timeless range
of mountains. If I tried to go back, it would take hours, and I
had no hope of following the trail. There was nothing I could
do. The only viable option was to go forward.

"I knew if I told you, you wouldn't have come," Dieter said.
"You're a criminal now, you might as well enjoy it."

I'd been had, and Dieter was successful in his effort to take
me on 'French leave.' While I was irate, I also rather liked that
it had happened, though worried. At least I would get to see
where Picasso had the artistic insight that would influence
him for the rest of his life. It was to have been one of the
themes for my article.

As we headed down the side of the ridge, Dieter began to explain why he had tricked me.

"Don't blame Peter, it wasn't his idea. You needed an adventure. They are out to get you, they will trap your soul, put a policeman in your head, and keep you there."

"Thanks, Dieter," I said with a touch of sarcasm.

But he had a point. It wasn't only the police, or the Count, controlling what I thought and did. I had begun to trap myself. So maybe it wasn't such a bad idea, if I got away with it.

As it turned out, Josep had arranged for a van to pick us up at the base of the ridge. Going the rest of the way on horseback would have taken at least another day, but now it would only be about an hour. In Gosol, we could eat, look around a little, and then get back here by three or four in the afternoon. The horses would have had a chance to rest for the ride back, and it was the safest way to cross the border.

Gosol was a small mountain village, and while tourists were now a primary source of income, it had not changed much in size or appearance since Picasso, and his mistress Fernand Olivier, made the trek by mule in 1906.

"This is where Picasso stayed," Peter said as we pulled in front of a small hotel. "I know the owner, whose grandfather was the proprietor, smuggler, and all-around character when Picasso was here. Picasso liked the guy, they spent a lot of time together, and he painted his portrait."

The grandson, and owner, came out and hugged Peter. In their youth, they worked in the mountains together.

"Come in, come in. So, this is the criminal, glad to meet you," he said, shaking my hand and obviously aware of the scheme.

We had a small table at the back of the dining room, and the walls were lined with memorabilia. Old rifles, oil lamps, colored glass bottles, spurs, and pictures of men in traditional dress standing in front of pack mules. There was also a painting of a bald, high cheek boned man with a wide grin and astonishingly white teeth. While it was a copy, every art history student knew the picture.

"That's my grandfather by Picasso," the grandson said with admiration. "And here's a photo of him, and my father as a boy, with Picasso. Oh, the stories they could tell. Let me show you where they stayed. We have kept it the same."

The room was small and spare. I could now understand why Fernand, who loved fine perfumes and the comforts of Parisian life, was miserable in the place.

"The locals were not used to visitors from Paris then, and were offended that they were not married. One night a few rowdies were haranguing them from the street, then Picasso came out with his pistol, and started shooting," he said laughing. "They were really blanks, but it created quite a stir."

I soon discovered the Cathars were featured in some of Gosol's cuisine. They were vegetarians, and we ate a traditional meal of carrot and chickpea soup, vegetarian meatballs, and finished with spice cake. The son kept filling our glasses with Catalan wine until we almost needed four legs to walk straight.

We visited the local church containing the Romanesque frescos, with their primitive, flattened images of saints and symbols that captivated Picasso. I initially tried to keep a low profile as we walked through the village, worried about my "criminal" status. However, I was assured there were so many tourists that no one was ever questioned. Besides, I wasn't under investigation in Spain. I was free.

I made some quick watercolor studies of the church and the hotel. The steep cobblestone streets led the eye naturally through the buildings and up into the mountains beyond. I tried flattening the paintings like Picasso and began to understand why he had been so inspired.

"Picasso of the Pyrenees," Peter said, looking over my shoulder. "I like yours better than his."

As we got into the van to leave, the son handed Peter a bottle of wine.

"This makes the rocks softer," he said with a grin. "An old

mountain trick."

I then handed the grandson the painting of the hotel as a thank you gift. His face changed as he looked at it.

"I'm going to hang this above where you sat," he said. "Someday you will be famous, and I can tell a story."

"I just hope the French police don't find it," I said.

"Don't worry, we know how to get you away," he replied with a grin that made him look just like his grandfather.

Back in the mountains, the horses were waiting. This time, I was given a different one, but it was as unfamiliar with the trail as the other. Josep was soon taking us back through the mountains laced with limestone cliffs and spires that eons of rain and snow had made to appear like melting ice cream cones frozen in time.

It was dark by the time we approached Josep's home. Suddenly I saw fires on the peaks of the mountains around us. The others didn't seem to notice, and I began to wonder if I was having a hallucination. Maybe there had been something in the food.

"It's Midsummer's Eve," Peter said behind me. "It's a Catalan tradition to light bonfires on the peaks to celebrate the Summer Solstice, welcoming the longest day of the year."

"Are we in France or Spain?" I asked, but more entranced at the magical sight.

"Andorra, it's its own country. So you are still a criminal," Dieter joked. "But Josep's home is on the border with France, so once we are there you are back in prison."

While we continued down, I had time to reflect. I was changing in ways I barely understood. It had nothing to do with Cathar trails, ancient languages, or even the writings. It had to do with something new. I just needed a little more time.

CHAPTER TWENTY-NINE

After we arrived at Josep's place and were putting the horses in the barn, I heard Josep, Dieter, and Peter, laughing amongst themselves.

"What did I miss?" I asked as I pulled the saddle off my ride.

"It's your horse," Dieter said.

"What about it?"

"Didn't you notice?"

"You mean that it didn't know the way?"

"Do you know why?"

"Because you wanted to kill me?"

"No, because it was smuggled. We dropped one off in Spain, and picked up another for here," he said, laughing harder than I'd ever seen him. "Josep figured if we got caught, you'd be the one riding the stolen horse."

I was still a criminal, and still rather liked it.

On the return to Peter and Marianne's home, Peter apologized. He explained that since France and Spain had become part of the European Union, border checks were almost a thing of the past, particularly where millions of tourists came and went. It was difficult to control in the mountains anyway and not cost-effective. Moreover, while Andorra was its own country, the smallest in Europe, and not part of the EU, its government was partly French and partly Spanish under a very old agreement.

"There was no risk. We would not have put you in that situation," he said. "We did use an old smugglers route, however, just to be sure."

"I'm glad we didn't see anybody on the trail," I remarked. "And by that I mean tourists."

Peter slapped me on the shoulder and said, "Let's get home,

my butt is sore."

The women had saved us supper, and Artemisia was in the yard playing with Sophie. We broke open the bottle of wine the grandson had given us. While we were away, they had gone to the cave and enjoyed the hot springs. Marianne had told Juliette what was going on.

"Our little French friend was here," Juliette said, sitting down beside me.

"You saw him? He was following us?" I said as my heart sank at the thought.

"We saw his car drive-by shortly after you left, but he must have run into trouble because a while later a tow truck drove up the road, and came back hauling his car. If he followed you, he didn't make it very far."

I could only imagine him hitting the ditch in that little Renault on that rough road.

"The front was caved in," Juliette continued. "And the bumper hanging off."

"Didn't anyone warn him?" Peter said deadpan.

"We waved as he passed," Marianne said, taking a sip of wine.

"Was he wearing his seatbelt?" Dieter remarked. "I hope not."

We all looked at each other and smiled. While I was still concerned, the dark spell over my time had been broken.

"So, what's next on your agenda for me?" I asked.

"Tomorrow is a free day for you," Dieter said. "I have some work to do with Peter, but we should be done by evening."

That was welcome news. I wanted to spend time with Juliette.

As we cleaned up from dinner, with Dieter again washing the dishes, I went to get my computer, which I had also put in Juliette's room. Artemisia was on the bed admiring some rocks and leaves she had collected from around the cave. I sat down on the bed and asked her how her day had gone.

She picked up one of the rocks, handed it to me, and then

put a leaf on top. It was like a game. I put a rock on top of the leaf, and she put a leaf on top of my rock. We kept stacking until it toppled over, and then did it again. As we were playing, Juliette came into the room.

"So, how was it?" she asked.

"It was quite an experience. They had me coming and going, but it was good. I needed that."

"You smuggled some horses I hear," she said with a smile.

"I'm a natural, never gave it a thought."

We kissed lightly, and Artemisia put her head in Juliette's lap.

"She had a good day but was a little scared of the cave," Juliette said. "She didn't go into the hot pool."

"Yeah, I can imagine," I said, putting my hand on Artemisia's head, and it felt as warm as if she had gone in the water. "Is she running a fever?"

Juliette then checked.

"Maybe a little. I think I'll stay with her tonight."

We talked about our day's activities for a while, and I took the computer case when I left.

"I just want to make a few notes. I might be able to turn this trip into a story yet."

Going into the living room, I asked Peter if he had Wi-Fi or Internet access.

"Yes, let me get you the code."

As I opened the computer case, the same flash drive that had fallen out of my car at the hotel fell out again.

"That's funny," I said.

"What's that?" Peter asked.

"This flash drive keeps falling out. It happened in the hotel parking lot, too."

"Let me see that," he said, stopping to examine it. "Are you sure this is yours?"

"Yeah, I mean it looks like mine."

"Come with me," he said. "I want to check something."

In his office, he had an array of screens, keyboards, control pads, and computers. It was a full production studio.

"Wow, I didn't know you did this," I said.

"I have a degree in computer engineering, that's how I made my living. I work remotely now, though I'm pretty well retired," he explained.

He pulled out a separate laptop, and turning it on, he brought up a screen that looked a little like what air traffic controllers use to monitor flights. He plugged in the flash drive, and long lines of code began appearing across the screen.

"Just what I thought. This is Trojan. Someone was trying to hack your computer."

"Really?"

"I'm sure you've heard about it. Someone places a flash drive where the target is likely to pick it up. They plug it in, and voila, their computer and everything connected to it is compromised. The hacker can see and control everything without you ever suspecting."

"God damn," I said, realizing not only me but the entire computer system at the magazine could have been hacked.

"Maybe it is your little friend," he said. "Hmm, it's an older version, not very sophisticated, but effective if you don't have the right security."

"So, you didn't just infect your computer?"

"No, this one isn't connected to anything in here, and it's well protected. I only use it for this type of thing, and to catch hackers and stuff. It's kind of a game."

"It's no game for me," I said. "Can you tell who it is?"

"Maybe, let's see how good they are."

As he began tracing it back, he found it went to a large business complex in Toulouse. He couldn't tell which office, but he looked up the companies located there for a possible clue, and found the Count controlled the firm that controlled the complex.

"Bingo," he said. "I can't be sure, but I would bet that's it."

"That little...." I muttered, again feeling like a pawn in a game.

"What do you think I should do?"

"Nothing," he said casually. "Just don't plug it in. This goes on a lot more than most people know. It's not just governments and hackers doing the dirty work anymore, it's companies spying on each other."

"Really?"

"Yeah. In China it's a standard business practice, has been for years, everyone does it. They wonder why Americans get so upset about it."

It was news to me, but I was glad Peter found it, and his casual attitude was reassuring.

"Here," he said, unplugging the flash drive from his computer and tossing it to me. "Keep it as a memento."

"I didn't tell you this, but someone stole my briefcase out of our car."

"I know, Juliette told us last night. Why do you think I went the back way? It's not a shortcut," he said with a wink.

So it had been planned. I just shook my head. They really were covering my back.

"Juliette asked us not to tell Dieter," Peter added.

"Yeah, he doesn't tell me everything either," I said a little wryly. "But I suppose we can tell him now."

With this new information reeling in my head, I went to Juliette's room to see if she was still up. I put my ear to the door and heard nothing. I peeked in, and I could see her and Artemisia curled up together, sound asleep. I quietly closed the door and headed to my tent to join them in dreamland. Sophie was lying by the fireplace and picked her head up as I passed.

"Night Sophie," I said, scratching behind her ears.

She rolled over so I would rub her belly, exposing the tender scar on her side, a white ridge against the grey and black fur.

"Thanks for keeping watch."

Outside, the stars felt so close that I could reach up and grab one as they danced across the sky. I could almost hear them sing. I crawled into my sleeping bag, and my butt was sore, too.

That night in my dream, I was still riding the swaying horse, only this time it wasn't in the mountains, but on a white sandy beach, with a turquoise ocean blending into a cerulean sky. Soon a bank of dark clouds rolled in, obscuring everything until I couldn't even see the ground. Behind me, something I could only feel began to chase me, and as I urged my horse to run faster and faster, its hooves lifted off the ground, and we were airborne. I emerged from the thick layer of clouds, and the sun was shining warm and bright. Whatever had been looming below couldn't break through the shadows into the light. I was flying free.

It was one of those vivid dreams I remembered upon waking, and I wanted to get it down. However, as I began writing, I found I was not describing the dream but something else.

"The Creator who made this world comes in our sleep, and tells us not to be afraid of the dark, but dream in it.

Where were you when the wings of your consciousness wove the form of your being, and the light in your eyes was the sun, the moon, and the stars?

Hear the words from your deep well.

Pray tell."

'What is this?' I asked myself. It was so unlike anything I had ever written that it was almost as if I wasn't the one writing. Reading it over, it sounded like a message. Then I had the urge to write more.

"When man was formed of the dust of the ground, the dust was not the same as we know it now.

The earth was alive, a living body, the radiant flesh of a planet. Water ran with joy, and the air was filled with wonder. Is this so hard to believe? The memory lingers in our very bones."

I thought, 'Why am I writing like this?' But it was flowing, and I let it continue.

"Is this the Creator people once worshipped in ways we cannot anymore remember? A voice where the silence between words is more potent than those spoken? It is not easy to forget when that sound barrier has been broken."

And finally, it was like I was being left with a question or challenge.

"Are the blessings of the gentle rain, and rays of a joyous sun, too much for that courageous heart which beats in the golden cauldron of your chest?"

'Wow,' I thought, 'is this like the muse the Greeks spoke about or the Oracle at Delphi?' Yet, I wasn't in Greece, and this wasn't Delphi. Then I remembered Marianne saying oracles were in other locations, too. The writing didn't seem to rise to a mythic level, but I would have to ask her about it, although the idea was a little farfetched.

Then I remembered the letter to Mary, "The Truth is not found by logic and reason alone…"

After getting dressed, I went into the house and found Marianne, Juliette, and Madeline with their hands resting on Artemisia, who was sitting on the couch.

"Is she OK?" I asked, a little puzzled.

"She is feeling a little under the weather," Juliette said.

"This is an old healing technique," Marianne explained.

As I stood watching, I realized they weren't touching Artemisia. Instead, their hands were a few inches over her.

"Why don't you join us?" Marianne said. "You have a sense for this."

"Do I?" I replied, a little surprised at the invitation.

"Yes, you showed it with Sophie."

"I didn't heal Sophie," I answered.

"No, but you knew what was needed."

Curious, I came over and copied what they were doing.

"Do you feel anything?" Marianne asked.

As she said it, there was a tingling sensation in my fingers. It was subtle but distinct.

"See?" Marianne said. "Just hold them there."

After a moment, the women backed away, leaving me as

the only one with Artemisia. Everyone was quiet, and in a few minutes, Artemisia fell asleep. Juliette picked her up and went to lay her down in the bedroom.

"You're very good," Marianne said.

"You mean at putting her to sleep?" I asked, not quite knowing what I was good at.

"She had tossed and turned all night, and needed rest. You helped her."

Juliette came back and sat down beside me. She gently took my hands in hers and examined them.

"Nice hands," she said.

I remembered Marianne saying the Languedoc had been a center for the healing arts in the Middle Ages, and that women and men were respected equally in the field. I wondered if this was like laying-on-of-hands.

"There's something to it," Marianne said. "But a lot depends on the person. I think you have the touch. Madeline does, too. Here, let's do something."

Marianne had us sit facing each other and holding our hands, palm to palm, a little distance apart. Soon I could feel slight pressure, like two magnets close to each other.

"Hmm," I said. "That's interesting."

"You should try it again sometime," Marianne said. "Maybe with Juliette."

I rather liked the idea, or maybe it was just doing it with Juliette.

Peter and Dieter were in the computer den, and I shared my dream writing with Juliette, Marianne, and Madeline.

"So, what do you think of it?" I asked.

"It's the most beautiful thing I've ever read," Madeline said.

"You should write more," Juliette stated.

"It does read a little inspired," Marianne commented. "Have you thought about going into the cave?"

"I remember what you said before about oracles. Is that what you are suggesting?"

Marianne's eyes lit up.

"You remembered, that's a good start," she said. "But, no. I wasn't thinking of you going in there to write. I was thinking you might like to explore it a little more. You know there are seven chambers."

"I thought there were only two, that's all I found. I even touched the end."

Marianne smiled.

"There are seven. You need to find the other five. I can help you, but only so much. Some of this you will have to do for yourself," she said somewhat mysteriously,

It was the same as what Karl said when I asked him about the more "important parts" of the Great Pyramid.

"I'd love to visit the cave. I've been looking forward to it, actually."

"OK, let me get a few things, and we'll go."

"Right now?" I asked, a little surprised.

"Right now," she said. "Oh, and put on swimming shorts, and maybe bring a towel.

While she was gone, I was searching my memory as to how I had missed the other chambers. It had been dark, but I had felt around, and there was no sense of another opening. Finally, Marianne came back with a sealed wooden tube, and a bone tied to a leather loop, like a necklace.

"Let's go," she said. "I'll explain these when we get there."

It was all a little cryptic, but I had come to trust Marianne and her rather esoteric ways. Beneath that, she was practical and solid as a rock. Juliette and Madeline came with us, along with Dieter. I noticed I was the only one in swimwear and everyone else was fully dressed. I assumed they had been in the pool yesterday, and Dieter was probably just along for the hike. Artemisia was still sound asleep, and Peter offered to watch her.

When we arrived at the cave's mouth, Dieter asked us to wait. He pulled out a woven braid of what he said was sweetgrass. It was Y shaped, like a tuning fork, or the letter Y. He said it came from Scandinavia.

"Your ancestors," Dieter remarked, looking at me.

He lit it and asked each of us to stand in the fragrant smoke, which curled over us, only to be gently drawn into the cave entrance.

"This is for purification," Dieter explained. "Did you know sweetgrass is the only plant used in common for ceremonies by indigenous people in Europe and America? It's native to both places."

I already had a sense that this would be more than cave spelunking or a dip in the hot springs. However, I decided that I wasn't going to ask any questions and just watch, listen, and go along. I wanted it to be my experience.

We then crawled through the cave entrance and into the first chamber.

"This is where the people lived," Marianne explained. "When it was first discovered by previous owners of our house, the entrance had been artificially blocked. Who knows when that was done, maybe 10 or 20,000 years ago? Anyway, they found things like stone flakes, shells, and bones. What was most interesting was a whistle made from an eagle bone, others that have been found in caves around Europe."

"On a hike a few years ago, Peter came across the bones of a dead eagle, and he made a copy of the whistle," she continued. "Here's what it sounds like."

She raised the bone she had been carrying up to her lips and blew. It was sharp, shrill, and sweet. My senses were transported back in time.

"Let's go to the next chamber," she said.

We all climbed up, and the light from the cave mouth receded until it was pitch black. Once in the larger chamber with the hot springs pool, Marianne lit a small lantern. The water was calm and reflected the light almost like a mirror. The walls sparkled, and I could now see they rose about 15 feet and ended in a domed roof.

"This is where they stored things, bathed, got water in winter, and their heat except for cooking," Marianne continued.

"It was also used as a living quarters. Not bad, eh?"

"I always said you should live here," Dieter remarked.

"Peter isn't so keen, you know, his electronics and stuff," Marianne replied

I was dying to ask where the other five chambers were, as I couldn't see any other openings even in the light. But more, something in me wanted to stay silent, and wait and see.

"The next five chambers were the realms of the ceremony leaders, and no one else was allowed in them unless it was for special purposes," Marianne said. "Bjorn, this is where your adventure begins. You have to find the next entrance."

I was a little dumbfounded.

"Before you do though, I want to give you these."

She handed me the wooden tube sealed with wax, and the eagle bone whistle from around her neck.

"When you find each chamber, light a match and blow the whistle," she instructed. "You'll notice there are four holes in the whistle. Blow a different hole in each chamber. In the fifth chamber, you can blow them all. There are also only five matches in the tube, so don't waste them. They are water-proof and really make a flame, so be careful."

"I'm supposed to lead you?" I asked, still not sure what she was expecting me to do.

"No, you're going alone."

"What?"

"Yes, this is your journey."

Dieter slapped me on the shoulder, Juliette hugged me, as did Madeline, and without another word, they left me in the dark.

CHAPTER THIRTY

After they were gone, I lay down on the sandy floor, trying to assimilate their sudden departure and everything else that had happened over the past few days. I wondered if I was being tricked again, and whether I should simply stay for a while and then go back out. I had no idea where the entry to the next chambers was, and now that I couldn't even see my hand in front of my face, it was all but hopeless.

I put my head against the back wall and shut my eyes. I decided I was going to give things a chance to settle down. I was soon asleep. When I woke up, I was a little unsettled. It was pitch black, and the air was moist and warm. However, my head was clearer.

I had no idea how long I'd slept but guessed it was less than an hour, not that it mattered. Then, as I considered what to do, it occurred to me that Marianne had me wear swimming shorts.

Without any other idea, I rolled over and tested the water. It was hot, but not excessively. I lowered myself into the pool, and as I felt around for handholds my arm slipped. There was nothing where there should have been a wall. Startled by the void, I pulled my hand away. Then I stuck it back in, reaching as far as I could. It was open. Then I tried putting my legs in, and still no wall.

Could it be the entrance was underwater? The thought seemed realistic, but also risky. I couldn't see a thing, and if I became stuck or injured, I could drown. Still, it seemed to be the only possibility.

I took a few deep breaths and went under. The opening was narrow but spacious enough for the first four or five feet. I pushed myself back out to get another breath. My heart was pounding at the exertion and the thought of going further. Not wanting to wait and talk myself out of it, I took another deep breath, but then stopped. If I did this, and it worked, I wanted to have the matches and whistle. I felt around where I'd put them, and they were in easy reach. I put the whistle around my neck and gripped the match tube in my left hand.

Taking another deep breath, I pulled myself into the opening with a shove. My hands were stretched out in front of me, feeling for any obstacles. Very quickly, I was far enough in that I might not be able to get back out, and the water was becoming hotter. I began kicking hard, banging my feet against the wall, and trying to pull forward with my right hand.

I was becoming desperate and started to think what would happen if I died in here. Not only the pain of the final struggle, but about my mother and father, Juliette, Artemisia, and all my friends. I could almost see the expression on their faces and my cold, lifeless body. I kicked even harder, and then something changed as my hands no longer touched anything but water. I'd reached an open space. Then my shoulders slammed against stone. The opening was too narrow.

I pushed against the barrier, collapsing my shoulders to make myself as narrow as possible, with my legs churning. I started wiggling in a serpentine motion and felt a small slip, so I struggled harder. Suddenly my who body slid forward. I was free.

My lungs were burning, and I had lost all sense of direction, but swinging my legs, my feet touched rock. I quickly crouched and pushed off, not knowing if I'd hit open air or a wall. When my head breached the surface, I took my first breath.

I floated on the surface as my gasping subsided until I realized the water was scalding. Anxiously I reached around for some way to get out. Thankfully I felt a ledge close by, and I yanked myself out, flopping onto a stone bank. The pain on my skin was all I was aware of as I waited for it to subside, and nothing else mattered. My mind was blank.

Slowly, I began to notice the sound of my breathing, and water trickling into the pool from somewhere, also that I was buck-naked. Coming through the constriction, my shorts had peeled off. However, the whistle had managed to stay around my neck, and the matches were still clenched in my fist. I was now deep inside the cave. Why didn't Marianne tell me? What am I doing here?

The first thing I needed to do was get my bearings and hopefully find a way out or into the next chamber. I prayed it wasn't underwater, too, or that I'd have to go back the way I came in. I only had five matches, and with the possibility of four more chambers, I'd have to make each one count. Why hadn't Marianne had given me more?

I struck the first match, and it burst into a furious flame as Marianne had cautioned. I was temporarily blinded but quickly looked around. The cavern was much larger than either of the first two. Though oblong, it was at least 30 feet high and equal to that distance around. At one end was an opening that hopefully led to the next cavern.

I took in all I could in the minute or so I had of flame. The place was magnificent. Firelight sparkled off the stone, and columns ascended like in a cathedral, but natural and wild in their design. Then the match dimmed and burned out. I was back in black.

As I sat there, with the image of the cave slowly fading in my mind, I thought of the whistle. Not knowing what else to do, I covered three of the four holes, as Marianne had instructed, took a deep breath, and blew. The high-pitched sound ricocheted off the chamber walls. I blew it again, and again the sound penetrated every niche and corner. It was unlike anything I had ever experienced, an echo of an ancient memory

I blew it again, then again, and yet again, setting up a rhythm that not only filled the cavern but my whole being. It became trancelike and yet wakeful, as the whistle's pitch was too sharp to be somatic.

After a while, I stopped. As the sound receded, it was as if the silence had been activated. In fact, the whole chamber felt alive. I could hear Marianne saying, 'mother earth", and then what I had written in the morning popped into my head.

"The earth was alive, a living body, the radiant flesh of a planet. Water ran with joy, and the air was filled with wonder. Is this so hard to believe? The memory lingers in our very bones."

It was like the cave talking. I shook my head, thinking that might be a little much. However, I could feel it in my bones. I lay down and closed my eyes. The earth was alive.

I was too energized to rest, but I wasn't ready to leave either. The experience was too fresh. I discovered the darkness not only took away sight but time, too. I was content to be there without trying to formulate thoughts or ideas, and I knew I could find my way to the next opening.

When it felt right to leave, I began crawling along the stone floor. There seemed to be a path in the uneven stones. My thoughts had become simplified and focused. The world became my hands and knees on stone and anticipation of what was immediately in front of me. Then I came to what I perceived to be the entryway. The air here was much cooler than the hot humid atmosphere by the pool.

As I went through, it was like entering a different world again. While I couldn't see anything, I knew something had changed. My mind cleared of the rush and heat, and I had a feeling of beginning. I was making progress.

Crawling along, I came to a low ledge and decided it would be a place to stop and assess the next move. However, I raised the whistle to my lips and blew using the second hole before I did. The piercing, sweet sound echoed differently than before. I blew it again and found this chamber had another tone. It was a little muted, closer, and more human.

I struck my second match. Again I was temporarily blinded by the blaze, but looking around, I saw the cavern was lower, and more irregularly shaped. There were ledges of various heights, and large and small stalactites and stalagmites protruding throughout.

I noticed short black marks on the walls, some with angles, some in pairs, which were obviously manmade, and more than I could count. One wall had a large cleft, and sitting inside on a stone outcrop was a voluminous form like a large Venus of Willendorf. It was naturally created, but the similarity to the 25,000-year-old figurine was remarkable.

As the match was sputtering down, I saw a dark area toward the end of the chamber, which I hoped led to the next one. Then complete blackness again. Distracted by the Venus form and the black marks, I had failed to survey a way to the opening. However, I knew there were obstacles, and the total loss of sight was disorienting. I was hesitant to use another match as I had no idea what lay ahead. Now I wished I'd asked more questions, like why she didn't give me more matches.

The cooler air felt soothing on my red-hot skin. I started to worry about becoming too chilled, but it was just the medicine I needed for now. I was in no hurry, and I began to move slowly forward to avoid losing all sense of perspective and direction. It was hard, though, as I had to navigate around and over rock outcroppings, and soon I was completely lost. I stopped before making it worse.

As I sat there, I told myself to stay calm and relax in the space rather than fight it. After a few moments, I took the whistle and began to blow it in a rhythm, as I had in the other chamber. The piercing sound filled the room. I found myself standing up and gently tapping my feet to the beat. The sound became like a chant, and I continued for a long time. At one point, I imagined I was doing it to honor the Venus mother, and at another the spirit of the place, and perhaps even summoning the Oracle. I also thought it was a little crazy.

When I stopped whistling, I had a better sense of direction, and making my way along, I was discouraged when I found myself right back where I started. However, I continued to resist lighting another match and consoled myself with at least knowing where I was. Yet, having gained some idea of what was around me, I was able to slowly make my way to the next entryway.

The air coming through the new opening was even colder, and I was hesitant to go in. I took a few steps and immediately banged my shin on a protruding rock. When the pain subsided, I reached for my matches as I had to see what I was getting into. Striking the match, I immediately realized this would be much more difficult, if not impossible, in the dark. While there was something of a pathway, it went up at least 25 feet through jagged stone outcrops and walls, only to vanish into a gap between two pillars that led to who-knows-where.

Then I saw the painting. It was a life-size ocher-colored horse, outlined in black with white face markings and red spots on its hindquarters. It seemed to move across the wall in the firelight. Then the match went out, with the image still burning in my brain.

The path was strewn with sharp stones, which slowed progress and threw me off balance as I began. Finally, I edged around a large rock on the left side of the cave, only to smack my head on a stalactite, jamming my shoulder into a rough boulder as I lurched back.

I began to doubt this was the way to the pillars. I felt with my hands and could tell the path took a curve around, which then led into a wall. I was boxed in.

I cursed myself for ever coming into the cave, but then I remembered the horse. If I was right, it was directly above me. I reached high and felt a ledge. It must have been where someone stood to do the painting. I pulled myself up, scraping my elbows and knees, and managed to get onto the platform. I lay down to catch my breath, hurting and spent.

I was shivering, staring into the darkness. If the air was cold, the stone was colder and sapping my strength. My only option was to light another match, and that's when I realized they weren't in my hand. I had been so distracted I had failed to notice. Now I was faced with searching for them, if I could even find how I got here.

Sliding down off the ledge I twisted my foot just enough to wonder whether I'd sprained it. Getting down onto my hands and knees, I crawled around searching for the container, hoping it hadn't rolled into a crevice, and afraid I was getting even more lost. Finally, after what seemed beyond time, I made it back to the entrance of the previous chamber. I was seductively drawn to the warmer air.

I had no other option but to turn back. I was tired, cold, burnt, and hurt, and at least I knew the way. However, when I started to go, my foot struck the wooden tube with the matches. I had put it down when I saw the horse. While it was too little, too late, I could at least light the next match, see the horse again, and have just enough left to find my way back to the cave entrance.

As I stood up to leave, I heard the sound of a stone bouncing off stone. When I turned, it hit me between the shoulder blades and knocked me forward, slamming my chest into the doorway. I couldn't tell if I'd been cut, and my fingers were still too numb to feel if I was bleeding. Through the shock and pain, I felt a surge of anger, and the impression that something wasn't right. It felt harsh and unfair. I said, 'No way I am turning back now.' I was determined to make it through the challenging chamber.

Retracing the rocky path, I reached the horse ledge again and pulled myself up. This time I crawled further along until it slanted upward and then around a hairpin turn. That led to the stone columns marking the cleft that I prayed went to the next entrance. Squeezing through the gap, I inched forward, rubbing against the narrow walls. Finally, a warmer draft brushed against my face, and I knew the new entrance was ahead. I slumped down. How long I stayed like that, I couldn't tell and didn't care. I was empty.

The warmth finally beckoned, and I forced myself to my

feet. Then, as an act of defiance, or maybe victory, I put the whistle to my lips, and locating the third hole, I blew. The sound of an eagle cry poured throughout the chamber, and I could almost see the pale horse looking over its shoulder, and with a burst of speed, it leaped forward off the wall and into infinity.

In the new cavern, I sensed more open space around me. I was becoming aware of the way of caves, blinding by darkness but seeing with other eyes. I took a deep breath and struck the third match. The flame was again brilliant, but more I was astonished to see the chamber dancing with paintings in the unsteady light. There were horses, fish, bison, lions, black marks, and a stick-drawn image of an eagle. I turned in a circle to take it all in. As I did, I could see the floor was more level than the previous chambers and the low entrance into the next one. I felt like dancing, and then the light went out.

I sat down with all the animals and figures around me, invisibly there, like in a dream. However, I was shivering almost uncontrollably. The air wasn't as cold, but the stone was as chilled and draining the little energy I had left. I also didn't want to leave. The paintings felt like friends, each with a different voice, speaking other things.

At one point, I noticed there was someone else in the room. In one sense, I knew no one was there, but I could see him in my mind's eye. He was standing next to me wearing a dark coat and hat. His countenance was not unpleasant, even handsome, and of a deeper, tanned, complexion.

'Who is he?' I thought. 'What is he doing in here?'

And then I realized it was Death.

"Am I going to die?" I asked.

"Yup," he said.

"Is it going to be soon?"

"Yup."

There was nothing fearful or threatening in his voice.

"Is there anything I can do about it?" I asked after reflecting for a bit.

"Not really," he said.

But I noticed it wasn't a definite no.

"What would I have to do?" I ventured.

"Change," he said.

I knew he didn't mean a change of job, or career, or where I lived. He meant a much more substantial change. I would have to change myself.

The vision passed, and I was back on the cold floor, shivering, and about to move to the next chamber. I lifted the whistle, and finding the fourth and last hole, I blew, singing to the animals, to the vision, to whatever was to come next.

As the echo faded, I made my way to the next entryway, and hopefully, the last cavern. I felt fresh air. It didn't have the heavy dampness of the cave, but as if it came from the outside. I looked, but there was no sign of light coming through anywhere, but maybe it was night. I had no idea of the time or even what day. Assuming Marianne only gave me five matches because this was the end of the journey, I struck the last one.

The space was smaller, more like the front of the cave. As my eyes adjusted in the firelight, I could see the walls had also been painted, but these were very different. They were covered with red dots, and at my feet was a Y-shaped sweetgrass braid like the one Dieter had, which I quickly lit before the match sputtered out.

Using the dim light from the braid, I looked for a way out but couldn't find any. I stomped my foot in frustration, and suddenly the cavern was filled with a deep booming sound. Taken aback, I stamped again, and a bass sound filled the space once more. Then I realized a resonant chamber lay below, making the floor into a giant drum. I began walking in a circle, pounding with my feet, entranced by the red dots flickering in the light of the glowing braid. I raised the whistle and blew all four holes.

The effect was almost more than I could take. It was deep

and wonderful. The echoing boom and pitched whistle went into my body and came up to the top of my skull, bouncing back down to my feet, passing through my soul, the air redolent with sweet fragrant smoke. Then a shaft of light came down from above and surrounded me. Astonished by a vision turning into reality, I looked up, and there were Marianne, Juliette, Dieter, Madeline, Peter, and Artemisia all staring down at me with big grins. They had uncovered a hole in the ceiling, letting in a beam of sunlight. I blew the whistle as hard as I could.

CHAPTER THIRTY-ONE

"Tie it on!" Dieter shouted as a rope came dropping down, followed by a rappelling harness.

It felt like I was ascending as I rose into the light.

"Welcome back - to the real world," Peter said as I stood up. "You have a problem wearing clothes?"

Artemisia's eyes were open wide, and I looked down at the harness around my naked waist, with the rope trailing away like an umbilical cord.

"Maybe I should take this off," I commented sheepishly.

"You've just been born," Juliette said laughing, and then she hugged me.

"And put this on," Madeline said as she handed me the towel I had left at the hot pool, but also not looking away.

"Welcome home," Marianne said simply, holding my gaze, and I knew she understood.

"Let's eat," Dieter said. "It's tradition."

I had been in the cave overnight without any food or drinking any water. Despite being tired, dirty, and aching, after coming out, I felt rejuvenated.

"Twenty-four hours," Peter said. "It's the same time of day as you went in."

It was a little hard to believe, but I didn't doubt that much time had passed. I needed a shower and clean clothes, but first, we went to the patio. The table was loaded with food. Marianne, however, handed me a cup of broth.

"Here, this will bring you back," she said. "It has a few things in it to help your system adjust."

She was right. I wasn't ready for a substantial meal yet. As they were conversing around the table, I still felt far away, and when I did respond, it was like someone else talking from a distance. I thought I had an obligation to be around, but what I wanted was to be alone for a while.

"Why don't you clean up and change," Dieter suggested. "Then go for a walk, or find someplace."

"There are towels in the shower," Marianne said.

I went to my tent for clean clothes, and I felt a little hand in mine as I went back to the house. Artemisia was walking with me as if it was the most natural thing in the world to do. When we reached the door, she let go and returned to the table. The innocence of the act struck a deep chord.

I washed, changed, and went out the back door. I didn't go very far and sat down in a small grove of apple trees. I wasn't trying to understand and was content to let it come in its own time.

When I returned, Peter greeted me.

"Juliets," he said, pointing to the trees. "The apples are Juliets."

"No kidding?"

"It's a relatively new variety," he remarked with a slight wink.

After having had some time to gather myself, Marianne explained a little about the cave.

"Remember when I said the five other chambers were only used for ritual purposes? No one knows for sure, it was 10-20-30-40,000 years ago, probably more, and it's not like they left a manual. But some Native cultures have maintained their traditions for thousands of years, amazingly enough, and I see similarities, like the use of eagle whistles."

"The hot pool is for purifying and cleansing, too, and not just the body. Then there is the Venus room, as I call it. I'm sure you saw the Earth Mother, the feminine, followed by the rough room. That chamber is not supposed to be easy, and you had to sacrifice something there, probably discouragement. After that the picture room, where you saw the whole world, and yourself. And the last, well, you were free."

"What were the red dots, if I could ask?"

"Likely made by Neanderthals, the first artists, and the oldest."

"And the black lines all over the place?"

"My guess is commitments. 'Here I am, and this is what I'll do.' It was serious."

Listening, I was amazed at how much she knew. But, then again, if what she said was true, I was only the latest in a very, very long line, even going back to when the earth was not like we know it now.

"It was initiation," she concluded. "Not into a tribe, or belief, so much, but what it means to be a human being. Everyone's experience is different."

"Why didn't you tell me this before I went in?" I said, shaking my head.

"You didn't ask."

Later that day, I caught up on what had happened when I was in the cave. Dieter and Madeline had to leave in the morning, as Madeline needed to get back to work. Juliette also felt it was time to return to Toulouse; and, while her break was short, it marked a start to the separation from William.

"Are you going to stay in Toulouse?" I asked.

"Probably not. I think it's best if I return to the States. I don't want to remain here, it's time to move on."

"It's going to be quite a change, particularly for Artemisia," I said.

"That's why it's good to do it now, the sooner the better," she replied. "I have support from my family. It's the right thing to do. Besides, you are there."

Our relationship was moving faster than I expected, but we both understood the direction it was heading.

"It is easier for me to move there, than for you to come here," she continued. "Besides, we also need time to get to know each other a little more, don't you think?"

I felt some of the tension release. I had mistaken her directness as pushing, when in fact it was more an expression of desire. Underneath was a practical assessment that an overseas relationship was not the best if we were serious about each other.

"It would be good if we were close," I surmised.

"I'd like that," she said. "Let's be together tonight. Artemisia wants to sleep in a tent."

This was going to be a different kind of challenge than the cave.

I spent the rest of the afternoon by myself. I didn't have much to say, and my experience underground had left me quieter. I was feeling a power that went deeper than the mind. I had never been as aware of it as I was now. Perhaps I'd been fearful the darkness needed to be constrained. But the power wasn't dark, just strong, and didn't need to make a lot of noise.

"It's been good having you here," Marianne said at supper. "I really appreciate you showing us the letters. You will handle them in the right way, whether you believe it or not. You are the right person to have found them."

"Be careful. There are some unsavory characters out there, as you know," Peter said, tapping his fingers on the table as if it was a keyboard.

"I'll let you know," I said. "It's been good."

Juliette put her arm around my shoulder.

"I'm going to go to America," she suddenly announced. "We're going to get married."

Everyone started at her comment, not knowing if she was serious.

"Well, maybe not right away," she added cheerfully. "First, Bjorn has to stay out of prison."

"I'll toast to that," Dieter said.

I could only shake my head.

Artemisia, meanwhile, had taken no notice, as she was more occupied with slipping food to Sophie under the table. I was feeling better about the state of our relationship all the time.

Before we went to bed, Juliette took me aside.

"I don't want to make love tonight, not that I wouldn't like to, but it seems you are in a very different place."

"I am," I said. "I want to be together though, and like the idea of Artemisia being there."

"It should be an interesting experience for her. She's never camped out before."

Peter had an extra sleeping bag and pad for Artemisia, who came out of the house in pajamas, wearing hiking boots, and carrying her knapsack. She arranged everything in a corner of the tent, then nestled into the sleeping bag and went right to sleep.

Juliette looked at her in surprise.

"I thought she might take a while to settle down. But look at her."

"She's a natural," I said. "And besides, you're here."

"It's you," she replied, poking me in the ribs.

We started to wrestle, but we both stopped when it started becoming intimate. At first, I couldn't sleep, but then drifted off as if I was back in the deep darkness of the cave.

I woke as the pre-dawn sun was beginning to glow on the horizon. Juliette and Artemisia were still asleep. I quietly slipped out into the cool morning air. Walking back to the apple tree I sat under the day before. I was listening for that inner voice.

I began reflecting on what had happened since finding the fleck of light in the library at St. Sernin. Discovering the letters, meeting Yoseph and Karl, learning about the Cathars and their sacred texts, coming here with Dieter, the Pentagram, the time in the cave, everything. They were like markers on a map, red dots tracing a journey, but to where?

I had a sense it was all of those things, and yet none of them. It wasn't that kind of journey, but to a memory of something.

Then I remembered my experience outside the hotel, where I heard a voice, the one that could speak the unknown name 'I am', and ask and answer questions I never knew I had. Slowly,

I was realizing it wasn't an outside voice, it was my voice, there was no separation. It had always been there, waiting, as behind a wall, and then it opened in ways I could not have imagined.

Is this what Karl was talking about with the letters, and a meaning of 'Ena na'? If so, nothing would ever be the same. Then I remembered my conversation in the cave. This was change.

Suddenly there were people behind me. When I turned to see, Artemisia and Juliette were sitting a few feet away. I had been so lost in thought I had not heard them come up. I wondered how long they'd been there.

Juliette smiled.

"Are we bothering you?" she asked.

"No, I think I was done."

"Was it good?"

"It was."

They came down and sat beside me, Juliette on one side, Artemisia on the other. We stayed until the sun crested the hill, and then holding hands, we walked back to the house.

"Did you know the apples in these trees are called Juliets?" I remarked.

"Were they tempting you?" she replied. "In that case, we need a bushel."

Artemisia had managed to keep her stick from Montsegur and was waving it at the tree.

"I want one," she said, clear as a bell.

Juliette and I looked at each other.

"We already have one," I remarked holding Juliette's gaze, and Artemisia cocked her head.

"They need to ripen," Juliette told her, and then looking at me, "It's just the beginning."

CHAPTER THIRTY-TWO

As we packed up the tent and gathered our things, Marianne came to me with a present.

"A gift," she said, handing me a small box. "It's a reminder."

Inside were four objects, a small red pyramid, a pink stone in the shape of a heart, a piece of bone, and a lens.

I hugged her.

"I wish I had another painting to give to you," I said in thanks.

"You gave us something more," she replied. "Besides, I have a whole cave full."

"The best in the world, Paleo-Picassos as Peter might say," I added.

We were to follow Dieter and Madeline back to Toulouse, taking the road from Rennes Le Chateau through Limoux rather than Montsegur.

"It's faster," Dieter said. "And besides, I think you have had your cave experience."

After saying our goodbyes, we saw no sign of the French cop as we drove to Rennes. We had planned to stop at Sauniere's church so Juliette and Madeline could see it, but Artemisia waved her stick and did not want to get out of the car. Dieter took that as a sign, and instead, he went into the liquor store and bought another case of sparkling wine.

"It's good to get it at source," he said, smiling as he put it into his trunk. "We'll have some when we get home."

"We might need more than a case," Juliette quipped.

The drive back was uneventful. Artemisia played in the back seat with her stones, leaves, and stick, and then Juliette's phone rang. It was her husband.

I couldn't hear, but I knew from her expression it was serious. She listened for a few minutes without saying anything.

"We'll talk about it when I get back," she finally said and hung up.

"He says no," she said with her lips pursed, eyes angry, and beginning to tear up.

Artemisia stopped playing and sat quietly with her hands in her lap. After a while, Juliette reached over and rubbed my neck.

"I don't want to discuss it here," she said. "I'll take care of it."

She then turned to Artemisia.

"Don't worry, honey, everything's OK," but she knew it wasn't.

The rest of the drive was sullen, though we tried to make light of it. The midday traffic was modest as drove into Toulouse. When we turned onto Dieter's street, a black limousine and three police vehicles were parked in front of his house. Dieter had arrived before us and was arguing with two officers in the driveway.

"Uh oh," I said. "This doesn't look good."

"Should I drive away?" Juliette asked.

"No, that would just make things worse."

My adrenaline was beginning to kick in, but I needed to stay calm. I saw Consulate Randy Chamberlain and Magistrate Genseau standing by the black car, along with the French cop.

"Pull over here," I told Juliette when we were across the street from Dieter's house, and I almost regretted not driving past.

I quickly got out of the car, and after looking both ways, walked over to the group of officials.

"So, what's going on?" I asked.

"You need to come with us," Chamberlain said. "We'll explain in the car."

"Am I under arrest?"

"Just get your things," he said. "And bring your computer, phone, camera, and anything that might have to do with the letters from the Lautrecs."

That gave me a clue, but I still didn't know what was going on, and whether I was going to jail.

"I have everything here in the car."

Genseau directed one of the officers to accompany me. Meanwhile, Juliette had remained in the car with Artemisia.

"What's happening?" she asked me through her open car window.

"I don't know, but I have to get everything out of the car," I said, my hands beginning to shake a little. "You're going to need to open the trunk."

Artemisia looked at me through the car window, her face was calm but a little excited.

The trunk lid popped up, and as I gathered my things, the officer took the computer, camera bag, and painting knapsack when I pulled them out. I carried my other items, making sure I left nothing behind. As I turned to say goodbye to Juliette, I felt a hand on my shoulder. Another officer had come over and was shaking his head.

"I love you," Juliette called out as I was led back across the street.

"Are these all your things?" Chamberlain asked.

"Yes, except for my rental car."

"Which one is it?"

"It's parked in front of you."

Dieter, meanwhile, had calmed down but was still talking.

"You can't take him like this," he was saying. "This is my home. I want to see a warrant."

Two officers stood beside him but made no moves to restrain him.

"Please, get in the car," Chamberlain said, holding the door open.

"I'll get you a lawyer," Dieter shouted. "Don't worry, we'll get you out."

I was just glad he hadn't done anything to get himself arrested.

The car was a limo, with the back seats facing each other.

Chamberlain and the French cop sat on one side, while Genseau and I sat next to each other, with a third officer on my other side. As we pulled away, the driver turned and looked, Chamberlain nodded, and a dark divider window rose behind him, sealing us off from the front.

"I'm sorry we had to do it this way," Chamberlain began. "But you have to leave the country. We're taking you to the airport."

"Right now?" I said in surprise.

Right now," he said. "It's the best we could do to save you from being charged."

"But I didn't do anything," I began to protest.

"If you refuse to go, you might be facing manslaughter, grand theft, violation of the antiquities act, and breaking a court order, among other things. You could be spending over 20 years in prison."

The weight of the law landed on my shoulders. I had no choice.

"We will need to take your computer, your phone, your camera, the letters you stole from the Lautrecs, and any record or copies that you might have made of them, including the phone numbers and emails of people you sent them to or may have seen them.

"I think you might already have some of that," I said.

"What do you mean?" Chamberlain asked.

"Someone stole my briefcase that had the translation of the letters in it."

Chamberlain looked at Genseau.

"When did this happen?" Genseau asked.

"Three nights ago. It was in Rennes Le Chateau. The trunk lock of the car was jimmied, and my briefcase was stolen. Nothing else was taken, and my camera and computer were right there."

"I'll look into it," Genseau said, glancing at the French cop.

"The Lautrecs have sole possession and control of the letters, and will prosecute to the full extent of the law anyone who violates their rights. Is that clear?" Chamberlain continued.

"Yes, I think so," I said, still absorbing that Genseau had told the Count about them.

"It better be more than just 'think so'. Is that clear?" Chamberlain said.

"Yes," I said. "You know the computer, phone, and camera are not mine, they belong to the magazine. They let me use them for the assignment."

"We have contacted them," Genseau said.

My heart really sank. I would never work for them again, and who knows what else.

"And the rental car?" I asked.

No one said anything, except the French cop gave me a subtle cursed smile. It was then that I noticed he had a black eye and a bandage around one hand.

"You might want this, too," I said, reaching into my pocket and pulling out the flash drive. "Someone tried to hack my computer. It is a Trojan, so don't plug it into anything you don't want infected."

Genseau took the device, looked at it curiously, and put it in his pocket.

The French cop had been glaring at me, but his eyes lowered after I mentioned the flash drive. I suspected he might be in trouble, particularly when they find out what was on the drive, and that it was tied to the Count. But I didn't have time to dwell on that at the moment.

"So, where are the letters you stole?" Chamberlain asked.

"I didn't steal them, they were handed to me by the aunt."

"The aunt whose death you caused," he replied.

"I didn't do that either," I said, but somehow it made me sound like I was guilty.

"Where are the letters?" he asked again.

"They are in my knapsack. Be careful with them, they are really delicate."

Chamberlain knocked on the divider window, and it

263

lowered. He asked the driver for trunk access. A door opening to the trunk parted behind me, and the officer reached in and pulled out my knapsack.

"Wow, pretty fancy," I said in surprise, but no one laughed.

I reached into the knapsack and took out the letters' leather case. When I opened it, I could barely smell the sweet scent of beeswax and wondered how long they would last in this toxic atmosphere. As I was giving it to Chamberlain, Genseau reached over and took it instead. Briefly, all our hands touched, and at that moment, I felt a spark exchanged.

"Here's what we've worked out," Chamberlain said, suddenly looking slightly unsettled. "You will be escorted to the plane, and flown to Denver. Once in the United States, you are free to go, but you are not to return to France under any circumstances. If you do, you will likely be arrested and charged. It was a difficult negotiation, I hope you can appreciate that."

"Do you have your passport?" Chamberlain then asked.

"It's right here," I said, removing it from my pocket.

"Let me have it," he said.

I hesitated.

"It's OK," Genseau said to me. "He's not taking it away."

I handed it to Chamberlain, who scanned something into his phone, but didn't give it back. I looked at Genseau.

"You can return it to him," Genseau told Chamberlain.

I didn't know what was going on, but I was beginning to understand whatever had been worked out Genseau was still in charge, though probably under pressure to go along with some scheme involving the Count and the Consulate. I remembered Chamberlain saying my situation was threatening a significant international arrangement of some kind, which I assumed involved a lot of money.

When we arrived at the airport, the officer sitting next to me took my bags, and Chamberlain got out to escort me through the terminal. Genseau remained in the car, and as I began to leave, he patted the seat as if I should stay for a moment.

"I hope things work well for you," he said.

"Thank you," I replied, and as I moved to get out, he stopped me again.

"How was Gosol? I've always wanted to visit."

So he knew and hadn't had me arrested.

Chamberlain was becoming impatient, but I could tell he wasn't going to interrupt the Magistrate who, on the other hand, was being very deliberate and taking his time.

"Have a good flight," he finally said, letting me go. "Maybe we'll meet again."

It sounded prophetic, and I could tell he didn't mean it in a criminal sense.

Chamberlain was gesturing to hurry along. We did not go through the regular inspection stations, but into a side door and a back security area. Uniformed officers watched as we went by, Chamberlain flashing his credentials. He led me through the airport, up the boarding ramp, and right to the plane door.

"You've caused us a lot of problems, you're lucky to even be getting on this plane," he said harshly, and then in a change of tone. "Have a good flight."

He started shaking his head after he turned and walked away, almost as if he hadn't intended to say that last little bit. I smiled to myself, but then it hit home, I had lost the letters. Walking back to my seat, I felt surrounded by a grey weight of sadness

I was given a row to myself at the rear of the plane. My back was to the lavatory, and I was cramped. I could tell the stewards were watching, as their service was curt, unlike the other passengers.

I had no cellphone, and even if I did, I'd had no time to call Juliette, Dieter, or anyone. I didn't even have their phone numbers anymore. Everything had happened so fast, like a puzzle falling off the table, I was unable to catch all the pieces.

As the non-stop flight lifted into the air, Toulouse quickly vanished in a bank of clouds, which soon turned into the

Atlantic Ocean, and later the green hills and crowded communities of the east coast, which became a quilt of squares and circles beyond the Mississippi River. Finally, landing in Denver, we taxied around the tent-like terminal, the Rockies poking up on the horizon to the west.

There was no consular agent to meet me at the gate, no escort to the baggage claim, and no limo waiting to pick me up. I was as anonymous as anyone else on the shuttle ride to the long-term parking lot. The only person who spoke to me was the driver, sporting a scruffy beard, ponytail, and dry sense of humor.

"How's the weather?" I asked.

"Getting some rain," he answered.

"Good for the cows," I remarked.

"Good for the fish," he replied.

I had planned to be away much longer, and thankfully the parking fee was low, as the magazine wasn't going to pick up the tab. I was soon on the road, the traffic thinning from three steady streams of cars and trucks into two lanes of open-highway in Wyoming. I had deliberately closed myself off, not wanting to think of what lay ahead or my feelings about what lay behind. In other words, I was numb.

With rolling prairie for miles around, and a few scattered ranches and towns, I could feel the loneliness, and it fit my mood just fine.

Driving the switchbacks up to my rented mountain cabin, it felt like I was flying again as the snowcapped Bighorns came into view in the distance.

I was alone, and there wasn't much to do around the cabin once I was back. So I shopped for some groceries, went for walks, and didn't even bother to turn on the lights, letting my rhythm be by the sun.

I thought of trying to find Juliette's number, and Yoseph's bookstore, but something inside had gone dark. I let everything go.

THIRTY-THREE

One morning, after about a week had gone by, I heard a thump on my roof, and I went out to see what had fallen on it. As I stepped back to get a better view, my phone rang. How coincidental, I thought, as it was the only spot where I had cell phone reception. I didn't recognize the phone number and wasn't going to answer, but I pressed the on button anyway.

"Bjorn,"

I would have recognized that voice anywhere, like a beautiful cloud in a blue sky. It was Juliette. I felt a knot in my throat.

"Are you there?" she asked after a pause.

"I am," I said, trying to sound normal.

"Where have you been? I've been trying to call, it's like you dropped off the end of the earth."

"It's Wyoming," I remarked.

"It's good to hear your voice," she said.

"And yours."

She then explained that Dieter was fit to be tied after I was taken away, and they threatened to arrest him.

"No one would tell us anything. We spent days trying to get some information. Dieter thought they'd taken you to a black site prison or something. Then, finally, we learned they had flown you back."

"They took the phone, computer, camera, anything that I could communicate with, and so I lost all your numbers," I told her. "Frankly, I began to think the whole thing was over, you, Wendy at the magazine, my friends."

"Never," she said. "But have you heard the news?"

"What news? I haven't heard or watched anything."

"It's about the Count."

"Did he die?"

267

"No, he is going to show the letters. He's going to unveil them at the Louvre!"

"What?" I said in disbelief, but suddenly feeling life-blood returning to my body.

"The Louvre! I have to admit when he does something, he does it big. It was that letter, the special one that nobody can translate. Something happened when he saw it. He said his heart melted. Can you believe it?"

It took a minute to grasp what she was saying, but I knew what he had experienced. The Count had withdrawn the allegations, and the Magistrate closed the investigation finding no grounds for charges. Furthermore, the Count apologized to Juliette for what he had done and invited us to the Louvre opening as his guests.

"Oh, and he wants to give you a pre-exhibit in the library."

"Only if he personally greets me at the door," I said, and she laughed.

"Also, William and the Count have had a parting of the ways. No surprise there. He's decided to go back to Belgium and won't fight the divorce."

As it turned out, a major exhibit of the Lautrec's private art collection had already been in the works, and the letters were now the blockbuster feature. Negotiations were also underway to bring the show to the US in a significant cultural exchange. This was the multi-million dollar venture and big diplomatic arrangement that Chamberlain was trying to save by sacrificing me.

After we hung up, I was still in a daze. The earth had revolved a little more during the call, but my world had turned completely around.

Then the phone rang again.

"How would you like to go to France?" Wendy began.

ACKNOWLEDGEMENT

I would like to thank: Lou Rotola, Karen Snyder, Cindy Pillmore, Hailey Ellingham, Helen Dziemidko, Astrid Bjorlo, Uranda, Martin, Steve Weber, Ruud West, Jon Shanker, Liz and Steve Ruhl who put up with my late night pacing, and the Nakoda and Aan-iiih people.

Made in the USA
Monee, IL
07 November 2022

17312784R00163